"How good it is to see you again, and looking so well,"

he said softly, whilst all the time peering down intently at each delicate feature in turn, as though to assure himself that the boy-girl who had trailed about after him over the estate like some adoring puppy all those many years ago, and this self-assured young woman now standing before him were indeed one and the same person.

Their years apart had undoubtedly been good to her. There was no sign now of the pretty plumpness of youth. Bright blue eyes considered him levelly above high cheekbones. The small, straight nose and the contours of her perfectly molded mouth had not changed, as far as he could tell. Only the firmness of the jaw-line seemed more marked, and there was a suspicion too now of determination in the set of the slightly pointed little chin.

"You look very well, Beth, my dear. Very well indeed," he assured her, releasing her hands the instant he felt her attempting to withdraw them.

"And so do you, Philip," she returned, bestowing a smile upon him that emphasized wonderfully well those beneficial changes in her appearance….

* * *

The Transformation of Miss Ashworth
Harlequin® Historical #253—February 2009

ANNE ASHLEY

was born and educated in Leicester. She lived for a long time in Scotland, but now lives in the West Country with two cats, her two sons and her husband, who has a wonderful and very necessary sense of humor. When not pounding away at the keys of her word processor, she likes to relax in her garden, which she has opened to the public on more than one occasion in aid of the village church funds.

THE TRANSFORMATION OF
Miss Ashworth

ANNE ASHLEY

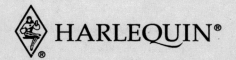

TORONTO • NEW YORK • LONDON
AMSTERDAM • PARIS • SYDNEY • HAMBURG
STOCKHOLM • ATHENS • TOKYO • MILAN • MADRID
PRAGUE • WARSAW • BUDAPEST • AUCKLAND

Recycling programs
for this product may
not exist in your area.

ISBN-13: 978-0-373-30562-9
ISBN-10:   0-373-30562-1

THE TRANSFORMATION OF MISS ASHWORTH

Author Note

When I first began to write Historical romances for Harlequin Books, I did so by writing six books, all of which were linked by one or more characters. I have once again returned to a linking theme with my next two novels.

In each story one of the main characters, one male, one female, has been involved in the Peninsular Campaign. Their reasons for going out to Portugal and Spain were vastly contrasting, and both are changed by their experiences.

Both stories begin in September 1814, after our hero and heroine have returned to England, at a time when Napoleon is still in exile on the Isle of Elba, and people believe the conflict with France is finally over.

Observing the courtesies practiced during the Regency period, and ladies first, *The Transformation of Miss Ashworth* centers on Miss Bethany Ashworth's story.

I hope you enjoy it.

DON'T MISS THESE OTHER
NOVELS AVAILABLE NOW:

Chapter One

September 1814

With a heartfelt sigh Miss Bethany Ashworth transferred her gaze from what had once been very familiar countryside indeed, and focused her attention on her sole travelling companion.

'I'm so weary, Ann,' she revealed softly, 'so very tired, now, of it all.'

The admission was instantly acknowledged by a soft smile, which managed to combine both affection and sympathy. 'Hardly surprising, my dear. We've both done more than our fair share of jaunting about Europe during these past five years or so. And speaking for myself, I've found this last journey from Paris particularly trying.'

'It isn't the travelling I find irksome,' Beth revealed, once again turning her attention to the view beyond the window. 'It's my own indecisiveness, not knowing my own mind, that I find so confoundedly bothersome.' She gave vent to a shout of self-deprecating laughter. 'I've frequently deplored the lack of resolution displayed by so many of our sex. Yet here I am now, in-dulging in just such a weakness myself! I shall have to take myself roundly to task, and do some very hard thinking in the not-too-distant future.'

Brown eyes betrayed a degree of concern. 'Are you trying to say you now regret your decision to return, here, to your childhood home? I remember, after your dear papa passed away, you were quite undecided.'

'No, I don't regret that,' Beth answered, before a faintly enigmatic smile curled what more than one gen-tleman in recent years had considered a perfectly shaped feminine mouth. 'It might yet prove a means to an end. But whether I shall choose to remain indefi-nitely is quite another matter. Thankfully, we shan't be forced to stay should we become restless. Which should come as no great surprise to either of us, considering the life we've led in recent years. And Papa, bless him, has ensured I'm no pauper. I could reside permanently in the capital should I choose to do so. Perhaps not in one of the most favoured locations, but at least at an address that is not frowned upon. But, no, Ann, I don't regret returning to the house I grew up in,' she reiter-ated, her mind turning to more mundane, practical matters. 'And providing the indispensable Rudge has done his job, it will provide us both with a very com-fortable abode for as long as we choose to stay.'

The older woman appeared a good deal easier having learned this. 'Well, I for one am very much looking forward to residing in your childhood home, and putting down roots. I'm seven years your senior, remember, and rather weary now of the nomadic life, even if you are not.'

'In that case, my dear Ann, I shall do my utmost to speed up our arrival,' and, so saying, Beth pulled down the window to instruct the post-boys to turn off the road directly ahead.

The chaise then drew to a halt before a pair of impressive wrought-iron gates. One of the post-boys gave a blast on his horn to alert the gatekeeper to their presence, and a few moments later a small, stocky figure emerged from the lodge, looking anything but pleased at being summoned so summarily.

'And what be your business 'ere at Staveley Court, may I ask?' he demanded to know, the sight of a post-chaise-and-four seemingly having made no impression upon him whatsoever.

'My business is my own affair,' Beth called, half-smiling, thereby alerting the gatekeeper to her presence. 'So just you look lively, and unlock those gates and let me pass, George Dodd, otherwise I might well be tempted to play the talebearer and have a word with your master when next I see him.'

For a full half-minute the gatekeeper peered between the iron bars at the hatless young lady staring back at him from the chaise window, before his craggy, weather-beaten face eventually broke into a near-toothless grin.

'God bless my soul! As I live and breathe, if it ain't you, Miss Bethany! And after all these years an' all!' he exclaimed, throwing wide the gates without further ado, and then moving as swiftly as his arthritic, bow legs would carry him to the side of the vehicle.

'Never thought to see you back 'ere again,' he declared, his beady-brown eyes betraying a suspicion of tears as he stared up at a face he well remembered.'

'How are you, Dodd? she asked gently. 'Still suffering with the old joints, I see.'

'I do well enough, miss. All the better for seeing you. And I fancy I won't be the only one, neither. The master be up at the 'ouse. Come back from Lunnon weeks back.'

All at once Beth's radiant and unforgettable smile began to fade. 'Truth to tell, Dodd, I'm not here to see your master. I've been travelling for the best part of three weeks, and thought to make use of the short cut across Sir Philip's land. But I don't want to get you into trouble.'

'Bless you, Miss Beth, you go right on ahead. Master wouldn't mind you crossing 'is land, that I do know.'

Staveley Court was not so much distinguished by its size as by its architectural splendour, and the magnificence of its surrounding park, which could be viewed unrestricted from most every room in the house. Consequently Lady Chalford had had little difficulty in following the progress of the post-chaise-and-four from her brother's west-facing library window.

'You didn't mention at luncheon that you were expecting visitors, Philip. I wouldn't have taken my customary afternoon nap had I known. You may as well make use of me during the time I'm here. At the very least I could have made your visitors welcome.'

The shapely hand moving back and forth across the page did not falter even for an instant, as the recipient of this disclosure confirmed his only caller that day had been his steward in the forenoon.

Lady Chalford's brows came together in rare show of disapproval. 'In that case, dear brother, someone is once again taking advantage of your good nature. I've told you before, Philip, you are far too tolerant in many respects, too complaisant by half! It's common knowledge that, since the war, pockets of unrest have sprung up all over the country. Why, look what happened to you earlier this summer. Someone tried to take a pot-shot at you. And it's of no use your pretending otherwise! You simply cannot afford to let strangers trespass on your property, even if they are travelling in a post-chaise-and-four.'

Completely unruffled, Sir Philip Staveley signed his name with a flourish, before rising to his feet and joining his sister at the window. 'I would be extremely surprised, Connie, if that shooting accident was anything other than just that. Remember, it took place on my land. In all probability the culprit was one of my neighbours' over-enthusiastic sons discharging his gun without due care. And as for that carriage... I very much doubt all the occupants can be total strangers, otherwise entry would have been barred, most especially by Dodd on the east gate. Furthermore, that conveyance, unless I much mistake the matter, has travelled some distance, possibly from London.'

Lady Chalford turned her head to stare up at her much taller brother, thereby instantly revealing a similarity or two in their profiles. Both had inherited certain Staveley facial characteristics—the long, thin aristocratic nose, not to mention clear, grey eyes.

Unlike his sister's, however, Sir Philip's orbs had once betrayed a disarming twinkle that a great many members of the fair sex had found most winning. His hair, a shade or two darker than his more mature sibling's, swept back in soft waves from a high, intelligent forehead. A firm jaw-line, a shapely yet not overgenerous mouth, and a pair of gracefully arching brows above those thickly lashed eyes were all features worthy of note; and although he might not have been considered strictly handsome by the more fastidious among his class, a great many discerning female members considered him most attractive.

Which was more than could be said for his sister, whose youthful bloom had long since faded, and whose thickening figure betrayed the fact that she had presented her spouse with several pledges of her affection during fourteen years of marriage. Notwithstanding, even her fiercest critics would never have stigmatised Lady Chalford as an ill-favoured woman. In fact, when animated, as now, she still held an appeal to a certain number of the more mature members of the opposite sex.

'You're bamming me, Philip!' she chided gently. 'How can you possibly deduce that?'

'By using my eyes and brain, Constance,' he returned, slanting a mocking glance down at her. 'Firstly, not many can afford the luxury of travelling in a post-chaise-and-four. Those in these parts with funds enough to do so, like myself, own their own carriages. Secondly, the majority of the larger houses in the locale lie to the north and east of my property. Furthermore, there is only one house situated on the western boundary whose owner has been absent for any length of time, and whose return might well be undertaken in a hired carriage.'

Lady Chalford's jaw dropped perceptively, a clear indication that her mind had woken up to a startling possibility. 'You don't suppose, do you, that young Bethany Ashworth has returned home after all these years?'

Unlike his sister, Sir Philip betrayed no emotion whatsoever as he said, 'Naturally, I shan't know for sure, until I've consulted with Dodd. All the same, it's a distinct possibility. Augustus Ashworth, together with his associates and members of his family, was among the favoured few who attained permission from our sire to take a short cut across the park in order to reach the village more quickly.'

As the post-chaise at last disappeared from view behind a screen of stately elms, Sir Philip moved across the room in the direction of a small table upon which several decanters stood. 'Common report would have me believe the shutters have been removed from the Grange's windows these past three weeks or more, and that a couple of village girls have been hired to work in the house. Seemingly someone, I know not who, has been buying in supplies of food, and making use of several local tradesmen in order to make the house ready for habitation.'

'It stands to reason, then, that Bethany must be returning home,' Lady Chalford concluded, after having accepted the glass of ratafia her brother held out to her. 'What other explanation could there possibly be?' she asked, rearranging her skirts as she made herself comfortable in one of the chairs.

Seating himself opposite, Sir Philip gazed across at his sister with lazy affection. Fond of her though he had always been, he had never rated her capacity for understanding very highly. At the same time he did appreciate her finer qualities. For instance, she was, basically, a very kind person, never one to bear a grudge or utter a deliberately unkind remark. Moreover, as she had never attempted to make unreasonable demands on his time, he was able to ignore for the most part her less favourable traits when she did choose to inflict her company upon him for a prolonged stay.

'Several, my dear,' he responded, after fortifying himself from his glass. 'Dodd, as I mentioned before, must have recognised at least one occupant of that vehicle, otherwise he would not have allowed entry. It might have been Beth, of course. Or it might easily have been the late Colonel Ashworth's man of business, who could well have received instructions to ensure the house is in good order for a new occupant.'

He couldn't forbear a smile at his sister's look of utter bewilderment. 'Evidently you hadn't considered the possibility that Beth might have chosen to sell the house in order to live elsewhere, possibly abroad,' he went on. 'After all, she's lived away from these shores long enough. And now I come to think about it, when last I saw Lady Henrietta Barfield during the Season she mentioned something about her niece's intention to remain in Paris for a while.'

All at once Lady Chalford was silent, clearly in a world of her own, before surprisingly announcing, 'Do you know, Philip, I always considered her actions most strange.'

Philip paused in the act of raising his glass to his lips again to gaze across indulgently at his sibling. Clearly her thoughts had spun off at a tangent. In which direction, however, was anybody's guess.

He wisely took the precaution of taking a further fortifying mouthful from the contents of his glass before asking, 'Are we referring to Beth, now, or Lady Henrietta?'

'Why, Bethany, of course!' his sister exclaimed, clearly amazed at having been asked the question in the first place. 'I never quite understood why she went to live with her mother's relative in Plymouth. Surely Lady Henrietta Barfield was her favourite aunt?'

'That I couldn't say with any conviction,' Philip responded. 'After her mother's demise, she certainly spent time with her father's sister. And it's also true to say that Lady Hetta, taking an active role in Beth's upbringing, was a more frequent visitor to the Grange than any other relation. But you must remember that Colonel Ashworth was summoned urgently to London in the spring of '08, and soon afterwards set sail with Wellesley for the Peninsula. Poor Beth was hardly granted much time in which to consider where she wished to reside. And who knows, maybe she felt that Lady Henrietta had interfered in her life quite enough. Or maybe she just didn't wish to be an extra burden on the Barfield family at a time when they were fully occupied with matters relating to Eugenie's future.'

At mention of his deceased fiancée, Lady Chalford shot her brother an anxious glance from beneath her lashes. It was rare, indeed, for him ever to allude to that period in his life, let alone his engagement to Lord Barfield's beloved eldest daughter. During the past years, whenever the topic had been raised within her hearing, he had never been slow to change the subject.

Notwithstanding, this knowledge did not deter her from saying, 'But that is precisely what I find so puzzling. She and Eugenie were so close—more like sisters than cousins, I seem to recall someone remarking once. One would have quite naturally supposed that Beth would have wanted to be with the Barfields at a time of such celebration.'

All at once it seemed as if her brother's face had been cast into shadow, his lids lowering like shutters, concealing any emotion mirrored in his eyes.

'As I said before, Constance, I'm sure Beth had her reasons for choosing to live with her late mother's aunt. You may be lucky enough to satisfy your curiosity if she has, indeed, returned,' her brother replied, with the all-too-familiar hint of finality in his tone that revealed clearly enough that he considered the topic at an end.

When residing at the Court Sir Philip generally kept country hours, and the following morning proved no exception. As his sister preferred to break her fast in her bedchamber, he enjoyed the leisure of a solitary breakfast, before setting off on horseback for the prearranged meeting with his steward.

It was a common sight to see the master of Staveley Court out and about at an early hour, astride one of his prime horses. From a very young age he had betrayed a keen interest in husbandry, and, since coming into the title, some seven years previously, his love of the land had not diminished in the least.

He concerned himself with every aspect of the day-to-day running of the estate, and the welfare of his tenants, who farmed his many acres of West Country land. His steward knew well enough that he could consult with his master on any problem, no matter how trivial, and made a practice of doing so quite frequently. All the same, as their meeting the day before had been fairly lengthy and involved, their business that morning was soon concluded, leaving Sir Philip with ample time to do as he wished before he need return to the Court for luncheon.

Finding himself close to the eastern boundary of the deer-park jogged his memory. Consequently, he turned his fine gelding in the direction of the gatehouse to discover one of his oldest employees busily working in a small vegetable patch.

'Morning to 'ee, sir. Be 'ee wanting me to give the lads a 'and wi' the logging again this autumn?'

'Only if you feel up to it, Dodd,' Philip answered, thereby betraying the affection in which he held this particularly loyal estate worker. 'The reason I'm here is to ask you about a certain post-chaise-and-four I spied crossing the park late yesterday afternoon. The occupant made no attempt to come up to the house. Was it from this gate entry was gained?'

'God bless you, sir, 'twere indeed! And 'twere none

other than Miss Bethany 'erself come 'ome after all these years, would you believe!' The old man removed his hat to run a hand over his balding pate. 'What a sight for sore eyes she be, too, sir. Didn't suppose you'd mind 'er taking liberties, not Miss Bethany,' he added, casting a questioning glance up at the tall figure on horseback.

The assurance was not long in coming. 'Of course I don't object. But remain vigilant, Dodd. Miss Ashworth is by no means the only one to have returned from across the Channel in recent times,' he said, recalling his sister's fears. Which were not without foundation, as it happened. 'There's much unrest about the county at present, many who harbour bitter feelings now the war with France is at an end, and they have come home to find no work.'

Sir Philip took a moment or two to appreciate the picturesque landscape, where no firearm had been discharged in anger, as far as he was aware, since the Civil War, when his ancestors had stood firm against the Roundheads for several days before finally being defeated. Then his mind returned to more recent events, and the arrival home of someone he'd known almost since the day of her birth.

All at once he was consumed with curiosity, a rare experience for him these days. 'What is she like, Dodd… Miss Ashworth? As you had no trouble recognising her, I can only assume she hasn't changed much.'

'Changed some, sir. But not so much that I didn't know 'er after a second glance. I mind she's a deal leaner than of yore. Not much flesh on the bone from what I could see. But the smile ain't changed, sir. I'd know that smile of Miss Beth's anywhere. Light up the dullest day, so 'twould!'

'Yes, yes, you're right,' Philip acknowledged, his

mind's eye conjuring up images from the past. Memories, almost forgotten in recent years, came flooding back of a girl dressed in breeches, galloping, astride her horse, across the estate at his side. She had been more boy than girl in those years before Lady Henrietta Barfield had taken a very necessary hand in her niece's upbringing. The transformation from sad romp had eventually been achieved. He seemed to remember that before she had left the Grange she bore all the trappings of a young lady; suddenly recalled, too, that he had not altogether approved of the changes that had taken place in her. But that was then, he reminded himself. What was she like now? Might she be a wife and mother?

For some reason that escaped him completely, he found the thought faintly disturbing, and consulted once again with his gatekeeper. 'Was she travelling alone, Dodd, or with a protector?'

The old man shook his head. 'That I couldn't say for sure, sir. Being a mite on the short side, as yer might say, I can't see into carriages none too well. But, I mind there were someone else in there with 'er, lurking in the shadows.'

Quickly taking his leave, Philip headed back towards the Court. He was halfway along the sweep of the drive when a second surge of curiosity, not untouched by tangled threads of lingering disquiet at the thought of Beth being married, gripped him, and he turned his mount, and headed across the park in a westerly direction.

Nestling just beyond the boundary wall in a picturesque, shallow valley was the thriving community where a good many of his estate workers resided. Neat rows of lime-washed cottages lined the main village street, and led up to the tiny church, where the Staveley family had for generations always worshipped. Beyond the church, several much larger brick dwellings had been erected during the latter half of the previous century. The Grange, the grandest of the newer buildings, was set in a large garden and was shielded from the road by a substantial yew hedge.

It had been a number of years since Sir Philip had had reason to visit the house. He could see at a glance, as he turned his fine bay hack into the driveway, that the property was showing signs of neglect. The garden, although far from overgrown, was nowhere near as neatly contained as he remembered, and the house, too, clearly demanded attention in several areas.

After securely tethering his mount to the hitching post, he wasted no time in making his arrival known. His summons was answered promptly enough by a middle-aged woman whom he had known since boyhood, and who didn't attempt to hide her delight at seeing him.

'Why, Sir Philip! It's been a mort of years since you stepped into the parlour here at the Grange. Come in, do, sir,' she invited. 'Miss Beth will be that pleased to see you, I'm sure. She shouldn't be long. Be out with that man of hers at present. But she promised to be back in good time for luncheon.'

'Man…?' Philip echoed, once again experiencing the strangest gnawing sensation in his abdomen.

'That's right, sir, Mr Rudge. Takes proper good care of her so he do. Hardly ever lets her out of his sight, so I understand. They be out now looking at horses over Markham way, it being market day. But Mrs Stride be here. Nice lady she be. I'm sure she'll be happy to bear you company until the mistress returns. If you step inside, sir, I'll make you known to the lady.'

Still trying to assimilate what he had discovered, and not put his own wild interpretations on the scant information, Philip entered the, now, slightly faded front parlour to discover a woman seated by the hearth, and looking so completely at home in her surroundings that one might have been forgiven for supposing she were mistress of the house.

As she set aside her sewing, and rose to her feet, he judged her to be of a similar age to his sister, though wearing rather better. The instant she spoke, inviting him to sit down and offering refreshment, it was evident, too, that she was an educated woman of no little refinement; and one who, moreover, betrayed no diffidence whatsoever at finding herself in the company of a peer of the realm. All of which only added to the puzzling questions swirling round his head.

'You must forgive me, ma'am, for calling so soon after your arrival here. Only I allowed avid curiosity for once to override basic good manners. Miss Ashworth and I knew each other so well at one time that I wished to renew the acquaintance without delay.'

'I know she will be delighted to see you, Sir Philip. She mentioned yesterday, when we took a short-cut across your land, that you would forgive such a liberty in one whom you had known since she was an infant.'

Heartened by the fact that Mrs Stride had not attempted to correct him after he had referred to Beth as Miss Ashworth, Philip took a moment to sample his wine and study the handsome woman seated opposite. 'Forgive me, ma'am, for asking, but would I be correct in assuming you're not even distantly related to Beth?'

'You would indeed, sir,' she instantly confirmed. 'I am, to all intents and purposes, a hired companion. But you will never get Beth to admit as much. My late husband was a major in the army, and lost his life at Talavera. It was while I was attempting to attain passage back to England that Colonel Ashworth engaged my services, after his daughter's unexpected arrival in the Peninsula.'

Sir Philip's ears instantly pricked up at this. 'Unexpected…?' he echoed.

The widow appeared nonplussed for a moment, then she shrugged. 'I believe I'm right in thinking the Colonel wasn't expecting her. But it was some years ago, and my memory is a trifle hazy. Many letters from home were never received, so perhaps it was merely that he wasn't sure when to expect her.

'He certainly never seemed displeased by her presence,' she continued after a moment's consideration. 'That I can tell you with complete conviction. Quite the opposite, in fact! I believe he derived great comfort from having his daughter with him. And, of course, he always made sure she was well protected.' She shook her head and smiled. 'Not that Beth needs much protection. As you are possibly aware, she can ride and shoot as well as most men. Which, she assures me, was the result of a somewhat unorthodox upbringing.'

'Unorthodox in the extreme, ma'am,' he concurred, smiling as he was assailed by further memories. 'Encouraged by a doting father, she scandalised half the county by her tomboyish behaviour.'

'But not you, sir, I think,' the widow remarked, after staring across at him intently.

'How very perspicacious of you, ma'am,' he responded, not attempting a denial. 'No—in fact, in many ways I thought it a great pity that the Colonel permitted his sister to interfere to such an extent in his daughter's upbringing. Under Lady Henrietta Barfield's guiding hand much of Beth's natural charm simply disappeared.'

Clearly Ann Stride was amazed to hear him say this. Before she could voice her surprise, however, the door was thrown wide, and the young mistress of the house stood framed in the aperture.

For several long moments no one spoke. It was evident to Ann, at least, that her dearest friend had been apprised of the precise identity of the caller awaiting her in the parlour, for no vestige of astonishment whatsoever was apparent in her face. In fact, her expression remained so impassive that it was impossible to judge just what was passing through her mind, as her visitor rose at once to his feet and her vivid blue eyes scrutinised him unashamedly from head to toe.

Sir Philip, on the other hand, appeared, if not precisely stunned, certainly taken aback. And favourably so, Ann suspected. At first glance his shapely brows had risen sharply, then, with the self-assured air of a gentleman of breeding and aplomb, he moved languidly towards the door, hands outstretched to capture both of Beth's.

'How good it is to see you again, and looking so well,' he said softly, whilst all the time peering down intently at each delicate feature in turn, as though to assure himself that the boy–girl who had trailed about after him over the estate like some adoring puppy all those many years ago, and this self-assured young woman now standing before him, were indeed one and the same person.

Their years apart had undoubtedly been good to her. There was no sign now of the pretty plumpness of youth. Almost half a decade spent out in the Peninsula, suffering privations he dared not even imagine, had helped to hone her face into something quite out of the common way. Bright blue eyes considered him levelly above high cheekbones. The small, straight nose and the contours of her perfectly moulded mouth had not changed, as far as he could tell. Only the firmness of the jaw-line seemed more marked, and there was a suspicion, too, now of determination in the set of the slightly pointed little chin.

'You look very well, Beth, my dear. Very well indeed,' he assured her, releasing her hands the instant he felt her attempting to withdraw them.

'And so do you, Philip,' she returned, bestowing a smile upon him that emphasised wonderfully well those beneficial changes in her appearance, before brushing past and turning her attention to the other occupant of the room.

'How often have I remarked, Ann, that the passage of time is grossly unfair to favour for the most part the male of the species, though overindulgence can be disastrous for members of both sexes. And talking of which…can I tempt you to remain a little longer, Philip, by refilling your glass?'

He readily agreed. Ann, on the other hand, refused, and begged to be excused a moment later in order to search the workbox in her bedchamber for a certain shade of thread better suited to the fabric she was sewing.

Once again smiling, only wryly this time, Beth watched her leave, before returning her attention to her guest, and tutting loudly. 'Really, I think I must have a word with dear Mrs Stride. If she wishes to be considered my companion, then she will need to take her duties a deal more seriously from now on. To leave me ensconced with an eligible bachelor…what can she be thinking of!'

He had no difficulty recognising that age-old glint

of mischief dancing in her eyes, so wasn't unduly taken aback when she added outrageously, 'Of course, she might have wisely perceived that I was in no danger. But she might at least have considered you, Philip. An eligible baronet is fair game, and it isn't totally unknown for me to act on impulse. Just think what a scandal we'd cause if I were to take it into my head to importune you.'

For answer he threw back his head and laughed heartily, something he had done so very infrequently in recent years. 'I was wrong. You haven't changed much at all.'

'I wouldn't go so far as to say that. People do, you know,' she countered, after collecting his glass. 'Can I tempt you to join me in a measure of port?' The slight frown of disapproval bent in her direction was patently not lost on her, for she added, 'No, not considered a lady's drink, I know. Unfortunately I picked up the habit whilst abroad, and got my darling Rudge to return to Portugal in order to obtain a couple of dozen cases of the stuff, before setting sail for home.'

'And dare I enquire who "darling Rudge" might be?' Philip asked, watching her lower herself with a grace that was wholly natural into the chair opposite.

'For want of a better description, I suppose you might say Amos Rudge is my major-domo.' Leaning back in her chair, she appeared completely at ease in the company of a gentleman whom she had not set eyes on in six long years. 'He's a trifle rough around the edges, it must be said. The Lord only knows what callers to the house will make of him. He's not above telling someone he doesn't like the look of to clear off in no uncertain terms. Used to be dear Papa's batman, as it happens.'

At mention of the late Colonel, Philip immediately offered his condolences. Which were sincerely meant, for not only had he respected his late neighbour, he had genuinely liked him too.

'I understand it happened towards the latter part of the campaign,' he added, when she regarded the contents of her glass with a pensive expression on her face, though blessedly with no suspicion of tears.

'Yes, he was shot in the back whilst out on a scouting mission for Wellington, shortly before the army crossed into France, and died a few days later. But I'm not sorry it happened that way,' she surprised him by admitting. 'I had been informed by one of the army surgeons a few months before that my father was in the first stages of the wasting disease. He died serving his country. He would have wanted it that way. He was buried in Spain. And I remained with the army until we reached Paris. I believe he would have wished that too.'

Once again she relapsed into silence for a few moments, whilst all the time regarding him steadily over the rim of her glass, before adding, 'Yes, sadly we have both lost loved ones during these past years, Philip. It was very many weeks before the sad news of Eugenie's death reached us. Papa did write on behalf of us both. I hope you received his letter?'

Beth continued to regard him keenly. Although the heartfelt sympathy he had shown when speaking of her father was still there, lurking in the depths of his eyes, she could detect, amazingly enough, absolutely no other very evident emotion hidden in those grey depths. It was really most strange. She would have expected to see something…anything to betray his own deep sorrow. But there was nothing.

'I did write to my aunt and uncle, of course, during the time I was out there in Spain, keeping up with all their news as best I could,' Beth went on to reveal, more in an attempt to bridge the lengthening silence than anything else. 'I will say one thing for Aunt Hetta, she's nothing if not a pragmatist. Grieve over the loss of her eldest daughter she undoubtedly did, and always will, I do not doubt, but it clearly didn't deter her from doing her absolute best for her other girls. Three married daughters now—some achievement!'

'Indeed, yes,' Philip agreed, a suspicion of a smile tugging at his lips now. 'Life goes on, as the saying goes,' he added, finishing off his port, and rising to his feet. 'And speaking of which, would you and Mrs Stride care to dine with us at the Court on Friday evening as, judging by your attire, I assume you consider your period of mourning at an end?'

'Us...?' Beth echoed, swooping down on this surprising disclosure.

'Connie intends staying with me for a few weeks, playing hostess.'

'Has she brought the family with her?'

'Good God, no!' Philip shuddered at the mere idea. 'I might be an indulgent brother, Beth, but not to that extent. The whole brood, five of 'em at the last count, decided to come down with a string of childish ailments that continued throughout the spring and most of the summer, resulting in their mother's total exhaustion. She's taking refuge with me at the Court for a few weeks' well-earned rest. Or at least that's what she's putting about. What she's really determined to do is ensure my thirtieth birthday doesn't pass without celebration.'

Beth frankly laughed as she, too, rose to her feet to bid him farewell. 'Oh, well, in that case we'll be delighted to accept your invitation to dine.'

'Excellent!' He appeared very well pleased. 'Only a small affair, you understand? But it will offer you the

opportunity to reacquaint yourself with a few neighbours, and meet some new ones too.'

With that, he captured her hand, and, before she
could withdraw it from his grasp, he had brushed his
lips lightly across the skin.

Chapter Two

At the click of the door Beth abandoned her position by the window, from where she had been following her esteemed visitor's progress along the short sweep of the drive, until he had disappeared from view. She wasn't remotely surprised to see her good friend return to the room, just as she hadn't been particularly surprised by her feeble excuse to leave it a short time earlier. Ann was nothing if not highly perceptive. She would have judged in a trice that the rapport between the master of Staveley Court and the mistress of the Grange had once been, perhaps, a trifle stronger than that of merely affable neighbours, even though Beth had done her utmost to keep her feelings well under control the instant she had discovered the identity of the unexpected caller.

She continued to do so now, as she slanted a mocking glance on her way back over to the decanters. 'My paid companion you might wish to be termed, but pray abandon any desire to become a duenna. I should dismiss you in a trice for rank incompetence.'

Far from chastened, Ann frankly laughed. 'But, my dear, I could see you were in no danger! I believe I recognise an honourable gentleman when I see one. And such a handsome one, too!'

Beth paused in the act of refilling her glass to consider for a moment. 'Do you think him handsome?'

'Why, yes! Don't you?'

'Not particularly, no. Attractive, certainly,' Beth answered, as candid as ever. 'But I have always considered him completely trustworthy. And I cannot imagine my opinion on that will ever change.'

'And, of course, you have known him well enough to have formed that opinion of his character. Yet, when you took the liberty of crossing his land yesterday, and touched upon your relationship with the eligible Baronet, you gave me every reason to suppose you had never been anything other than amiable neighbours.'

Although the accusation was clearly discernible, Beth wasn't unduly troubled by it. 'And so we were, Ann dear. Here, pass me your glass, and I shall refill it with that revolting concoction you choose to tip down your throat!'

Once comfortably settled in their respective chairs again, Beth made no attempt to divert her companion's mind by raising a different topic. Instead, she tried to explain her past relationship with the Baronet more fully by first reminding Ann of certain convivial evenings enjoyed out in the Peninsula in the company of Colonel Ashworth, and other distinguished officers.

'So, having heard him, on more than one occasion, reminisce about my childhood,' she continued, 'you must have gathered I had had something of an unorthodox upbringing.'

'Oh, yes, I do recall your father mentioning on more than one occasion that you were something of a tomboy, shamefully going about in breeches.'

Beth gurgled with mirth, genuinely amused. 'Yes, and it was all very well for him, years afterwards, to lament over my deplorable behaviour, but let me assure you, at the time, he actively encouraged me to behave like the son he'd never been blessed to have.' She considered for a moment. 'Had my father been next in line for the title, instead of the youngest of three sons, I think maybe he might have remarried at some point and tried to beget a son himself. But as it was…'

Settling herself more comfortably in the chair, Beth allowed her mind to wander back over the years yet again. 'You'll remember me telling you that my mother died when I was very young. My recollections of her are distinctly hazy, merely flashes of memory concerning sweet perfumes and gentle words and caresses. My recollections of my father in my formative years are, by contrast, most vivid. He taught me to ride. Astride, I might add. When I was seven years old and he wished to purchase a side-saddle for me, I quite naturally recoiled in horror at the mere thought. So he bought me a suit of boy's clothes instead.

'Don't be fooled by anything you might have heard him say out there in Spain,' Beth advised, smiling fondly. 'Believe me when I tell you he felt so proud that his little girl was a bruising rider, and had learned to shoot as well as he could. He rarely objected when I escaped from my long-suffering governess to accompany him out. And so it followed that whenever he was invited to join a shooting party in the locale, or went fishing with neighbours, I, too, went along. Philip frequently accompanied his father, and so, naturally, we became very well acquainted. I always looked forward with much pleasure to those times when he came home from school and, later, university. I regarded him as…possibly…a surro-

gate brother then, and followed him about everywhere.'
Smiling still, she shook her head. 'He, poor boy, must
have found me such a confounded nuisance, but he was
always so very patient with me.'

Pausing to reduce the contents of her glass, Beth
took a moment to collect her thoughts. 'Of course such
a state of affairs couldn't possibly continue. Dear, dear,
the granddaughter of an earl, no less, going about in
breeches…?' She raised her brows in mock horror. 'It
was not to be borne! Eventually my father's only sister,
the only member of his family, incidentally, with whom
Papa ever had any dealings during the vast majority of
his adult life, succeeded in forcing him to acknowledge
the error of his ways, and in persuading him to pack me
off to an exclusive seminary in Bath, where her own
eldest daughter was a pupil.

'I must confess I did somewhat resent Aunt Hetta's
interference at first,' Beth went on to reveal. 'And woe
betide the woman if she ever attempts to meddle in my
affairs again!' A reluctant smile then tugged at her
mouth. 'To be fair, though, I'm forced to own she was
in the right of it on that occasion. Eventually even I was
brought to acknowledge the fact that I simply couldn't
go on behaving in such an outrageous fashion, especially if I ever hoped to make a suitable marriage. And
besides—' she shrugged '—the few years I spent at the
seminary weren't so bad. My eldest cousin and I were
much of an age, and of course we'd seen each other on
several occasions before then. But at the seminary we
shared a room and became the very best of friends,
more like sisters than cousins. At least, that's how I
eventually came to look upon Eugenie.'

The widow thought she could detect just the faintest
trace of bitterness in Beth's voice, and was frankly

puzzled by it. Although Beth could never have been accused of boasting about her more illustrious family connections, she had on several occasions during the past five years mentioned her cousin Eugenie, always with affection, and always with much regret at her passing.

'I seem to recall your saying you kept in regular contact with that cousin in particular,' she remarked, in an attempt to discover a little more about this period in her dearest friend's life.'

'Yes, we exchanged letters on a regular basis and, as Papa had become increasingly less remote as the years had passed, at least where his only sister was concerned, we visited Lord Barfield's mansion in Surrey at least once a year. Then, quite out of the blue, shortly after Eugenie had enjoyed a very successful first Season in town, Aunt Hetta professed a desire to accompany her eldest daughter here. The visits quickly became more frequent, every three months or so. Foolishly I imagined my cousin instigated those frequent journeys into the West Country for the sole purpose of seeing me.' The shout of laughter that echoed round the parlour held a distinctly hollow and bitter ring. 'How wrong can one be! The main reason for the regular visits was to remain in close proximity to a certain eligible young bachelor who had paid her no little attention during her weeks in London the previous year.'

Ann sympathised. 'Little wonder you felt so aggrieved, my dear.'

'Yes, and much more than you realise. I also foolishly imagined that Philip's visits to this house were prompted by a desire to keep in regular contact with his childhood companion, not to moon over the beautiful girl with whom he had fallen head over heels in love.'

Rising to her feet, Beth went to stand before the

window once more, and after a significant silence, when the only sound to be heard was the crackling of the logs on the fire, she at last conceded, 'But perhaps I'm doing Philip an injustice to speak so disparagingly of him. Little wonder he fell so hopelessly in love with Eugenie. Believe me, Ann, she was the most beautiful girl imaginable—golden blonde hair, big, bright blue eyes, and the sweetest of dispositions.'

The sigh she uttered seemed to hang in the air for a long time before she added, 'Although I was blissfully ignorant of it at the time, Waldo Staveley persuaded his nephew to wait until the following year before making anything official. Philip, seemingly, must have been content enough to follow his uncle's advice. Which was understandable in the circumstances. He was very young, not four-and-twenty, and he was having to accustom himself to a vast number of responsibilities, as he had only months before come into the title. None the less, one cannot expect to keep things secret indefinitely and eventually word leaked out that an engagement announcement would be forthcoming in the spring of the following year.

'During this period, Papa sailed for Portugal with Wellesley in the summer of '08, as you know, and there was no possibility that I could remain here at the Grange. Foolishly I felt hurt, and harboured far too much resentment towards Eugenie and her mother to stay with them for the duration of Papa's absence, and so I inflicted myself on my mother's maiden aunt, who still resides in Plymouth. I was brutally aware, of course, that I would be expected to travel to Surrey for the engagement party the following year. As the months passed, and the date for the celebration loomed ever nearer, in sheer desperation I sought a way out of my predicament, and managed to attain passage on board a ship bound for Portugal, just a matter of a week or so before the engagement was made official. Great-Aunt Matilda suspected nothing until she discovered the note I had left her, poor darling. She must have been desperately concerned, even though I assured her I was sharing a cabin with the wife of an army surgeon, eager to join her husband out in the Peninsula, and would therefore be adequately chaperoned for the duration of the voyage.'

'Even so, you took a desperate risk, my dear—a young girl, just turned twenty, travelling without a male protector,' Ann pointed out.

'True,' Beth was obliged to agree. 'But at the time to have remained seemed a far worse fate.' She shrugged. 'Her numerous letters since would suggest Great-Aunt Matilda has long since forgiven me for the distress I caused her. Lady Henrietta Barfield is a different matter entirely. Although she did eventually bring herself to write to me, the few letters received during the intervening years have contained precious little warmth.'

Ann stared intently at the figure still standing at the window. 'And do you still feel resentment now?'

Beth turned to stare out at the slightly neglected garden once more. 'Not towards my Aunt Hetta, no,' she at last revealed. 'Perhaps a little towards Philip, still. But I hope I didn't allow it to show.'

'I could detect nothing of the kind,' Ann assured her.

'Good—because we have been invited to dine at the Court on Friday, and it would be the height of bad manners to reveal the least animosity towards one's host, don't you agree? Besides which, I am determined to put such youthful grievances behind me!'

Ann offered no response. She merely turned her

attention to her sewing once more, her brow furrowed by a thoughtful frown.

Philip arrived back at the Court to discover his sister seated close to the parlour fire, also plying a needle. Unlike the lean yet shapely women with whom he had conversed a short time earlier, Lady Chalford was not given to indulging in any form of strenuous exercise, if she could possibly avoid it. And it showed!

'Ahh, busily occupied again, I see!' he quipped, making a beeline for the table on which recently refilled decanters stood. 'Can I tempt you to join me in a glass of madeira before luncheon, m'dear?'

'Yes, I rather think you can, Brother. I'm quite fatigued after all the embroidering I've been doing during your absence.'

Living up to his reputation for gentlemanly conduct, he refrained from comment, and merely apologised for deserting her for the entire morning. 'But as the business with my steward was accomplished swiftly, I took the opportunity to call in at the Grange in order to welcome Beth home personally.'

Happily abandoning her sewing, Lady Chalford accepted the glass of madeira, while favouring her brother with her full attention. 'Well…?' she prompted, after he had quietly settled himself in the chair opposite. 'What is she like? Did you find her much altered?'

Philip took a few moments to contemplate the contents of his glass, his mind's eye conjuring up a clear image of a pair of clear, azure eyes, set in a finely boned face. 'Yes, some…and the changes are not merely physical, either. I detected a certain reserve in her now that might almost be taken for aloofness.'

Although not known for being particularly perceptive, Lady Chalford on this occasion could easily see something was troubling him. 'Do you mean she didn't seem pleased to see you?'

'Oh, no. No, I wouldn't go as far as to say that, exactly.' Frowning more deeply, he shook his head. 'Perhaps I just imagined it, or am being too sensitive. After all, she's a woman grown, not the lively girl she once was, given to displays of adoration. And, of course, she was bound to have changed after what she's experienced during these past years.'

Lady Chalford uttered a sound that was suspiciously like a snort. 'Well, if she did suffer hardship, she has only her late father to blame. What on earth possessed Colonel Ashworth to send for his daughter, do you suppose? If he had placed her in his sister's care, I'm sure Lady Henrietta would have been only too happy to chaperon her for a Season. It would have been the ideal time to bring Bethany out. Once the event to celebrate your engagement was over, that is.'

As always, she cast her brother a searching look in an attempt to gauge his reaction. On this occasion, however, his expression gave absolutely nothing away. It was almost as if he had not heard. 'Bethany might well have been married by now had she remained in England.' A thought suddenly occurred to her. 'Or is she married?'

'No, she isn't,' he eventually revealed, frowning more deeply than before. 'Which is most surprising, because there's no denying she's become a most attractive young woman, quite strikingly so. But what puzzles me even more is why she took it into her head to join her father in the Peninsula in the first place. Beth's companion inadvertently revealed something that has given me every reason to suppose that Augustus Ashworth didn't plan for his daughter to join him out there.'

He shrugged, straining the material of his impec-
cably tailored jacket across much-admired shoulders.
'No doubt we'll discover the truth in time, possibly
even this coming Friday, as I've invited Beth and her
charming companion, Mrs Stride, to join our small
dinner party.'

Philip favoured his sister with a prolonged stare.
'And have a care, Connie,' he warned. 'Unless I much
mistake the matter, Beth looks upon this woman as
rather more than a companion. I know you are far too
well bred to make any guest of mine feel ill at ease, but
you do not always put a guard on that tongue of yours.'

Lady Chalford clearly bridled at the accusation, yet
possessed sense enough not to refute it, and merely
said, 'Well, if I'm being forced to play hostess to a man
of Bathurst's stamp, I'm sure I can be civil to a hired
companion.' Her grey eyes were suddenly lit by a catlike
gleam. 'In fact, the companion might turn out to be a
blessing in disguise. I was wondering who to place next
to Mr Charles Bathurst at table, as you will insist on
inviting the fellow to dine.'

'An excellent notion!' Philip announced, completely
impervious to his sister's attempts to provoke him. 'And
it might not be such a bad notion to place Bethany on
my affluent new neighbour's other side, for unless her
character has changed out of all recognition, and I don't
suppose for a moment it has, she wouldn't care a jot if
she was seated next to someone who for the first twenty
years of his life was considered a bastard!'

Although having had the advantage of becoming re-
acquainted with Bethany, and therefore having already
appreciated the quite apparent physical changes in her,
even Philip found himself almost gaping when she

entered his drawing room with her companion early on Friday evening.

A gentleman of no little experience in such matters, it was evident to him that both ladies were dressed in creations clearly fashioned by a leading modiste, and possibly purchased during their recent and quite lengthy sojourn in the French capital. Bethany's gown of king-fisher-blue silk clung to her slender figure in gently flowing folds. Long evening gloves, satin slippers and the ribbon entwined through a coiffeur of intricately arranged dark-brown curls were all dyed the exact same shade as the stylish dress. Only the simple string of pearls adorning her throat and the pearl-drop earrings provided some contrast. From head to toe she was the epitome of serene elegance, and her companion's appearance, too, left nothing to be desired.

Leaving his sister still staring slightly open-mouthed, he set about playing the gracious host until dinner was announced by introducing the new arrivals to his other guests, some of whom were known to at least one of the ladies.

Although he had left most of the organising in his sister's very capable hands, Philip had specified which of his female guests he wished placed next to him at the head of the table. For reasons which escaped him still, he had refrained from choosing Beth as one of his close dinner companions. Nevertheless, throughout the meal he found himself frequently casting surreptitious glances in her direction in an attempt to assess her social skills.

No one could ever have accused her of being in the least shy when a child. She had simply oozed confidence in those early years of her life. Yet surprisingly enough when she had returned home after her final year at the seminary, he at least had detected tiny cracks of insecurity in her character. She had certainly been more at home on the hunting field in those days than in a fashionable drawing room. Now, however, there wasn't a sign of diffidence or awkwardness in her demeanour. She conversed easily with those sitting nearest to her, and paid particular attention to the wealthy newcomer to the locale.

Interested to discover what she thought of Charles Bathurst, he didn't encourage the gentlemen to linger over their port, and surprised the ladies by returning to the drawing room before the tea things had even been removed.

'Can I tempt you to take a stroll with me in the garden, Beth?' he asked her, easily prising her away from the other female guests. 'It's a fine evening, and there'll not be too many more to enjoy before autumn sets in.'

If she was surprised to be singled out for particular attention, she betrayed no sign of it, and appeared quite relaxed and content as she accompanied him across the terrace and down the steps to the formal gardens at the rear of the mansion.

'I'd quite forgotten how splendid the grounds are here,' she admitted, her expression openly admiring. 'Or maybe it's that I never fully appreciated the beauty of English gardens until I was denied the pleasure of being in one for so many years. The roses here in the summer must have been breathtaking! I'm determined the garden at the Grange will be as lovely as it once was when Mama was alive. Papa frequently remarked on how wonderful it looked during those few short years before he became a widower.'

Had it been any other female of Philip's acquaintance, he wouldn't have considered the remarks in the least trite, merely a well-bred young woman's attempts to maintain a conversation that was lacking any hint of contention and, in consequence, could offend no one.

Yet, because it was Beth, because it was someone who throughout childhood had possessed such a wealth of roguish charm, he had found the discourse commonplace, and could only wonder at himself for experiencing such a surge of dissatisfaction. What had he expected, for heaven's sake! She was no longer the adoring infant, only too willing to share confidences with someone whom she had looked upon as an indulgent big brother. Furthermore, this evident reserve in her now hadn't suddenly manifested itself overnight, he reminded himself.

Quickly casting his mind back over the years, he recalled the time when she had returned after the period spent at that Bath seminary. He remembered experiencing a sense of acute disappointment in Beth then, especially when she had attempted to ape the more ladylike behaviour of her beautiful cousin. Missish conduct hadn't suited her in the least. He recalled vividly now that he had found the totally feigned manners irksome in the extreme. It simply hadn't suited Beth at all to act the helpless, languishing damsel. It was different now, though, he realised. During their years apart she had developed her social skills, and her manner no longer seemed artificial. Undeniably it was some achievement, and one of which he would have wholeheartedly approved had he not the increasing suspicion that she was determined to keep him at a distance.

This strong impression was endorsed moments later, when they continued their stroll through the gardens, and Beth inadvertently stepped on a large pebble and momentarily lost her balance. Instinctively he grasped the upper part of her right arm in order to steady her, and just as quickly she wrenched it out of his gentle clasp, as though the heat from his fingers had seared through the material of the long evening glove, burning her flesh.

She recovered her poise almost at once, the frantic look of a creature caught in a trap instantly fading from her eyes. 'Forgive me, I'm not usually so clumsy.'

He experienced a stab of irritation at the needless withdrawal. Exerting the praiseworthy self-control for which he was much admired, he none the less suppressed his annoyance in a trice. 'On the contrary, I clearly remember you being exceedingly accident-prone as a child,' he countered. 'I distinctly recall rescuing you from countless scrapes. I was obliged to climb numerous trees in order to assist you down. I even plunged into the river, here, to save you on one occasion, when you ventured too close to the bank, remember? And ruined a pair of brand new boots for my pains!'

Philip could only stare in wonder as he watched a smile, full of that roguish charm he well remembered, light up her face like a beacon. He had seen it numerous times in his youth, and realised quite suddenly how much he had missed not seeing it in recent years. It worked on him like a physic, instantly lifting his spirits from the merely contented frame of mind he'd been in for far, far too long.

'Great heavens! I'd quite forgotten all about that!' Her spontaneous gurgle of mirth was further proof, had he needed any, that beneath the demur, ladylike surface trappings lurked, still, that impish and intrepid spirit of yesteryear. 'Poor Philip, you must have found my company confoundedly tiresome on occasions.'

'Far from it,' he was swift to assure her. Then, after

considering for a moment only, he quite deliberately added, 'Only after you'd returned from that seminary did I find your company less than agreeable.'

Study her though he did, he could detect nothing to suggest she was in the least offended by the disclosure. Her smile had faded in an instant, true enough, but her expression gave him every reason to suppose she was more intrigued than anything else by the candid admission, before she eventually asked, 'Why so?'

'Because I found your behaviour during those few years leading up to your eventual departure from the Grange quite artificial,' he told her bluntly, fervently hoping that by so doing it might result in a resumption, at least in part, of the relationship they had once shared, which had been based on mutual trust, deep affection and honesty.

He chose not to dwell on the reasons why he should wish for a resumption of their past close association as he gave voice to his earlier thoughts. 'You attempted to ape the manners of your cousin Eugenie, and it simply didn't work. It just didn't suit you to play the simpering miss.'

One finely arched brow rose, as blue eyes studied him keenly. 'I cannot recall you regarding Eugenie in the light of a simpering miss,' she reminded him, with just the faintest trace of pique in her voice. 'In fact, if my memory serves me correctly, I seem to recall your remarking once that her manners and conduct were beyond reproach.'

'And so they were,' he readily concurred. 'And perfectly natural too. From the cradle your cousin had been strictly reared. You were not. Eugenie's behaviour was scrutinised at all times for the slightest imperfection. You, on the other hand, were allowed to do more or less as you pleased. I thought at the time that it was not the wisest thing your father ever did, allowing his sister to persuade him to send you away to a school that was renowned for turning out débutantes who all behaved exactly the same. No doubt it was beneficial for some; for others, like yourself, it was nothing short of disastrous. The Colonel would have done better either to engage a stricter governess-companion to instruct you on how to comport yourself, or to send you to a school where standards were not so rigidly high. '

He watched as she turned her head and stared intently in the direction of the neat yew hedge that divided the formal gardens from the shrubbery. 'I'm sorry if I've offended you, Beth. Believe me, it wasn't my intention.'

'You haven't offended me,' she said at length. 'You've merely given me pause for thought. No doubt I shall mull over what you've told me at my leisure, and decide if there is some justification for the criticism.'

Once again he became the object of a level blue-eyed gaze. 'At the risk of inviting further criticism, dare I ask how such an arbiter of conduct in the fair sex rates my behaviour now?'

Although half-suspecting her of mockery, he decided to be totally frank. 'If what I have observed since your arrival here is a true representation of your character, and I would be most surprised if it was not, I should say you're a young woman who conducts herself to please no one but herself, who is now totally without artifice and who is more than capable, still, of exuding an abundance of natural charm, when the mood takes her.' He took a moment to slant her a quizzical smile. 'You certainly had Charles Bathurst clinging to your every word during dinner.'

'What utter rot!' she exclaimed, while eyeing him

uncertainly, as though unable to make up her mind whether his intention had been to compliment her or not. 'It was simply that, apart from Ann and myself, no one sitting close to him attempted to engage him in conversation very much at all. The vicar and his wife, seated opposite, apart from one or two polite exchanges, virtually ignored the poor fellow throughout the meal. And your sister didn't precisely exert herself to converse with him very often, either.'

'Mmm...I have frequently remarked upon it that dear Constance is not altogether wise on occasions,' Philip responded, as he began to guide Beth along one of the paths that led back to the terrace. 'There's some excuse for the vicar and his spouse, I suppose. They're good people, but the Reverend Mr Chadwick wouldn't wish to offend the more influential part of his congregation by becoming too friendly with someone who was considered a bastard by the vast majority of the polite world for the first two decades of his life.'

'Great heavens!' He had captured her full attention, and it clearly showed. 'I was wondering throughout dinner why it was I couldn't remember old Eustace Bathurst ever mentioning he had a nephew. Not that I ever knew the old curmudgeon very well, of course.' She frowned suddenly. 'But surely he must have acknowledged him at some point, otherwise why did he leave his property, not to mention all his wealth, to his nephew?'

'Poor old Eustace had been in an unenviable position,' Philip began to explain. 'I discovered from Uncle Waldo that not only was Eustace's brother a key player in the scandal that took place almost four decades ago, Eustace himself was on friendly terms with the sixth Viscount Litton who, incidentally, remained until his death Charles's mother's legal spouse. It appeared not to trouble Eustace a whit that his friend the Viscount, when in his cups, wasn't above beating his young bride unmercifully for the slightest misdemeanour. Like so many others, Eustace considered it a wife's lot to put up with a husband's—er—peccadilloes'

Disgusted, but intrigued, Beth demanded to be told more.

'It was after she had suffered a particularly vicious beating, that the young Viscountess was attended by the newly qualified Dr Cedric Bathurst. They fell in love, and as soon as the Viscountess was restored to health they ran away to live under assumed names as man and wife. Some few years later the Viscount succeeded in locating his errant wife's whereabouts. Charles had been born by that time, but even so the Viscount flatly refused to grant his wife a divorce, and made life so difficult for the couple that they were forced to flee yet again. Eustace had no contact with his brother at all during this period. In fact, it wasn't until after the Viscount's death, some fifteen years later, when Cedric had been able to marry the mother of his child, and had set up a very successful practice in Northamptonshire, that contact between the Bathurst brothers finally resumed. But even so mud sticks, and there are those still unwilling to recognise Charles Bathurst as his father's legitimate offspring and the rightful heir to Eustace Bathurst's fortune.'

Once again Philip found himself the recipient of an assessing blue-eyed gaze. 'But you are not of their number, I fancy.'

'Assuredly not!' he concurred. 'But sadly there are those in these parts unwilling to offer him the hand of friendship. I am hoping he can rely on your support?'

'That must rate as the worst insult you have offered me thus far!' she returned sharply, her dark brows having risen in feigned hauteur. 'Really, Philip, I'm astonished you felt the need to ask!'

For answer he gave a bark of appreciative laughter. Then, before she was able to do anything to avoid it, he entwined her arm securely round his and returned to the house to rejoin his other guests.

Chapter Three

Early the following week, while alone in the front parlour busily dealing with household accounts, Beth was informed that Sir Philip Staveley's sister had called. A few moments later the lady herself swept unaccompanied into the room, appearing, it had to be said, slightly put out.

'What a—er—very singular manservant you keep, Bethany, my dear,' she began, after accepting the invitation to seat herself in one of the comfortable chairs by the hearth. 'His odd manner gives one every reason to suppose that he isn't solely an indoor servant.'

'Rudge's coat buttons over many duties, Constance,' Beth confirmed, all at once realising what must have given rise to her unexpected visitor's odd expression when first entering the room. 'Although I wouldn't be without him for the world, even I must admit he lacks the natural aplomb and social graces of an experienced butler.'

She smiled wickedly as a thought suddenly occurred to her. 'Perhaps, if I'm feeling particularly vindictive one day, I might persuade your brother to have Rudge up at the Court for a spell so that he might pick up a few pointers from the very estimable Stebbings.'

As the teasing had clearly been wasted on her guest, who appeared quite nonplussed, Beth didn't attempt to explain she had been merely jesting. Instead, she glided smoothly across the room in order to provide her visitor with some refreshment.

'Would I be correct in assuming you imbibe the same revolting concoction as my good friend Ann?' she asked, holding up a certain decanter containing a clear liqueur flavoured with almonds.

'What...? Oh, yes, yes. A glass of ratafia would be most welcome.'

'Each to her own,' Beth murmured, providing herself with a glass of burgundy, before joining her guest over by the hearth.

'Is Mrs Stride not to join us?' Lady Chalford asked after gazing about the room in a decidedly vague manner. 'Such a charming woman, not in the least ingratiating. Yet, at the same time, one gains the distinct impression she's quite accustomed to socialising with those more fortunately circumstanced than herself.'

Although in her formative years she had been far better acquainted with Sir Philip than his sister, Beth knew Constance well enough to be sure that she was not in the least malicious by nature. There was no denying, though, there was a wide streak of quaint snobbery running through her, which had a tendency to surface from time to time.

Consequently, although she had no intention in taking up the cudgels on her friend's behalf, Beth was not slow to reveal, 'If I were to tell you that her maiden name was Carrington, and that she is closely related to the branch of that family owning many acres of Gloucestershire countryside, you'll perhaps appreciate why she's not overawed in polite company.'

Quickly realising she had captured her guest's full attention by what she had thus far revealed, Beth was happy to divulge more in the hope that it might pave Ann's smooth introduction into local society.

'It is true that her father, like my own, was a younger son, and therefore was obliged to make his own way in the world. He joined the church, and ended his days as a well-respected, if not particularly affluent, clergyman. Needless to say, Ann too was obliged to earn her own living at a young age, and thanks to both her parents' efforts received a well-rounded education. She eventually attained a post as governess with a family in Hampshire, where she met and subsequently married Major John Stride, who owned a modest property in the county.

'When he went out to Portugal with his regiment, Ann was happy to accompany him. Sadly he lost his life at Talavera. It was around that time I arrived on the scene.'

Lady Chalford gave a sudden start. 'Why, yes! I clearly recall darling Philip mentioning something about that only the other day—said something about wondering whether Colonel Ashworth had sent for you at all. My brother seemed to suppose it had been entirely your own decision to join your father out there.'

Beth attempted to hide neither her surprise nor her grudging respect. 'Well, well, well! The clever devil! I wonder how he managed to deduce that.'

'It is true, then?' Lady Chalford prompted, after watching closely as Beth, her expression revealing absolutely nothing at all, merely turned her head to stare intently at the logs smouldering nicely in the grate.

'Oh, yes, it's true, right enough,' she admitted at

length. 'Very few people know it, however. I don't think even Ann was ever officially informed, though she might have guessed, of course.'

Raising one hand, she waved it in a dismissive gesture. 'Still, we digress. Getting back to dear Ann's history—her husband was with Wellesley in India, and the, now, Duke of Wellington thought well of him. Needless to say, even though she was my paid companion, she was treated with respect by the vast majority of the more discerning officers. She most always partook of meals with Papa and myself and, in consequence, has rubbed shoulders with a great many younger sons of the aristocracy. Little wonder, then, that she isn't in the least diffident when in polite company.'

'Indeed, no,' Lady Chalford agreed, frowning slightly. 'But I still think it strange that she agreed to be your paid companion when she might have returned to her house in Hampshire, and lived a genteel existence in her late husband's home.'

'You say that because you don't know Ann very well,' Beth told her bluntly. 'Her husband, although a serving officer, was by no means a wealthy man, and did not leave his widow so very comfortably circumstanced. Besides which, the house is leased until the end of the year, and is presently occupied by a practitioner and his family. We've never discussed it, but I doubt very much whether Ann would wish to return there. Engaging in some genteel occupation for a few hours each week in order to enjoy a luxury or two wouldn't suit her at all. She is both energetic and resourceful.'

Raising her head, Beth stared at the wall behind her visitor's head, her mind's eye easily conjuring up images from the past, the vast majority of which were not so very pleasant.

'Having no desire to offend your sensibilities, ma'am, I shall say only this—my friend and I suffered hardship out there in the Peninsula. We witnessed many happenings to which any gently bred female would not normally be subjected. That said, I believe my years with the army were the making of me. Had I remained here in England, I would undoubtedly have eventually been coerced into marriage, more than likely a loveless union, and would by now be heartily bored with my lot.'

Lady Chalford's expression was all at once one of both shock and disapproval. 'But, my dear! It's every young woman's ambition, surely, to achieve a suitable match, and become a wife and mother?'

'Not mine, it isn't!' Beth returned bluntly. 'I might have thought differently at one time. Thank the Lord I've more sense now!'

Easily recognising the signs of mortification her plain speaking had aroused, Beth changed the subject entirely by asking her visitor if her call was merely social or whether there was a specific reason for the visit.

'As a matter of fact, I did wish to consult with you on a particular matter,' Lady Chalford admitted, after once again appearing slightly taken aback by the younger woman's blunt way of expressing herself. 'And so pleased to have this opportunity to speak with you in private.' She shot a quick glance across at the door. 'Are we likely to be disturbed, do you suppose?'

'Only by Rudge, if he takes it into his head to bring in more logs. But don't be alarmed. Despite his blunt manner, he's remarkably discreet,' Beth assured her. 'And Ann isn't likely to return much before luncheon. It just so happens the vicar's wife, having somehow discovered Ann was the daughter of a clergyman, approached her on the evening of your dinner party, and asked if she would kindly assist in helping to distribute clothes to the needy in the parish.' Beth cast a brief look at the plasterwork ceiling above her head. 'And she agreed, more fool her!'

'Well, it just so happens that that is what I wish to consult with you about.'

It was Beth's turn to be slightly startled, and she stared at her visitor in no little amazement over the rim of her glass for a second or two before fortifying herself from its contents. 'You wish to discuss the vicar's wife importuning Ann?'

'Oh, no, no! You misunderstand me, my dear. It was mention of the dinner party that jogged my memory. You see, I wanted to ask you about Philip. I couldn't help but notice you and he spent some little time together quite privately in the garden during the evening.'

Once again Beth was at a loss to understand what her visitor was attempting to convey. Disapproval, perhaps? 'What of it?'

'Well, I was wondering, you see, what you thought of him—his manner towards you, I mean?'

Just a ray of enlightenment at last began to dawn. 'Damnably insulting, if you must know!' Beth returned, at her most plainspoken. 'Had the crass impudence to accuse me of once having behaved like a simpering idiot, would you believe!' A vindictive glimmer all at once added an extra brilliance to her striking eyes. 'And I shan't forget it in a hurry, either, I can tell you!'

Lady Chalford gurgled with mirth. 'You jest, wicked girl! Philip is ever the gentleman in mixed company.'

'Ha! Much you know!' Beth scoffed, but then relented when her visitor appeared slightly put out by the slur on the Baronet's character. 'Well, I suppose he's your brother, so you're bound to think the best of him.'

'Oh, I do. I do,' she was speedily assured. 'And I'm so very concerned about him too.' A moment's pause, then, 'Do you find him much altered?'

'Well, naturally I do!' Beth returned in a trice, thinking the question faintly absurd. 'We've all changed in more than half a decade. The passage of time is kind to so very few.'

'Quite!' Lady Chalford acknowledged, frowning. 'But I was thinking not so much of physical differences as changes in his character, his manner. He has become so withdrawn, so insular since…since poor Eugenie's demise. Oh, I know he puts a brave face on it when in public, poor boy. But I have seen him, Bethany…have come upon him on several occasions since my arrival at the Court, just sitting there, studying the miniature of his late fiancée, which he keeps in the desk in his library. He always looks so forlorn, so lost, just staring down at the only remembrance he has of that lovely, lovely girl. But whenever I've attempted to console him, he sets me at a distance, and is distinctly aloof. I hardly dare mention Eugenie's name for fear of upsetting him, and on the rare occasion I do he invariably changes the subject.'

'How odd!' Beth was genuinely perplexed as she recalled Philip discussing Eugenie quite openly with her on the evening of the dinner party, and surprisingly betraying little emotion whatsoever. Perhaps, though, it wasn't sympathy he sought. Furthermore, he had never been one to wear his heart on his sleeve, she reminded herself.

'Your brother was ever the private man, preferring to keep his own counsel for the most part, at least in his private concerns. He wouldn't willingly betray his emotions in public, even in front of you, Constance. I do not doubt, though, he has suffered much over the loss of Eugenie.'

'Oh, he has!' Lady Chalford wholeheartedly agreed, taking a moment to dab at her eyes with the wisp of fine lawn swiftly extracted from her reticule. 'He has never so much as looked at another female since the tragedy occurred.' She coloured slightly. 'At least, he has taken little notice of any female who would make him a suitable wife...not until, that is, this past Season.'

All at once Lady Chalford brightened, betraying more liveliness of spirit than Beth had ever witnessed in her before. 'I do not know if you are aware of it, but your cousin Phoebe was brought out in the spring. And although, perhaps, not the instant success her eldest sister once was, she wasn't without certain admirers. Even Philip paid her no little attention. Hardly surprising, though, really. She bears a striking resemblance to Eugenie.'

'Really?' Beth said, mildly interested. 'The last time I saw Phoebe she didn't resemble her eldest sister very much at all. Quite the little brown mouse, in fact! But that was some years ago, now I come to think about it.'

'Then you are in for a surprise, my dear, for she does so now, as you'll discover for yourself next month. Your aunt and cousin are to attend Philip's birthday celebration, and are to put up at the Court for a few days. And that is where I am hoping I might count on your support.'

All at once alarm bells began to sound in Beth's head. 'How do you mean—count on my support? For what, precisely, may I ask?'

'In helping Philip see a little more of Phoebe by, perhaps, generously inviting your cousin and aunt to stay here, enabling them to extend their sojourn in the county.'

'Absolutely not! I shall not be made a convenience of a second time!' Beth could see at a glance that she had shocked her visitor by the vehemence of her refusal. Nevertheless, she had no intention of changing her mind.

'I'm sorry, ma'am, but it's simply out of the question. And you'll forgive my saying so, but I don't suppose for a moment Philip would thank you for interfering in his personal concerns. He certainly wouldn't appreciate me doing so, especially as we no longer share that close bond of friendship we once enjoyed. Furthermore, since I chose the Peninsula in preference to staying with her, the affection in which my aunt once held me has lessened considerably, if the letters I've received in recent years are anything to go by. If, however, she is now prepared to let bygones be bygones, and voices a desire to stay with me here at the Grange, then I shall be only too happy to invite her…next year, when I hope to have the entire house in good order.'

And with that Lady Chalford was forced to be satisfied.

Ann, returning in good time for luncheon, discovered her young mistress seated at the escritoire in the parlour precisely where she had left her some two hours earlier. The accounts book was opened at the exact same page, with few entries having been set down. The neatly stacked pile of bills by the slender right hand, did not appear to have decreased by very much, and there was clear evidence of a troubled frown lurking between the striking azure eyes.

'What is it, Beth dear? Are you feeling slightly put out not having accomplished your accounts this morning? Would you like me to leave you in peace to finish the task?'

So deep in thought had she been that Beth had hardly been aware of the fact that someone had entered the room. As always, though, the soft, understanding tones, successfully breaking through her reverie, had had an immediate calming effect upon her troubled spirits, at least up to a point.

'It's true I haven't done as much as I might have wished, but that's the fault of my unexpected visitor, Ann,' she informed her. 'All the same, I don't wish to be left alone. Come, let's sit by the fire for a spell, and you can tell me all about your morning and the interesting snippets you've managed to pick up at the vicarage.'

Ann frankly laughed, because she knew well enough that Bethany, being somewhat unorthodox in behaviour, neither indulged in gossip nor paid much heed to it. Notwithstanding, there had been one or two curious pieces of information discovered that morning that Ann thought might be of interest to her unconventional employer. Consequently she had no reluctance in revealing the disturbing fact that instances of robbery in the area had increased dramatically in recent months.

'Mrs Chadwick also said that even two or three of the larger houses in the village had been broken into in recent weeks. And, by all accounts, it's much worse in the local town, where men hang about on street corners, behaving in a distinctly offensive manner to those more happily circumstanced.'

Beth wasn't unduly surprised to learn this. 'It's only to be expected. Now the war with France is blessedly over, there are too many looking for too few jobs. The unrest will continue, and get very much worse while men are unable to support themselves, let alone feed their families.'

Ann nodded in agreement before she bethought herself of something else she had discovered that day. 'Are you by any chance acquainted with someone by the name of Napier? Mrs Chadwick seemed to suppose you were. Seemingly he's a close friend of their son, and has been a frequent visitor at the vicarage in recent years. Said something about him heralding from Surrey, and living quite close to Lord and Lady Barfield,' she continued, when Beth had merely frowned.

'Oh, you must be referring to young Crispin Napier,' she responded, after giving the matter more thought, and then shook her head. 'I haven't seen him since he was a boy. He must be in his early twenties by now.'

'That's right,' Ann readily confirmed. 'I've discovered he and the vicar's only son were at some school together, and have remained friends ever since. Apparently, Mr Napier is returning here next month for Sir Philip's birthday celebration. Which I find most strange in the circumstances.' She shook her head, clearly perplexed. 'Mrs Chadwick divulged something that gave me every reason to suppose that young Mr Napier, for some reason, isn't too fond of the Baronet. Apparently Sir Philip organised a shooting party soon after his return from London earlier in the summer, and invited a great many of his neighbours, including the Reverend and Mrs Chadwick's son and Mr Napier, who happened to be staying at the vicarage at the time. Seemingly Mr Napier wasn't too eager to join the party, and only did so to bear his friend company. So why do you suppose he was so keen to accept the invitation to attend the birthday celebration if he truly isn't so very fond of Sir Philip?'

'Seems odd, certainly, but I suppose young Crispin has his reasons. Furthermore, I expect Lady Chalford was responsible for issuing the invitation, and I cannot imagine he holds a grudge against her,' Beth responded, before she bethought herself of something else. 'And talking of Lady Chalford... It was she who paid me a visit this morning, and whilst here gave me every reason to suppose that her brother knew, or at least strongly suspected, that it was indeed my decision to join Papa in the Peninsula, and not he who sent for me.' Beth paused for a moment to search her friend's face. 'It must surely have been you who told him.'

If Ann was startled by the blunt accusation, she betrayed no sign of it. If anything, she appeared slightly bewildered. 'I might have done so,' she acknowledged. 'But I honestly cannot recall.' All at once her expression betrayed slight concern. 'Does it matter? Would you have preferred him not to have known?'

'To be perfectly frank...yes,' Beth admitted, having quickly decided it would serve no purpose to lie. 'It doesn't redound to my credit, you see, the way I behaved back then...the bitter resentment I felt towards him and Eugenie. Naturally, I should prefer that he never discovers anything about my feelings at that time. It's all water under the bridge now, after all.'

She looked up to discover herself being regarded intently, and felt obliged to force a smile, feigning unconcern. 'Not that I need trouble myself unduly about it. Philip might be as sharp as a tack, but it's unlikely I shall find myself in his company so frequently that I might inadvertently relax my guard and reveal my—er—once, less than charitable feelings towards him.'

Two days later, whilst visiting the local market town, Beth was obliged silently to own that she might have been a trifle optimistic in her predictions, when she espied none other than her most influential neighbour sauntering along the main street towards her. In an instant she accepted that it was too late to avoid the chance encounter. Furthermore, she wasn't so very sure she even wished to try, as he was accompanied by none other than Mr Charles Bathurst, a gentleman who had left a very favourable impression upon a certain discerning female, judging by the number of times his name had been raised in conversation since the evening of the dinner party at Staveley Court.

Beth chanced to glance sideways in time to catch a becoming hue rise in her companion's cheeks the instance Ann observed precisely who it was approaching.

'Here to replenish stocks?' Beth asked, instantly drawing both gentlemen's attention, thereby allowing her surprisingly flustered companion a little time in which to regain her poise. 'Or merely enjoying the bustle and atmosphere of a Markham market day?'

'Both,' Sir Philip revealed, his gaze fixed on the young lady whom he considered appeared particularly becoming that fine morning in a dashing bonnet trimmed with blue ribbon. 'Bathurst is here to cast an eye over a few beasts. I'm here, as you so rightly surmised, merely to soak up the atmosphere. I love market days…always have.'

Beth's smile faded very slightly. 'Yes, I remember. I frequently accompanied you here.'

It would have been at this juncture that she would have made some excuse to part company with the gentleman, had it not been for the fact that she was certain her dear companion felt no similar desire to go their separate ways. Consequently, Beth disregarded her own feelings, and asked the gentlemen if they would be so obliging as to escort them back to where their carriage awaited them at the town's most popular inn.

Although she might have preferred it to be quite otherwise, Beth wasn't unduly surprised to find herself squired by Sir Philip, leaving Mr Bathurst to engage, if her expression was any indication, a highly contented widow in conversation a few feet behind.

'Without wishing to appear vulgarly curious,' Philip began, determined, himself, not to walk along in stony silence, 'might I be permitted to know what has brought you to town today?'

'A surfeit of nerves, I'm ashamed to say.'

'Now, that I simply cannot believe!' he countered, totally unconvinced.

'Well, let us say a desire to take some necessary precautions prompted the visit,' Beth confessed. 'I wanted half a dozen hens. So I thought to get a couple of geese at the same time. I've been reliably informed, you see, that there have been one or two burglaries taking place in the village in recent weeks,' she added, staring across the street at where a small group of men just happened to be loitering by a low wall.

'Very wise,' he said, following the direction of her gaze, and frowning slightly as he focused his attention on one lean, unkempt man in particular. 'But wouldn't a dog serve the purpose better? You could keep it close by, in the house, if you chose.'

'True. But I haven't heard of any new litters being born in the neighbourhood. And I should want a pup,' Beth answered, glancing up at him and catching his frowning scrutiny. 'What is it, Philip? Do you recognise one of them?'

'I'm not sure. But one does seem vaguely familiar, though I cannot for the life of me imagine why he should be. He certainly doesn't work for me.'

'Funny you should say that, because I thought I'd

seen the short one, with the limp and mousy-coloured hair, somewhere before.' Frowning, Beth shook her head. 'If he's a native of these parts I cannot imagine where I might have come across him. More than likely, though, he's a survivor of the Peninsular Campaign. Trouble is, I nursed so many out there I have difficulty remembering each individual.'

'You nursed the wounded? Good gad!'

Philip had been unable to keep both surprise and dis-approval from creeping in to his voice, which instantly earned him a flashing look of mingled reproach and anger.

'What did you suppose I did out there, Philip?' she demanded to know, the perfect shape of her mouth marred by a contemptuous curl of the upper lip. 'Did you imagine me just sitting there beneath the shading branches of some exotic tree, fanning myself like a sim-pering idiot, while ignoring the blood bath that was each and every battle? Do you suppose I remained oblivious to all those whom the surgeons considered too badly injured to warrant attention? Do you suppose I gave a damn about my reputation when a life might be saved...? How little you know me!'

He felt hurt, and not just a little annoyed as well, by the derision so clearly discernible in her voice. Yet before he could formulate a response, Beth's attention had already been captured by another man, hailing her from the forecourt of the While Hart Inn. He then found himself on the receiving end of a prolonged stare that was no less insultingly assessing, though a deal less sinisterly threatening, than the one he'd received a few minutes earlier from the tallest of the loiterers in the street.

'Ah, Rudge! Were you successful in your endea-vours? Please tell me you were.'

'Aye, Miss Beth,' he answered, his expression softening noticeably. 'Half-a-dozen prime layers, if I'm any judge. The farmer's going to drop 'em off on 'is way 'ome from market later today, with a couple o' geese. Not that I don't think you'd be better off with a cur.'

Blue eyes began to twinkle with an impish gleam of bygone years. 'It might surprise you to know, Rudge, that you and Sir Philip, here, are as one in that belief.'

'Well, I never! Who'd 'ave thought I'd ever 'ave something in common with a nob,' Rudge responded, appearing anything but gratified.

Neither, it had to be said, was Sir Philip, who considered the servant insolent in the extreme, and in urgent need of being reminded of his place. All the same, he was in no danger of losing his temper, and when in the next moment Charles Bathurst captured his attention by inviting him and the ladies to dine at his home the following week, his annoyance was quickly forgotten.

That evening, however, while mulling over what had turned out to be on the whole a most unsatisfactory day, Philip could only wonder at himself for becoming so irritated over such a trivial matter as a servant's lack of deference. Finally, after quietly considering the matter, he was obliged to acknowledge what had truly annoyed him. It hadn't been Rudge's lack of respect so much as his mistress's behaviour a matter of moments before that had really stirred his ire.

He sought solace in the contents of the glass by his elbow, finishing half of it before forcing himself to acknowledge, too, that Beth's attitude towards him since her return was increasingly beginning to both hurt and annoy him in equal measures.

Yet how on earth did he expect her to behave? She was no longer the adoring little companion, willing to cling to his every word in the staunch belief that he could say and do no wrong. She was a young woman with a mind of her own. Moreover, unless he was much mistaken, she was a young woman who had witnessed, first hand, the very worst traits of mankind. Little wonder, then, that her time out in the Peninsula had changed her, made her perhaps a deal more cynical in her outlook, he reasoned.

But that still didn't account for her attitude towards him now. He had already gained the distinct impression that she was determined to keep him at a distance whenever possible. What was worse, he could almost feel a resentment in her towards him that bordered on dislike... But why? What had he ever done to engender these almost hostile emotions in her? And why should he suddenly feel so determined to eradicate those negative feelings completely, and regain that special place he had once held in her affections?

The door opening brought a temporary cessation to his troubled musings, and he raised his eyes to see his sister framed in the doorway. One glance was sufficient to convince him that she was doubtful about entering his private sanctum and disturbing him on an evening when he had not been the best of company, leaving her entirely to her own devices once dinner had ended.

Prompted by a guilty conscience, he bade her enter and join him by the hearth, even though he would have much preferred to be left alone with his troubling thoughts.

'I've been poor company today, neglecting you so. Can I tempt you to join me in a night-cap...? A glass of wine, perhaps?'

'No, I thank you, Brother,' she answered, though

readily accepting his invitation to seat herself opposite. 'I merely wished to ask if there's anyone else you wish to invite to the party? I've already sent out most all the invitations, and have received quite a number of replies already. But I was just wondering if there was perhaps someone else you might have forgotten?'

'No, I don't think so. I did glance through your list, remember?' He checked for a moment before raising his glass once again to his lips. 'You haven't forgotten to send Beth and her companion a formal invitation, I trust?'

'No, and I feel quite annoyed with myself. As it happens, I could have taken it over with me the other day when I paid a visit. But it quite slipped my mind. I must remember to send it tomorrow.'

'You didn't mention you'd paid a visit to the Grange, Connie,' he remarked casually, and saw at a glance that for some reason she didn't seem able to meet his gaze.

'Didn't I?' she returned, plucking at the folds of her skirt. 'Must have slipped my mind. You know what a scatterbrain I can be on occasions.'

He knew nothing of the sort. Although his sister could never have been described as a bluestocking, she was neither downright hen-witted nor forgetful. All the same he decided not to pursue the topic as it was evidently causing her some embarrassment, and asked, instead, if she considered Beth had altered very much over the years.

'Why, yes! I do, as it happens,' she answered. 'In looks she's much improved, a most attractive young woman, I should say, if a trifle on the slender side.' All at once she looked primly disapproving. 'I do think she's grown quite hard, though, Philip. Quite unbecomingly so, in my opinion! I asked her to do me the tiniest little favour, and she virtually snapped my nose off.'

Intrigued though he was, he had to delve deep into his reserves of self-control to stop himself laughing at his sister's rare show of pique. 'Don't worry, Connie, I shall take her roundly to task the very next time I see her for daring to ruffle your feathers so.'

'Oh, for heaven's sake, Philip, please don't do that!' she implored, having clearly taken her brother's mock-threat quite seriously. 'I could see on the night of the dinner party, when you returned after your stroll in the garden, how well you two still get on. You appeared so blissfully content in each other's company after your walk round the garden. I should hate to be the one to cause a rift between you. Besides, which,' she added, little realising that an arresting look had flickered briefly in her brother's eyes at mention of that particular interlude with Bethany, 'she had every right to refuse to invite her aunt and cousin to stay with her.'

After forcing his mind back to the present in order to digest everything his sister was revealing, Philip suddenly experienced the gravest misgivings. 'Pray enlighten me, Sister, as to why you should have wished Beth to invite her aunt and cousin to stay?'

No explanation was forthcoming. Furthermore, Constance seemed unwilling to meet his gaze once again, which only succeeded in arousing his suspicions even further. 'You would not, by any chance, be so foolish as to attempt to indulge in a spot of matchmaking where the youngest Miss Barfield is concerned?'

'Oh, but, Philip, you cannot pretend you don't like her. You paid her such attention during the Season,' she reminded him, meeting his gaze, if only briefly. 'She's such a sweet child, and so like Eugenie.'

Only by exerting a deal of control did Philip stop himself from indulging in a rare show of ill humour. But even so his sister was left in no doubt that he would brook any interference in his personal concerns.

'Even if Phoebe Barfield was the very image of her dead sister, which she most certainly is not, I would still never consider making an offer for her hand. And I sincerely trust, Constance, that you have never given the child, or her mother, for that matter, any reason to suppose that I might.'

The softness of his tone was a threat in itself, and resulted in only emphasising his evident displeasure. 'Of course I wouldn't dream of offering any encouragement to Lady Henrietta,' his sister responded, at last raising her eyes to meet his. 'It was just that I hoped… Oh, dear,' she continued, her voice betraying a slight tremor now. 'Bethany said you wouldn't appreciate any interference in your personal concerns.'

This succeeded in diverting his thoughts. 'Said that, did she…?' He was impressed. 'Evidently she's grown into a perceptive little minx.'

'Maybe,' Lady Chalford grudgingly acknowledged. 'But that wasn't why she refused. Said she wouldn't be made a convenience of again. Though what in the world she meant by such a thing is anybody's guess.'

'How very interesting,' Philip murmured, studying the remaining contents of his glass with narrowed, assessing eyes. 'Yes, most interesting.'

Chapter Four

Irritability, borne of a guilty conscience, had continued to plague Beth long after her return from the market town. A good night's sleep, followed by a morning ride across landscape bathed in pleasant late September sunshine, did little to lift her spirits. Not even her decision to take her manservant roundly to task for his impertinence towards their illustrious neighbour resulted in a lessening of her ill humour. In fact, the opposite turned out to be the case.

She eyed him with misgiving, as they turned their mounts into the driveway at the Grange. 'What do you mean…it was a kind of test?' she demanded to know.

'Just that, Miss Beth. Were judging 'is mettle, as yer might say.'

'Judging his…?' Beth raised her eyes heavenwards. The divine guidance for which she might have hoped, however, sadly did not manifest itself, and she was left having to accept that her trusted servant's somewhat unorthodox behaviour was a problem she must attempt to deal with alone.

'Rudge, you simply cannot go about being deliber-

ately discourteous to people with whom I am well acquainted,' she began, determined not to allow her affection for the man riding alongside lessen her resolve to
reprimand him. 'Especially not to such well-respected
peers of the realm as Sir Philip Staveley.'

'Well, he's still a man, ain't he?' he responded, appearing anything but chastened by the reproof.

'And what has that to say to anything, pray?' Beth
demanded, surprised by the response.

'Why, everything, as you're a woman, Miss Beth.
And a damnably 'andsome little filly, to boot! Which
only makes things worse, if yer follow my meaning.'

Once again Beth found herself momentarily lost for
words when she realised precisely what the devoted servant was insinuating. 'Rudge, you are labouring under
a misapprehension. Sir Philip isn't interested in me….at
least, not in the way you seem to suppose.'

Judging by his expression, the assurance had left
him totally unconvinced. 'Didn't look that way t'me,'
he countered, sniffing loudly. 'Mighty smitten, I should
say. Noticed a certain twinkle in 'is eye, so I did, when
he were looking at you. But as long as 'is intentions be
'onourable, all well and good.'

'Believe me, you could not be more wrong. Sir
Philip and I have been close friends for years. Were
close friends,' she amended, her voice annoyingly
impaired by a sudden obstruction in her throat. She
swallowed hard, determined to conquer the unexpected moment of weakness. 'He—he evidently still
holds me in some little affection. But that is all, I
assure you.'

'If you say so, miss,' he responded, evidently still
highly sceptical. 'I'll say this for yer nob friend,
though—reckon he'd 'ave made a reet fine officer. We

could 'ave done with a deal more of 'is stamp out there in Spain, I'm thinking.'

As Rudge had held so very few officers in high esteem, this was praise indeed. All the same, Beth refrained from attempting to discover just why Sir Philip had surprisingly risen in her servant's estimation. The conversation with him had unexpectedly unlocked bittersweet memories that had been successfully confined for so many years, and she craved solitude, to be alone with her thoughts.

Leaving her mount in Rudge's very capable hands, she rushed into the house, not so much as pausing for breath until she had reached the blessed solitude of her bedchamber. The window offered a splendid view of the extensive rear garden. Unfortunately it wasn't the clear evidence of improvements already made to several flower beds she saw, but flashing images from bygone years that filled her with such shame and bitter regrets that it was a relief when a young maid entered the room, thereby unwittingly breaking the painful mental connection with the past.

'Sorry to disturb you, ma'am,' she began, remaining diffidently in the doorway. 'Mrs Stride said as how she thought she'd heard you return, and I was wondering if there was anything you needed, or maybe you wished me to help you change out of your habit?'

'Yes, thank you, Meg. Come in and close the door.'

Beth had been very well pleased with the two village girls that Rudge had hired in order to help get the house into some kind of order before her own arrival. Meg's elder sister Amy was proving extremely helpful about the house, most especially in the kitchen, where she was beginning to display real flair as a cook; while Meg herself was betraying every sign of becoming a highly proficient personal maid, showing particular skill when dressing hair.

Beth had had no hesitation in offering both sisters permanent positions, and they had quickly settled into a routine that was resulting in a smoothly run household.

'Oh, I almost forgot, miss,' Meg announced, delving into the pocket of her apron to draw out a letter the instant she had helped her young mistress to change into a most becoming turquoise-coloured day dress. 'This came for you this morning.'

Beth recognised those bold sloping characters in a trice, and knew it had come from the Court, even before she had broken the seal to discover a gilt-edged invitation card bearing both her own and Ann's name tucked inside the letter penned by Sir Philip himself.

After reading it through quickly, she consigned it, together with the card, to the safety of her own pocket, and then took up her former stance by the window.

Although her mind had once again wandered back over the years, she was conscious still of what was taking place around her. She knew the precise moment when Meg had left the room, and was aware, too, when the door softly opened again a few minutes later, and her companion entered.

'Are you all right, dear?' Concern was discernible in Ann's voice. 'I thought you seemed a little subdued at breakfast, and when you didn't join me in the parlour after your ride, I thought perhaps you might be feeling a trifle unwell?'

Beth might not have been in the most convivial of moods, but she could not resist smiling at this. She turned her head briefly in order to slant the older woman a mocking glance. 'Have you ever known me succumb to trifling ailments?'

'Well, no,' Ann was obliged to concede. 'But I don't think you've been quite yourself since our return from Markham yesterday.'

Once again Beth couldn't resist a wry smile. 'My dear, I haven't been myself for a deal longer than that, believe me. And I've decided it's high time I grew up, and stopped behaving like a thwarted, spoilt child, and learned to appreciate what I've always had, and blessedly could still have now, providing I'm willing to put the past well and truly behind me.'

She turned her head again in time to catch her friend's bewildered expression. 'Oh, don't mind me,' she added. 'I'm merely on the verge of recovering from years of being blue-devilled. Was there some reason you particularly wished to see me?'

For a moment or two it seemed Ann was in two minds, not knowing whether to remain or make an excuse to leave. Then she said, 'Well, yes, but it's nothing of real importance. It's just that I was wondering whether you considered my gown of lavender silk appropriate to wear to Mr Bathurst's dinner party on Friday evening? It's not one of my best, I know. But I thought if I trimmed the bodice and sleeves with lace it would serve very well.'

'You don't need my advice on such matters,' Beth returned bluntly. 'Your taste is second to none. But have a care.' she added, after staring sombrely across the room in silence. 'We are sometimes guilty of imagining things that simply are not real…that could never possibly become a reality.'

Ann visibly stiffened. 'Is that meant as a warning to remember my place—that I should accept that I have been invited to the dinner party solely as your companion?'

'Not at all. Merely advice,' Beth assured her, turning

again to stare out of the window. 'We cannot always
attain what we most desire in life… And because of it,
we sometimes fail to appreciate fully just what is being
offered,' she added, sharing some of her earlier
thoughts.

The following morning, just as he was about to set
out for a meeting with his steward, Sir Philip was presented with a note by his butler. Unlike Beth, the day
before, he did not recognise the handwriting, and was
pleasantly surprised when he discovered the identity of
the sender.

When last he had seen a sample of Beth's handwriting it had been a rounded, childish scrawl, bearing little
resemblance to the elegantly sloping characters gracing
the page in his hand. Yet another example of how much
she had changed over the years. It was just a pity that
the response was not what he might have wished. All
the same, she seemed genuinely sorry that she had been
unable to accept his offer to travel with him and his
sister to Charles Bathurst's home on Friday evening, as
she had already promised to take the vicar and his wife
to the dinner party in her own carriage.

'Will there be any reply, sir?'

Philip was mildly surprised by the question. 'One
isn't required, Stebbings. Why do you ask?'

The butler sniffed loudly. 'Because the—er—person
who delivered the missive by hand, sir, said he would
be happy to linger in the stable-yard for a while should
you wish to exchange a word with him.'

'Oh, he did, did he?' Philip guessed at once the
identity of the messenger, who had clearly not impressed the Court's rigidly correct major-domo. 'Don't
worry, Stebbings, I'll deal with the matter personally!'

* * *

As expected, he found Amos Rudge in the stable-yard, running a hand over the mount Philip had ordered to be saddled that morning. 'So why are you loitering here, you impertinent rogue? Unless I'm much mistaken, you knew very well there'd be no reply.'

Amos Rudge's initial response was to bestow a cheeky grin upon the master of Staveley Court. 'Now, come on, gov'ner, no 'ard feelings, eh? We both want the same thing, after all. And it ain't easy keeping an eye on Miss Bethany, as I reckon you knows very well yourself. But I promised the old Colonel on 'is deathbed that I'd 'ave a care for 'is daughter, until such time as someone more suited to the task comes along, as yer might say.'

Philip had no reason to doubt the servant's loyalty, even though his manners left much to be desired. 'Well, see that you do your duty, you scoundrel, or you'll answer to me!'

'Bless you, sir! You're a downy one and no mistake!' Rudge's response clearly showed he had taken the threat in good part. 'Said to the mistress only t'other day, when she told me to mind my tongue when you're about, you'd 'ave made a reet fine officer. You keeps yourself in 'and, and don't bridle easy. Say something else for yer, gov'ner. You knows a thing or two about 'orseflesh.'

It was evident to Sir Philip that he was by no means the only one who knew his way round a horse. His favourite bay hack could be temperamental on occasions, and was never at his best with strangers. Yet the unconventional servant had clearly won the animal's trust.

'You're no stranger to horses, either, are you, Rudge?' Philip remarked, the servant having surprisingly risen in his estimation.

'Grew up wi' 'em, sir. M'dad were 'ead groomsman at a fine 'ouse in Derbyshire. I worked by 'is side as soon as I were old enough. Good days they were, sir. Then the old master ups and dies without warning, and the new owner brought in 'is own people, and turned my old dad and me out o' the cottage.'

There had been not a trace of bitterness in the servant's voice for the way he had been unfairly treated, merely sadness, and once again Philip experienced a further surge of grudging respect. 'So, what happened to you both?'

If Amos Rudge was surprised by the peer's show of interest, he betrayed no sign of it, as he divulged, 'Dad didn't last long afterwards, and I just drifted, doing odd jobs, not settling anywhere. Did things I'm not proud of, neither. Then I decides to take the King's shilling. Was wounded soon after my arrival in Portugal at Oporto. And that's when m'luck changed, as yer might say. While I were recovering from m'wounds, I were consigned to Colonel Ashworth, as 'is batman, like. We rubbed along together from the first, and so 'ee arranged things so that I stayed with 'im.'

The servant paused to rub his fingers back and forth across the bristles on his chin. 'Funny 'ow things turn out, sir. Never thought I'd end up serving a young lady.'

'And one who will no doubt be wondering what's become of you,' Philip returned, feeling guilty for keeping the man from his duties. 'Come, mount up and we'll ride along together. I'm meeting my steward over at the western boundary.'

Beth's party was the last to turn into the gateway leading to Mr Bathurst's home on Friday evening. She had neither planned it that way, nor did she hold herself in any way responsible for the tardiness of their arrival. In fact, had she wished to apportion blame, she could, with some justification, have pointed the finger of guilt in her companion's direction, for Ann Stride, behaving quite out of character, had been in a nervous, indecisive state for most of the day.

Firstly, she had been unable to make up her mind whether to wear the lavender-coloured gown, which had been beautifully adorned with lace trim across the bodice and sleeves, or a gown of amber silk, purchased in Paris earlier in the year. When finally she had accepted advice and made the selection, Beth had then inadvertently made the situation worse by suggesting that Meg be allowed to dress her companion's hair for the occasion, which had resulted in further time-wasting and indecisiveness about the style.

Beth shot a quick sideways glance at her companion, as the carriage at last pulled up at the front entrance of the fine country property. Silently she was forced to acknowledge that, maybe, all the fluster had not been in vain. Had it been Ann's ambition to look elegant, yet quietly refined, then she had succeeded wonderfully well. There was nothing about her to suggest that she was attempting to appear what she was not by aping those more fortunately circumstanced than herself. Beth could only hope that her dear friend would exert the same praiseworthy discretion over her emotions.

The truth of the matter was of course that, as yet, neither of them knew Charles Bathurst very well. On the surface he seemed the perfect gentleman, polite and dignified. He appeared genuinely wishful to further his acquaintance with Major Stride's attractive widow. Which would have been in no way remarkable, considering Ann was both quick-witted and charming. All the same, it was quite possible that, being new to the area, and knowing few people, he had included Mrs Stride as a dinner guest merely to make up numbers at his table, and for no other more personal reason.

As she alighted first from the carriage and led the way into a house that she had entered only once before in her life, Beth was prepared, at this stage, to keep an open mind where their host was concerned. Although he displayed real discretion by greeting each member of her party with equal warmth, he succeeded in surprising Beth somewhat by choosing to escort her personally in to dinner. She was even more surprised to find herself placed next to him at table. The biggest shock of all, however, came when a certain other lady seated herself very regally in the significant position at the opposite end of the table.

'Great heavens! How on earth did you manage to persuade Lady Chalford to act as your hostess?' Beth demanded, astonishment overriding discretion for a moment. 'Oh, I'm so sorry,' she apologised in the next breath, 'that was not very tactful of me.'

'Perhaps not,' he agreed, 'but beautifully candid.'

Beth decided in that moment that she liked Charles Bathurst very well, and could quite understand why her good friend had fallen victim so quickly to the large gentleman's dignified charm.

'I wouldn't be in the least surprised to discover that a brother's gentle persuasion might have had some bearing on the matter.' He cast her a decidedly lopsided grin. 'But I'm far too diplomatic to attempt to discover if my suspicion is correct.'

'You might be, but I'm not!' Beth returned bluntly, much to her host's intense amusement. His spontaneous rumble of laughter induced most everyone at the

table to stare in their direction, Sir Philip included, who
favoured them both with a brief, assessing look.

'I believe you and I have a mutual friend, Miss
Ashworth,' the host remarked, successfully capturing
her full attention once more, and she could see at a glance
there was not a trace of amusement left in his eyes.

'Several by now, I should imagine,' Beth returned,
looking at the various people enjoying the delicious dinner
with them, and surprisingly discovering a certain pair of
unsmiling grey eyes still staring fixedly in her direction.

'No one here, ma'am. I was referring to a certain
major in his Majesty's Army.'

After easily detecting the note of suppressed concern, Beth once again favoured the host with her undivided attention. 'I've rubbed shoulders with numerous
majors in recent years, sir. Which one are you referring
to in particular?'

'Major Darcy Wood.'

'Yes, I know him,' she acknowledged, following his
lead by speaking in a hushed tone that did not carry
very far.

'I know I should not ask this of you, Miss Ashworth.
But would you grant me a few moments in private,
later, when we might slip away unnoticed?'

Beth was far too intrigued to permit accepted codes
of conduct to prevent her from having her rampant curiosity satisfied, and readily agreed.

Having always been able to carry a tune, Beth wasn't
averse to taking her turn at the pianoforte later that
evening, and amused every gentleman present, and
several of the ladies too, it had to be said, by singing a
rather saucy ditty she'd learned whilst out in Spain. She
then rendered her place to Mrs Chadwick, and whilst

the vicar's wife was holding most everyone's attention by her peerless performance on the keys, Beth noticed the host attempting to catch her eye.

Instantly responding, she slipped quietly into the hall and accompanied him across to the library, where he didn't hesitate to close the door behind them, once they were safely inside the book-lined room.

'Do not be alarmed, Miss Ashworth. My intentions are entirely honourable, I promise you.'

'If I thought otherwise, I wouldn't be here,' she returned in her usual no-nonsense fashion, which instantly won her yet another appreciative smile.

All the same, Beth wasn't fooled. She had witnessed on more occasions than she cared to remember the suppressed tensions in men on the eve of battle. She could sense the anxiety in Charles Bathurst now, even before his forehead was creased by a troubled frown, as he took up a stance before the fire.

'Where to begin?' As he seemed to address the question more to himself, Beth offered no response. Then he asked, 'How much do you know about Darcy Wood?'

'He never spoke much about himself as far as I can remember,' Beth replied, with total honesty, for she could see no reason to lie. 'He always struck me as a very private man. One might almost say reclusive. Which is perhaps not so surprising, considering the duties he performed out in the Peninsula, the very dangerous work he undertook.'

Belatedly accepting his request to be seated, Beth chose the winged chair closest to the hearth, and to him. She felt not a whit alarmed to be in such close proximity. She experienced only concern to see him looking so obviously troubled as she said, 'You know, I suppose, that Major Wood was on Wellington's staff,

one of his Exploring Officers. One of the very best, in
fact…if not the best. He would be absent for weeks at
a time, more often than not riding alone deep into
enemy territory. He's an extraordinarily brave man. I
happen to know for a fact the Duke thought highly of
him, as did my own father, who undertook similar, invaluable work.'

He stared down at her intently, his gaze unwavering.
'But you know nothing more of him than that?'

'Nothing of his life before he arrived in the Peninsula,
no,' she confirmed, 'save that his mother was French,
and that she had taught him to speak the language like
a native. I gained the distinct impression he was extremely fond of his mother. What he felt about the other
members of his family, I have no notion. He never spoke
about them, as far as I can recall.' When he didn't attempt to respond, she asked the question foremost in her
mind, 'Is he in some kind of trouble? I never saw him
again, after we had crossed into France, and I did
wonder what had become of him, but nobody seemed
to know.'

'That much I can tell you,' he declared. 'He remained
in Spain. He was safe there.'

Beth was puzzled. 'Safe…? So he is in some kind
of trouble?'

For answer he brought his fist down hard on the
mantel-shelf, making her start. 'Yes, Miss Ashworth,
you might say that. You call him brave; I call him foolhardy. But he was ever so, confound him!'

His testiness was followed by a long sigh. 'Just over
a week ago I received a communication from him to say
he was back in this country. I cannot express how deeply
troubled I felt. I made a brief, overnight stay in the
capital, and did my best to persuade him to return to

Spain, but he wouldn't even consider it. Stubborn fool! Maintained he had responsibilities he must shoulder himself, and wouldn't hear of me attempting to deal with the matter on his behalf. But at least I managed to persuade him to delay his pressing business for a while and leave the capital as soon as may be and stay with me. I reasoned that he was less likely to be recognised down here…except, perhaps, by you, and Mrs Stride, of course, who have seen him in recent years.

'Whilst dining with him on the one night I spent in London, I happened to mention your name, as I knew you too had been in Spain,' he continued when Beth merely stared up at him, waiting patiently to learn more. 'I also mentioned that you had recently returned to your family home, and he said he looked forward to renewing his acquaintance with you, declaring you were someone he could trust.' He regarded her sombrely for a moment, before adding, 'I shall do my utmost to try to keep his presence under my roof a secret for as long as possible. But I'm nothing if not a realist, Miss Ashworth. My friend was ever reckless, careless of his own safety, even as a boy. You yourself know only too well the dangers he faced out there in the Peninsula, when he went off on one of his missions. Can you imagine a man like that tamely remaining hidden within these walls, even though he will be offered every inducement to do so?'

'No, sir, I cannot,' Beth answered truthfully, while subjecting him to one of her level, penetrating stares. 'And as yet I am at a loss to understand precisely why you should feel the need to keep him hidden from the outside world.'

'Because some eight years ago the man you know as Major Darcy Wood was accused of the most heinous crime and taken into custody. He subsequently escaped, and with my help fled to Ireland, where he remained safely hidden for three years, before going off to Spain.'

His gaze was no less probing than her own continued to remain. 'By telling you this I am placing my trust in you also, Miss Ashworth. But if you do not wish to involve yourself in this sad affair, I shall quite understand, and shall only beg you not to reveal what you have learned thus far, not even to your estimable companion.'

'Pray continue,' Beth prompted, and then watched as he transferred his gaze to some spot behind her head. His brow became deeply furrowed as though he was attempting to put his troubled thoughts into some kind of order, the smile of respect he had bestowed upon her moments before having disappeared completely.

'I've known the man you know as Darcy Wood since he was a boy. I'm several years his senior. None the less, he was one of the few who offered me the hand of friendship in my youth.' His smile this time was distinctly rueful. 'I believe Sir Philip has revealed my somewhat— er—unorthodox beginnings, Miss Ashworth. So I imagine you can appreciate just how much I valued the fellowship of someone of Darcy's standing.'

Beth raised her brows at this. Evidently Major Wood's position on the social ladder was far higher than she had supposed. She would have liked to know precisely who he was, but decided not to press for more information than Charles Bathurst was willing to reveal at the present time.

'My father's property in Northamptonshire was situated on the southernmost side of Darcy's home, adjacent to its boundary, in fact. So as you can imagine we saw a great deal of each other in our formative years. Even when I left the family home, and went to London to study law, Darcy frequently stayed with me whenever he visited the metropolis in preference to remaining in his family's town house. Which reveals clearly enough the relationship he had with other close members of his family.'

Beth nodded. 'Evidently not good.'

'That, my dear ma'am, is an understatement. It was common knowledge that he loathed his father and elder half-brother. So when they were found by the aged butler one morning, brutally murdered in a downstairs room, and Darcy was discovered in the room directly above, lying on top of the bed, covered in blood, and with a bloodstained sabre discarded only feet away, there were those quick to point the finger of guilt squarely in his direction.'

Beth almost found herself gaping. 'You do not mean to tell me he was seriously suspected of having committed the crime…? Why, it beggars belief! He might be reckless on occasions, but he's no fool. Had he murdered two members of his immediate family, he wouldn't have stayed around very long afterwards.'

'That was precisely my own thought at the time. Unfortunately there was a wealth of evidence against him,' Bathurst revealed. 'The butler overheard a fierce argument, which resulted in Darcy storming out of the house the evening before, just prior to a certain cousin arriving for dinner. The cousin confirmed there had been an atmosphere about the place, and that his uncle had been threatening to disinherit his younger son. As for Darcy himself, he spent the entire evening at a local inn, swigging down pots of ale and I know not what else. Several people came forward to say he had left in the company of one of the family's grooms and his father's steward, who'd also both been drinking there that evening. The steward, having somehow learned of the family argument earlier in the evening, said they had managed to sneak Darcy back into the house by way of a side entrance, and up to his room without anyone else seeing them. Apparently Darcy had been in a belligerent mood, and was still cursing his father when relieved of his boots and jacket.'

'So it is assumed that he went back downstairs at some point and, still in a drunken rage, committed murder.' Beth sighed. 'Well, yes, I suppose it's possible. But I still don't believe it.'

Charles Bathurst looked grim as he nodded his head in agreement. 'He was arrested on the evidence of the steward alone, who continued to maintain that Darcy was not so drunk that he couldn't have committed the crime. At the time there was no reason to suppose he might have lied. After all, what had he to gain by so doing? And the only other witness to the state of Darcy's condition on that fateful night, as far as anyone was aware at the time, was the young groom who, strangely enough, could not be found the next morning, and has never been seen since.'

After she had listened with interest to his every word, Beth wasn't slow to ask, 'You emphasised that that was the only information you had then. Has something come to light since?'

'Yes. But before I reveal more, I must digress a little.' He paused for a moment and reached for a decanter and, at her refusal, filled just one glass. 'When these events took place I was working and residing in London, as I mentioned before. Unlike my father, who was a fine practitioner, I chose to study law, which resulted in my living in the capital most of the time. So when both my parents passed away, sadly within months of each other, a matter of five years or so prior to these terrible murders, I considered it a needless expense to retain the family home, and so I sold it to another doctor, as it happens, who had one daughter. And this daughter, bless her, has proved invaluable!'

He took a moment to sample the contents of his glass. 'About a year ago she came to my chambers in the capital, demanding to see me. I was an extremely busy man during that period in my life, Miss Ashworth. I'm ashamed to say that, having been heavily involved in a difficult case at the time, I was reluctant to grant her an interview, but she persevered. The information she passed on enabled me to start proceedings to have all charges against my friend Darcy Wood dropped. Of course it has taken time. However, with the Duke of Wellington himself now a staunch ally, I am optimistic of a swift resolution. The Duke has already written a private letter to the Regent, asking for his help in order to clear the name of a brave officer who has risked his life on numerous occasions for King and country. It might only be a matter of weeks now. And I'm determined to prevent my friend from getting himself into more trouble in the meantime! Which, believe me, he's more than capable of doing.'

Beth would have liked to discover much more about the young woman who had come forward with vital information, but resisted the temptation to ask. The host had neglected his other guests quite long enough, and sooner or later their absence from the drawing room would be noted.

So she merely rose to her feet, assuring him that he might rely on her full support. She was slightly taken aback when his immediate response was to raise her hand and brush his lips lightly across the skin in what was meant, she felt sure, to be a simple salute of respect, and nothing more. She then felt mortified when she followed the direction of his slightly startled gaze to discover that a certain someone had surely witnessed the entire totally innocent little interlude.

Although she had quite failed to detect the click of the door, she was not deaf to the icy timbre of Sir Philip's voice as he said, 'I trust I do not intrude?'

It occurred to Beth, as she watched him saunter slowly towards her, his gaze containing no more warmth than his voice had done, that he wouldn't have cared a jot even if he had intruded on what might well have been considered a lovers' tryst.

'My sister requested I seek you out, Bathurst,' he explained, in the same frigidly polite tone. 'I understand you promised to partner her in a game of whist, and your presence is now required in the drawing room.'

'Of course,' he responded promptly, before turning once more to Beth. 'May I escort you back to your—'

'There's no need for you to trouble yourself,' Sir Philip cut in, his voice if possible icier than before. 'I shall look after Miss Ashworth.'

Beth had guessed by the way Charles Bathurst had released her hand so abruptly that he had felt slightly discomposed at being discovered closeted with one of his female guests. There was no sign of embarrassment in his demeanour now, however. If anything, the sudden glint in his eye suggested strongly that he was becoming annoyed by his well-respected neighbour's strangely cavalier attitude. So Beth decided it was time to intervene before either gentleman could say anything he might later regret.

'Yes, do return to your other guests, sir,' she urged, bestowing a glowing smile upon him that also managed to encompass a look of entreaty. 'I shall be perfectly safe in Sir Philip's care.'

A few moments later Beth wondered if she hadn't been slightly rash in this judgement, when her beloved childhood companion strode back across the room to close the door quite pointedly behind their departing host.

Then he turned and came slowly back towards her, the look in his grey eyes as cold as ever it had been in the past whenever she had done something to vex him greatly. 'What on earth possessed you to risk compromising yourself in such a fashion? Haven't you more sense, girl, than to permit a man to get you on your own?'

Had it not been for the resolve she had made just a few short days before, Beth wouldn't have troubled to keep a firm hold on her temper. She had decided, however, that never again would she be hostile or argumentative without good reason in the hope that maybe one day they might enjoy at least a semblance of that wonderful rapport of bygone years.

None the less, his lofty attitude had succeeded in irritating her, and even with the best will in the world she could not resist countering with, 'Seemingly not, otherwise I wouldn't have permitted you also to get me on my own.'

'I'll shake you in a minute, my girl!' he ground out between tightly compressed teeth.

'I wouldn't advise it, otherwise I'll be tempted to box your ears in retaliation,' Beth returned in a trice, before sensibly taking the precaution of whipping round the back of a chair for safety's sake as he took a threatening step towards her.

'This is no laughing matter, Beth!' he scolded, but in a voice that had been noticeably several degrees warmer.

'Too true, it isn't,' she agreed, feeling satisfied because she sensed she was beginning to coax him out of this rare lofty mood. 'I feel quite offended to think you believe me foolish enough to go off willy-nilly with a gentleman for no good reason. Mr Bathurst, however, had an honourable purpose in desiring a few minutes in private with me. He wished to discuss the present dilemma of a mutual friend.'

'That's all very well. But you are not in the Peninsula now, my girl, and your behaviour will not be so easily overlooked. Bathurst, might I remind you, is still a man,' he countered sharply, clearly nowhere near fully appeased.

Her gurgle of mirth in response did little to placate him either, but she simply couldn't help it. 'How funny!' she declared. 'Rudge said the selfsame thing about you only the other day.'

There was a distinct twitch at one corner of his attractive mouth. 'Impudent rogue!'

Suddenly serious, she regarded him soberly. 'Did he apologise to you? I told him he should…though afterwards I felt such a hypocrite. After all, I snapped your nose off a short time before your first encounter with him for absolutely no reason whatsoever.'

All at once every vestige of annoyance disappeared from his expression as he held out both arms. 'Oh, come here, Beth,' he coaxed, and then clasped both her hands, when she immediately obeyed, holding them fast against his chest.'

For several moments he stared down at her upturned face, studying each fine feature in turn. 'Friends again?' he murmured.

'Friends,' she managed softly in a voice that in no way resembled her own, and then had her hand raised yet again.

Only this time when masculine lips made contact with her skin, she had to exert every ounce of control she possessed not to wrench herself away and flee the room.

Chapter Five

Guests began to arrive during the second week in October to celebrate Sir Philip's birthday. A number of strangers were seen, dressed in their finery, parading through the village during subsequent days. One person, however, had been noticeably absent from the district, a circumstance that had given rise to a deal of speculation in some quarters, and had been a source of acute annoyance in another.

'The vicar's wife was remarking, only the other day, that Lady Chalford seems quite put out by her brother's continued absence,' Ann remarked, as she set yet another perfect stitch in the fire screen she was embroidering. 'Quite understandable, really. Why on earth should he decide to absent himself from the Court at such a time, do you suppose?'

Behind the covers of her book Beth successfully concealed a smile. She had wondered how long it would be before Ann attempted to satisfy her curiosity on the closer relationship that had clearly developed between the Baronet and her employer.

Since the evening of the dinner party, Beth had discovered Ann staring at her with a speculative glint in her intelligent dark eyes on numerous occasions. It had come as no very great surprise. Ann was nothing if not observant. She wouldn't have overlooked the absence of her employer and host from the drawing room that evening. Whatever wild speculation or negative feelings arose from their joint departure had possibly been tempered by Sir Philip's behaviour during the latter part of what had turned out to be a most convivial evening, enjoyed by all.

From the moment they had returned to the drawing room together, Sir Philip couldn't possibly have been more attentive towards his friend of yesteryear. He had encouraged Beth to sing a duet with him, something they had done on numerous occasions in the past. He had then gone on to persuade her to remain seated at the pianoforte, and had invited several others to join them round the instrument.

During the days prior to his leaving Staveley Court, he had called at the Grange twice: once to invite Beth to ride with him over the estate, something that they had also done times without number in bygone years; and once during an evening, when he had extracted a firm promise from her to partner him in at least one dance of his own choosing at the forthcoming ball.

Beth lowered the book. 'If you're asking me if I know where he's gone, then the answer is no. He chose not to enlighten me.'

One of Ann's brows rose in a quizzical arch, and her voice held a distinctly sarcastic ring too, as she said, 'Well, you do surprise me! If he was likely to inform anyone of his intentions, I would have wagered it would have been you. After all, you cannot deny you've become wondrous close of late.'

Only for a moment did Beth's gaze stray from the woman seated on the opposite side of the hearth. 'For many years we were wondrous close, Ann,' she reminded her. 'But your remarks are timely, none the less. We're no longer children. Philip simply cannot pay me the same kind of attention that he once did without, now, giving rise to foolish speculation.'

Her wicked sense of humour then came to the fore. 'After all, I haven't been in my estimable Aunt Henrietta's good graces for some considerable time. I should hate to plummet even further by being viewed as her daughter's main rival.'

Ann gazed thoughtfully into space, her brow furrowed, before asking, 'Do you suppose Sir Philip's intentions towards your cousin are serious? After all, there is some disparity in their ages—almost twelve years.'

'I haven't the faintest notion. We've never discussed the matter,' Beth answered with total sincerity. 'He hasn't so much as brought my youngest cousin's name up in conversation, as far as I can recall. That said, knowing him as I do, I cannot believe he would ever intentionally play fast and loose with a woman's feelings, especially one so young.'

'No, I cannot imagine him ever doing anything so deliberately hurtful either,' Ann agreed, as she studied Beth intently, searching for the slightest change in countenance that might offer a clue as to what was really passing through her dearest friend's mind. Her expression, however, remained inscrutable, giving absolutely nothing away during those moments before she rose to her feet in order to return her book to the shelf.

'It's quite possible, though,' Ann added, after staring thoughtfully at the slender, straight back, 'that he's attracted to the girl simply because of her resemblance to her dead sister, and for no other reason.'

'I sincerely hope that isn't the case,' Beth responded sombrely, 'if only for Phoebe's sake. Personally, I would wish to be admired for myself alone, and not because of some similarity to someone else. I should find that intolerable! Just as I would being for ever compared to some special someone.'

The housekeeper's entry to announce a most unexpected caller successfully put an end to the discussion. Beth turned and, even though she had been apprised of the visitor's identity, almost gaped in astonishment when the handsome young gentleman, more suitably attired for a saunter down some fashionable street in the metropolis than the country, came striding into the room.

'As I live and breathe!' she exclaimed, not attempting to hide her surprise, as she instantly stretched both hands out in welcome. 'How you've changed, Crispin Napier! I should never have recognised you had we met in the street. You're quite the Bond Street Beau, I see!'

Had he known that Beth was not a particular admirer of the exaggerated styles embraced by the dandy set, he might not have appeared quite so pleased by the greeting. Hair pomaded and carefully arranged to appear windswept, nip-waisted jackets in bright colours, high shirt-points combined with heavily starched and intricately folded cravats that prevented wearers from turning their heads were fashions she found absurd. None the less she could detect nothing artificial in his manner, nor anything lacking in his address as she introduced her companion and provided him with refreshment.

'So you're here to attend the ball,' she remarked, after he had revealed that the Reverend Mr Chadwick

and his good lady wife were once again kindly putting
him up at the vicarage. 'I seem to remember someone
mentioning you had been invited.'

'Staveley's sister invited me after she had discovered
I was here during the summer, and had joined her brother
in a shooting party. I accompanied Lady Henrietta and
her daughter down yesterday, as it happens.'

Beth's ears pricked up at this. She had had no notion
that her aunt had already arrived at the Court, and exchanged a look with her companion before enquiring
whether Lord Barfield had also accompanied his wife.

'No, my godfather's suffering from the gout at the
present time, and was obliged to cry off at the last
minute,' he revealed, before falling silent for a moment.
'Truth to tell, I don't think he's too disappointed having
to remain at home. He's not as young as he was, and he's
been forced to do a deal of entertaining and the like in
recent years in order to achieve suitable marriages for his
daughters. I think he was hoping it might be different
where Phoebe's concerned, that he wouldn't be obliged
to do quite so much jaunting about the country—er—this
time.'

Beth missed neither the sudden rise of colour in her
visitor's cheeks, nor the faintly embarrassed look he
cast in her direction, as though he had revealed more
than he had intended.

Easily suppressing the desire to quiz him further,
she helped him overcome his moment's embarrassment
by saying, 'Yes, I'd quite forgotten Lord Barfield is
your godfather, Crispin.'

She turned to Ann. 'Mr Napier's father owns a size-
able property adjacent to Lord Barfield's estate in
Surrey,' she explained. 'The families have known each
other for years and years. You and Phoebe were always

particular friends, I seem to remember,' she added, once again favouring her visitor with her undivided attention. 'She must have been pleased to have you, someone she knows and trusts, escort her down here?'

'Oh, yes, yes, she was.' Beneath the light-coloured jacket, a thin chest simply swelled with pride. 'I—I think I can safely say there's no one she trusts more.'

'I haven't set eyes on her in…oh, it must be seven, maybe eight, years,' Beth revealed, a seed of suspicion having firmly embedded itself in her brain. 'I expect she's changed a good deal from the girl I remember. In fact, I seem to recall someone mentioning only quite recently that she resembles Eugenie somewhat.'

'Mama has often remarked that Eugenie was quite out of the common way, and by far and away the only real beauty in the family,' he responded, his expression having turned distinctly mutinous. 'But I think Phoebe's dashed pretty too!'

'If she resembles her eldest sister, she must be,' Beth agreed, the staunch show of loyalty on the part of her visitor only confirming her suspicions. 'And a good sport, too, I seem to recall. Much more so than any of her sisters.'

'Too true!' he readily confirmed. 'Never gets on to a fellow if he's late or should forget an appointment altogether. Never complains if it should come on to rain when out riding, or if her skirts get muddied when she's striding about the home farm. We both much prefer the country.'

Beth's brows rose at this. 'You do surprise me, sir! You'd look quite at home in any fashionable drawing room.'

He didn't misunderstand. 'A chap has to dress, don't you know. And I must admit to liking a spell in town from time to time,' he confessed. 'Spent the entire Season there this year. But that was mainly for Phoebe's sake. Didn't want her to feel lonely or—or overawed by it all.'

Beth doubted that young Mr Napier's experience of town life was precisely extensive as, by her reckoning, he couldn't have been much more than two-and-twenty. All the same she refrained from teasing him, and merely said that she'd heard from Lady Chalford that Phoebe's first Season had been something of a success.'

'Yes, it was,' he agreed, not appearing altogether pleased about it. 'At least it was after Staveley paid her some attention. But as I mentioned before, ma'am, Phoebe's like me. We'd much prefer to be back in Surrey. Truth to tell, the only reason I accepted the invitation here was to bear her company.'

Resisting the temptation to point out that, as he was staying at the vicarage, it wasn't likely he'd be spending much time in Phoebe's company for the duration of their stay in the county, Beth exchanged a further glance with her companion before changing the subject entirely. She succeeded quite quickly in drawing her visitor out of his slightly sombre mood, and even extracted a firm promise from him, before he took his leave, to partner her in a dance at the forthcoming ball.

'Dear, dear…I feel there could be a slight—er—to-do in the offing if my ambitious aunt is not very careful,' Beth remarked the instant she detected the front door closing behind their visitor.

Ann did not misunderstand. 'He's certainly young enough to commit such a folly as an elopement, without considering the consequences. And he resents Sir Philip's interest in the girl. That much is quite apparent!'

'I have yet to be convinced that Philip has an interest,' Beth returned, rising to her feet in order to replenish the fire, and then staring meditatively at the flames as they began to lick around the edges of the logs. 'There are a few questions whirling round in my head at the present time demanding answers, not least of which is what Phoebe's opinion might be. The last time I saw her she was a mere child, still in the schoolroom. Does she have a sincere regard for the son of her nearest neighbour, I wonder? Or might she welcome a proposal from Philip? I shall perhaps discover her state of mind when I've spoken with her.'

Once again Ann's gaze grew intense. 'And would it disturb you so very much if Sir Philip's intentions towards your cousin were indeed serious?'

Beth's shrug of indifference was not wholly convincing. 'Why should it?' she countered softly, resuming her seat, but continuing to stare steadfastly down at the hearth. 'Of course I do appreciate that any union he contracted would be bound to affect his relationship with me. We would undoubtedly see much less of each other. Yet, marry he must one day if he doesn't wish the name to die out entirely. Apart from his Uncle Waldo, who's a confirmed bachelor, not to mention the wrong side of five-and-fifty, Philip is the last of the Staveleys. I assume he'll one day marry, if only to produce an heir.'

Ann looked up sharply at this, her brow furrowed. 'Do you honestly suppose he'd marry for that reason alone?' She didn't wait for an answer, and appeared decidedly unconvinced as she added, 'I personally do not suppose so for a moment, otherwise he would have contracted a union by now.'

'Oh, for heaven's sake, Ann!' Beth exclaimed. 'He's only just turned thirty. Hardly in his dotage! Time enough, surely, for him to meet someone with whom he could

happily share his life? Even though she would undoubtedly pale into insignificance when compared to Eugenie.'

'Yes, and that's another thing,' Ann returned, shaking
her head and looking, if possible, even more puzzled
than before. 'If Sir Philip is still truly pining for his lost
love, then all I can say is he's learned to conceal the fact
wonderfully well. I was studying him closely throughout the latter part of the evening at Mr Bathurst's home,
and a gentleman more at ease with life and himself I've
yet to meet.'

This certainly gave Beth pause for thought, and after
a few moments' deliberation, she was forced to agree. 'All
the same, as I've mentioned before, he isn't one to betray
emotion in public. He's always shown remarkable self-
control, and although I would never be foolish enough to
place too much reliance on anything Constance might
say, there will be one or two others present at the forthcoming ball whose opinions I value and who might well
be able to shed some light on Philip's true state of mind.'

Beth was destined not to set eyes on Philip again
until the evening of the ball, when she entered the hall
at Staveley Court and caught sight of him immediately,
dutifully standing beside his sister at the entrance to the
large drawing room, which had always functioned as a
ballroom on such occasions.

Dressed in a fashionable gown of dull gold silk, with
a shawl in the same material draped across her slender
shoulders, and with a spray of artificial cream flowers
nestling amongst the intricate curls of her carefully
arranged dark hair, Beth felt she was looking her best
for the evening, a belief that was confirmed by the look
of unalloyed admiration that sprang into the host's grey
eyes the instant they fell upon her.

'Perfection,' he murmured, bowing low over her gloved hand.

'I would never aim so high,' she returned, nothing if not a realist. 'But I look well enough, I think, and shall not disgrace you when we take to the floor later.'

'That you could never do,' he assured her softly before finally releasing her hand in order to allow her to greet his sister.

Refusing to read anything more in the tender greeting than the genuine admiration of a true friend, Beth strolled into the ballroom. Scanning the throng for familiar faces, she swiftly located the vicar's good lady wife.

'I do believe your bosom-friend is attempting to catch your eye, Ann. Will you go over and bear her company for a spell, while I seek out my formidable Aunt Henrietta? I shall need to come face to face with her at some point. As well get it over with now.'

Ann's expression immediately revealed her unease. 'Are you sure you don't wish me to accompany you?'

'Of course not, dear. There are those who might consider Lady Hetta something of a dragon. But she doesn't frighten me,' Beth assured her, half-laughing. 'Oh, dear Lord, and there she is! She's taken to sporting a lorgnette, of all things! Whatever next! You run along and enjoy yourself. I'll catch up with you later, after I've had a chance to test the water, as it were.'

Although she continued to search the room for other familiar faces, as she headed towards the corner where her esteemed aunt was holding court, Beth was instantly aware when that aid to vision became fixed in her direction. She didn't miss the momentary look of surprise either as she drew closer, and couldn't resist saying, 'Yes, I scrub up rather well these days, do I not, Aunt? And how are you? In fine fettle, I hope.'

Clearly a greeting lacking deference was something to which Lady Henrietta was unaccustomed. All the same, she merely said, 'I am well enough, Niece, and know already that you have not learnt to put a guard on that naughty tongue of yours.'

'Believe me, Aunt, I'm ten times worse than I used to be, and well past praying for now, I'm afraid.'

A giggle, only partially stifled, drew Beth's attention. 'Ah, and Cousin Phoebe! I'm delighted to discover what I've heard about you is true—quite grown up now, and as pretty as a picture!'

The girl blushed quite charmingly, and her mother was evidently pleased by the compliment too, for she instantly invited her niece to sit and bear them company.

Exerting praiseworthy self-control, Beth listened patiently while her aunt revealed the comings and goings of other members of her immediate family, extolling her youngest daughter's success during the past Season, as she did so, and hinting that she would not be averse to chaperoning Beth should she wish to enjoy what London had to offer the following year.

The instant Lady Henrietta's attention was claimed by a matron of similar age, however, Beth didn't hesitate to focus on the one member of the Barfield family who was of most interest to her at the present time.

From the moment Beth had seated herself, Phoebe had not uttered a single word. This in itself was not unduly surprising. Beth was well aware that all her cousins had been strictly reared, and knew better than to speak while their mother was in full flow, unless addressed directly. Yet there was something about her cousin that had already struck Beth as odd.

A girl just turned eighteen, blessed with a pretty face and trim figure, not to mention an enviable position on the social ladder, ought to appear very satisfied with her lot. It wasn't that she looked miserable, exactly. In fact, she was gazing about the room with interest. All the same Beth gained the distinct impression that she was here, primarily, at her mother's behest and through no real desire of her own.

'I had a visit from a mutual acquaintance yesterday, Phoebe,' she remarked, instantly gaining her cousin's attention. 'How Mr Napier has changed! I hardly recognised him.'

If Beth hadn't witnessed the effect herself, she would never have believed it possible. It was as if mention of that young man's name had instilled new life in her cousin. All at once she became thoroughly animated, eyes sparkling, face positively aglow.

'He said he'd call on you. I'm so glad he did.' Her smile faded very slightly. 'Poor Crispin! He'll have a poor time of it without his friend to bear him company, until it's time to return to Surrey.'

'You mean the vicar's son?'

'Yes, they were at school together, and have kept in close contact ever since,' Phoebe revealed. 'Crispin often puts up with his friend when he visits London. Mr Chadwick is studying law, and wasn't able to have a break from his studies this time.'

The fact that he had expected his friend to attend the ball was undoubtedly the reason why Crispin had originally arranged to put up at the vicarage, Beth reasoned. But once he had discovered his friend wouldn't be bearing him company after all, why hadn't he put up at the Court? Did his dislike of Sir Philip go so deep that he couldn't bear to be under the same roof as him for any length of time?

Thrusting the question to the back of her mind to

mull over later, Beth said, 'Well, no doubt you'll be able to make his visit more pleasurable by bearing Crispin company from time to time during your stay.'

The new-found liveliness virtually disappeared in an instant. 'No, I won't, unfortunately. Mama has several things planned for us whilst we're here. I believe Sir Philip has offered to escort us to Wells Cathedral, and one or two other places.'

'Then, let us hope you, at least, enjoy your time here,' Beth remarked, not wholly convinced that this would turn out to be the case. 'Sir Philip is a most accomplished and charming host. I'm sure he'll do his utmost to keep you entertained. And it isn't as if he's a complete stranger. You've known him for some considerable time.'

'Oh, yes,' Phoebe agreed, staring shyly down at the hands in her lap. 'He—he was particularly kind to me when I was in London earlier in the year. He never failed to stand up with me if we had happened to be attending the same function.'

Yes, but for what precise reason? Beth couldn't help wondering, as she studied her cousin intently.

No one could deny that Phoebe was well enough. Sadly, though, she was a pale imitation of her deceased eldest sister. She lacked Eugenie's natural flair for socialising. It was hard to imagine, moreover, that Eugenie had been no older than Phoebe was now when she and Philip had first met and had fallen so irrevocably in love. Yet Eugenie had been far more self-assured, more than ready to embark upon matrimony; whereas Phoebe still seemed more child than woman, diffident and lacking vigour. So what on earth was it that Philip saw in the poor child to attract him so?

As she caught sight at that moment of a gentleman with sandy-coloured hair, whom she hadn't seen in a number of years, purposefully heading in her direction, Beth chose not to dwell on the conundrum. She was pleasantly surprised by the way her aunt cordially greeted the new arrival, for he was none other than the brother of the man responsible for causing the death of her beloved first daughter.

'I'm under strict instructions to seek you out, Miss Ashworth, and bring you to a certain worthy,' he told her, offering his arm.

Beth didn't hesitate to accept his escort. A very close friend of Sir Philip, Simon Joyce had been a frequent visitor to the Court, and a firm favourite of Beth's from the very first time they had met.

'I would have recognised you anywhere, Simon,' she freely admitted, staring up at his fresh complexion, which still boasted countless freckles. 'You've changed so very little since the last time we met, here at the Court.'

'I'm afraid I cannot respond in kind,' he returned, smiling down at her in that wonderfully engaging way she well remembered. 'In fact, after staring hopelessly about the room for several minutes, I was forced to approach our mutual friend, and was advised to seek out the brightest of celestial bodies, a sun goddess, no less.'

Beth grimaced as she stared down at her golden-coloured gown. 'Sun goddess, indeed! Wait till I see him. But first, I'm in need of refreshment to fortify me, Simon. I'm absolutely parched!'

Easily catering for her needs, he relieved a passing footman of two glasses of champagne before steering her to a secluded niche. 'I'm pleased to have this opportunity of a private word, Beth,' he said, swiftly re-establishing that easy relationship they had enjoyed so many years before. 'The letter you wrote concerning my brother meant so very much to us all, especially Mother.'

All at once his expression was unusually sombre. 'Even though you quite failed to reveal the extent of your care during my brother's last days. That we discovered from his colonel.'

All at once azure-coloured eyes were dimmed by the shadow of bitterly unhappy memory. 'I did little enough,' she at last responded, her voice not perfectly level.

'Oh, no, of course not!' he mocked, his smile crooked. 'Little enough to take it upon yourself to have my brother Harry removed from among the dead and dying. Little enough to have extracted the lead ball from his abdomen yourself, because the army surgeon had been fully occupied in attempting to help those less criti-cally injured, who were considered to have a greater chance of survival. Little enough to have remained with him constantly until it had seemed he might recover.'

'But he didn't, did he?' Beth reminded him softly.

'No. But I cannot help asking myself whether it was his wound that killed him, or the fact that he'd lost the will to live because he couldn't forgive himself.'

Beth wished fervently that she could have supplied the answer, but she couldn't, and so shook her head. 'I didn't know, until he told me himself, that Harry had been tooling the curricle at the time. He openly admitted taking the bend too fast, thereby causing the carriage to overturn, resulting in Eugenie's death, and himself sus-taining little more than a few scratches. All the same, it was an accident, pure and simple, and might have happened to anyone.'

'Yes, it might so easily have been me,' Simon re-vealed, as he stared meditatively down into the contents of his glass. 'Philip and I had been in London, enjoying what remained of the Season, when he received that fateful letter from Eugenie, accusing him of neglect, because he hadn't been near her for several weeks, not since their engagement party, in fact. She begged him to spend a few days with her at her parents' home. So off we all went, a whole crowd of us, including my brother. I don't recall who it was who first suggested the race. But I do remember names being drawn out of a hat, and finding myself in the enviable position of having Eugenie bear me company in my curricle. Unfortunately I succumbed to a severe chill the day before the race was planned, and so my brother offered to take my place. He was competent enough at handling the ribbons, a little reckless on occasions, maybe, but not downright foolhardy or dangerous. The next thing I knew, poor Eugenie was being carried back into the house, her neck broken.'

Beth could only imagine the painful horror of it all, and was secretly glad that she hadn't been there. 'I'm certain my aunt and uncle never blamed Harry,' she finally said. 'When they wrote to my father they merely informed us that their daughter had died as a result of a tragic accident.' Beth glanced up at him briefly. 'And I'm sure Philip didn't blame your brother either.'

'No, poor Phil merely retreated into a world of his own,' he revealed, staring across the room at where their host was cordially welcoming some late arrivals. 'After the funeral, he came down here, not seeing a soul, hardly, for very many months. Even when he did eventually begin to socialise again, he always seemed a little aloof, deliberately distancing himself from those around him, not allowing anyone to get too close, not even his oldest friends. Until last spring, that is. He began to be more approachable then. And I must say, since my arrival here this time, I can detect a most marked change in him. Why, he's back to the Philip of old!'

'I wonder why, though,' Beth murmured, her eyes instinctively straying to that particular corner, where her Aunt Henrietta still held court.

Mr Joyce either did not hear, or chose not to answer. He simply removed the empty glass from her fingers, and placed it on the table conveniently situated behind, before fulfilling his mission. Then, before she knew what was happening, Beth was being squeezed against a great barrel of a chest, held fast in a pair of stout arms.

'As I live and breathe! Waldo Staveley!' she exclaimed, peering up at those wickedly glinting grey eyes, set in a round, fleshy countenance that could never have been described as being even remotely handsome, not even when the skin possessed a youthful bloom. 'At least I would be able to breathe, if you'd release your hold,' she amended, after he'd taken the liberty of placing an avuncular kiss on one of her cheeks.

For answer he rumbled with laughter, thereby inducing more guests to stare in their direction, before addressing the gentleman who had done him the service of discovering the whereabouts of his slender captive. 'Go away, Joyce. You may safely leave darling Beth in my care.'

'Doesn't appear that way to me, sir,' he responded ungraciously, but did as bidden.

'Impudent young pup! Always liked him. Just as I always favoured you, you little minx,' Waldo revealed before holding Beth at arm's length, the better to study the noticeable physical changes in her since their last encounter, many years before. 'There's not much meat on the bone now, I see.' He tutted, clearly not wholly approving. 'Still, you seem to please the boy well enough, and that's what really matters. And I must say you've turned into a handsome filly, much like your mother, I fancy.'

Drawing her down on to the empty chair besides his own, he encouraged her to talk, not about her time out in the Peninsula, but about what she intended to do with her life now.

'And from what Connie tells me, you've a companion living with you now. All very respectable, and all that, but damnably restricting for a girl of your temperament,' he remarked sagely, after she'd revealed her plans for the Grange. 'Marriage would suit you better.'

'It most certainly would not!' Beth returned in a flash, and then found herself being studied intently by those same small, round eyes that more often than not held a merry twinkle.

Nevertheless, no one who knew Waldo Staveley well was deceived by that air of lazy geniality he exuded. He was a remarkably astute man whose keen head for business had allowed him to command most any luxury throughout his life. Although he had remained a carefree bachelor, one would have been grossly in error to label him a care-for-nobody. He was immensely proud of the name he bore, and his attachment to his nephew was unshakeable.

'Well, maybe you'll change your mind in time,' he said, patting her hand. 'And it can be a big mistake to rush into things. A fellow's tastes can change over the years. So I don't see why it should be any different for the ladies. One can make some terrible blunders in one's youth. Much better to leave the important decisions until one has acquired a touch of know-how, as it were.'

Transferring his gaze, Waldo stared across at the entrance to the drawing room. 'Glad I managed to persuade that nephew of mine to bide his time. Honestly believe he's long since appreciated the advice I gave him, all those years ago, even though he's never come straight out and admitted as much, at least not to me.'

Beth was puzzled by the disclosure. Although she had discovered years before that Waldo had advised his nephew to delay the engagement, she couldn't understand why he should imagine Philip would still have appreciated the advice, given what had happened. Unfortunately she was denied the opportunity to query precisely what Waldo had meant, for at that moment the subject of the conversation, at last abandoning his position by the door, came striding purposefully across the room towards them.

'That's it!' Philip announced determinedly. 'Any more late arrivals and Connie can greet them by herself, as she's responsible for organising the confounded affair in the first place.'

Beth wasn't deaf to the clear note of dissatisfaction. 'If you were so against the idea of celebrating your birthday, why on earth did you allow your sister to have her way?'

Raising shapely brows, Philip gazed down at her in mock surprise. 'Isn't it obvious...? Because I knew it would offer me the golden opportunity to dance with only ladies of my choice... Shall we?'

He offered her his hand, his eyes sparkling with a wickedly challenging gleam, and Beth instantly appreciated the reason why. The master of ceremonies had, only moments before, announced the commencement of a set of certain dances.

Turning her head on one side, she peered up at him. 'Are you so determined to ruin my reputation?' she asked him sweetly.

'Would you care?' he countered, his eyes never wavering from hers for an instant.

She chose to be totally honest. 'No, not a whit.'

'That's my girl!' Philip approved, drawing her to her feet.

'But then she always was,' Waldo murmured, the instant the pair had walked hand in hand on to the empty stretch of floor allocated for dancing, a look of sublime approval lingering on his plump features.

Chapter Six

It was without doubt the most enjoyable evening she'd spent in some considerable time. Perhaps the most enjoyable ever, Beth was obliged to concede as she slipped between the warmed sheets of her bed in the early hours of the morning.

Philip, a stickler for observing the rules governing accepted codes of conduct, had behaved quite out of character. He would have been well aware that, although danced quite openly across the Channel, the waltz had yet to achieve universal approval here in England; young ladies, especially unmarried females, risked social ruin by performing the dance in public. Yet in a strangely devil-may-care frame of mind, he had quite deliberately thrown down the gauntlet, and her nature being what it was she hadn't hesitated in taking up the challenge.

For a full three minutes or so they had been the only couple on the dance floor, with all eyes following their every movement, and yet Beth hadn't felt in the least self-conscious. In fact, the opposite had been the case. She had felt elated, blissfully content to be swirling about the room with a gentleman who performed the dance exceedingly well. Her own performance had left nothing to be desired, either. Even though she said so herself, she had always shown grace on a dance floor; and early in the summer, when in Paris, she had been taught to waltz by an excellent French dancing-master.

Ann, brave soul, ably supported by Mr Bathurst, had been the first to join them, and soon afterwards several young matrons, some even partnered by their more sober-minded spouses, had finally plucked up courage enough to swirl about the room.

And was she now sorry she had flouted rules of accepted behaviour? The answer came hard on the heels of the question—no, not a whit! After all, what had she to lose if her actions should become common knowledge? She had no ambition to cross Almack's hallowed portals in order to find a husband, so there was absolutely no need to win the approval of those formidable high-ranking society hostesses. For a different reason entirely, though, she must be prepared to modify her conduct from now on.

The simple truth was that most people simply could never comprehend the camaraderie that had always existed between Philip and herself, and might put their own wildly foolish interpretation on the evident close bond between them. It couldn't be denied that several brows had been raised when Philip had again chosen her as his partner for the supper dance later in the evening; not to mention the several faces that had worn thoughtful expressions when he had entwined her arm through his in a very possessive fashion indeed in order to escort her in to supper directly afterwards.

There was no avoiding the fact that Philip had quite blatantly paid her particular attention, selecting only her to dance with twice. Although his reasons for having done so remained his own, Beth strongly suspected that they had stemmed from a desire not to raise false hopes in any one of the other young ladies present, and a sure knowledge that she would never misunderstand his clear preference for her company.

All the same, their evident easy relationship might be followed with keen interest in some quarters, and that would never do. After all, it would only take one unguarded look, one thoughtless gesture, and someone just might suspect the true state of her foolish heart, and realise that she had been deeply in love with Sir Philip Staveley for a very long time.

She closed her eyes in a vain attempt to suppress the raw ache borne of an unrequited love successfully concealed for so many years. The tears that might have lessened the pain never came, but she refused to wallow in fruitless self-pity. She had made her decision to remain at the Grange, to stay close to the man she loved, always to stand his friend no matter when or whom he one day chose to marry.

She had done just that during supper, when he had urged her to accompany him out riding the following day. 'I must escape the onerous duties of acting the genial host, if only for an hour or so,' he had confided, easily winning her sympathy and support.

Although she had agreed without taking time to consider, she had no intention of dashing a note off at the eleventh hour begging to be excused. But even so it was vital that she remain sensible from now on, she reminded herself yet again. Until all his guests had left, it might be advisable to stay well clear of the Court and those inquisitive eyes of friends and relations who had Philip's best interests at heart.

* * *

Beth was a little surprised to discover none other than Crispin Napier loitering in the stable-yard, when she, accompanied by the faithful Rudge, arrived at the Court mid-morning. It immediately struck her as odd that his expression seemed slightly furtive, as he moved away from the two mounts tethered to the hitching post, awaiting their riders. Beth, however, didn't dwell on the slightly odd expression as her attention had quickly been captured by the gorgeous chestnut filly standing alongside Sir Philip's favourite hack.

'What a beautiful creature!' she declared, slipping gracefully from the saddle without assistance in order to look the animal over more closely.

'Just what I was thinking myself,' Crispin readily agreed. 'Noticed 'em as I was about to set off back to the vicarage, and thought I'd take a closer look. This bay of Staveley's is a fine animal too.'

Beth favoured the young man with her full attention for the first time, clearly recalling as she did so that he had seemed in remarkably good spirits at the ball, particularly in the earlier part of the evening, when within close proximity to Phoebe. Yet today Beth sensed he wasn't quite so contented, even though he was doing his level best to appear cheerful enough.

'You evidently walked up from the vicarage,' she remarked, after staring about the yard in vain for a further mount.

'Well, as you probably know the vicar owns a one-horse gig, but keeps no animal suitable for riding. Besides, I thought Phoebe might like to take a stroll about the park, as it's such a pleasant morning, if a trifle fresh.' The show of cheerfulness was less convincing as he glanced at the filly and added, 'It would seem, though, she's made other arrangements.'

All at once Beth felt she understood why Philip had been so keen for her presence that morning. With her along to bear them company, he would have considered Phoebe adequately chaperoned. It was by no means the most flattering invitation she'd ever received in her life. None the less Beth couldn't help but be quietly amused at being designated the role of duenna.

She cast the young man before her a sympathetic smile, quite understanding his disappointment. 'No doubt Phoebe will accompany you out another day, Crispin. My aunt mentioned you're not travelling back to Surrey until the end of the week.'

'Yes, that's right. Time enough to get together with Phoebe before then, I suppose. And I did leave a note, as I was denied the pleasure of seeing her.'

All at once he seemed eager to be gone. Beth didn't attempt to detain him, and walked in the opposite direction, entering the mansion by way of a side entrance.

Her arrival had evidently been expected. The butler betrayed no sign of surprise when she emerged into the hall, and informed her promptly that her aunt had expressed a desire to speak with her before she set out for her ride, if at all convenient.

Beth couldn't help but smile as she followed the major-domo up the impressive main staircase to the upper floor. She had a fairly shrewd idea why her aunt desired an interview. It had to be said that her exhibition on the dance floor had not exactly impressed the more mature matrons present, several of whom had frowned dourly in her direction throughout the remainder of the evening. Although her aunt had not been so obvious in her disapproval, it was highly likely that she hadn't been altogether pleased either.

She discovered Lady Henrietta still abed, a frothy lace cap concealing her silvery-grey locks, and the remains of a breakfast on a tray close by. Clearly she had been enjoying a leisurely morning, no doubt recovering her strength after the previous evening's exertions. Beth judged by the alertness of her aunt's gaze that the rest cure was complete.

After instructing her personal maid to remove the breakfast tray, and return later after she had helped Phoebe to dress, Lady Henrietta patted the bed, inviting Beth to seat herself, whilst all the time scrutinising every detail of her niece's apparel.

'You look remarkably fetching this morning, Niece,' she announced, surprising Beth somewhat. 'But then you always did look well in tailored clothes, and that habit suits your slender figure admirably. Paris, I suppose, like that beautiful gown you wore last night?'

'No, Aunt. In fact, this was made for me by a seamstress in the local town. An admirable woman, very gifted. She stocks a large range of materials too.'

'Really?' Lady Henrietta took a moment to study the stylish apparel more closely. 'I shall ask Lady Chalford to take me to the establishment when we visit the town later this morning. That dark blue suits you very well. I might be tempted to purchase a few yards. Phoebe could do with a new habit. I noticed the other day hers was beginning to show signs of wear.'

'But it will do for today, surely?'

Lady Henrietta's brows rose. 'We didn't pack her habit, my dear, so she'll not be riding whilst here. Unlike you, Phoebe doesn't show to advantage in the saddle. She's happy enough when she goes out with young

Napier, but becomes nervous when riding with strangers, and as a result is prone to the odd accident. The last thing I want is for her to injure herself whilst we're here.'

'Indeed, no,' Beth agreed, whilst wondering which of the other female guests was to accompany them out riding that day.

Forcing this to the back of her mind to consider more fully a little later, Beth asked her aunt why she had requested to see her, and wasn't unduly surprised to have her prior assumptions confirmed in this matter, at least.

'Please do not suppose I mean to scold,' she continued, after pointing out the dangers of performing that very *risqué* dance in public. 'I merely wish to offer advice, and should be failing in my duty as your closest female relative if I omitted to do so. No one can deny you show as much skill on a dance floor as you do on a hunting field, my dear. You are amazingly graceful. I'm also fully aware that you're no longer a child, Beth, and are quite capable of making your own decisions. But you're still unmarried, and your age will not protect you if certain persons believe you are deliberately flouting accepted codes of conduct.'

Reaching out for her niece's hand, Lady Henrietta gave it an affectionate squeeze. 'And I do so want you to accompany us to London in the spring and enjoy your first Season.'

Her aunt seemed to suppose that she would automatically fall in with her wishes, just as her daughters had always done, and Beth discovered she simply hadn't the heart to disappoint her. Clearly Lady Henrietta was willing to forgive her for not attending Eugenie's engagement party all those years ago, and Beth was moved by the forbearing attitude. All the same, she was determined to make one thing perfectly clear at the outset.

'If I should accompany you to the capital next year, Aunt, it will be to enjoy the experience of a London Season, and see the sights. And maybe attempt to compensate for those years we spent apart. But it will not be to find a husband, I assure you.'

'Nonsense, child! You're an exceedingly handsome young woman. I wasn't blind to the admiring glances you received from several gentlemen present last night, including the host, I might add, who clearly admires you.'

'He admires my daring, you mean,' Beth corrected, refusing to read anything at all in her aunt's observations, and then rose to her feet. 'But I shall fall from favour if I force him to leave his horses standing too long. Perhaps you and Phoebe will find time to take tea with me at the Grange one afternoon during your stay?'

After placing a farewell salute on her aunt's cheek, Beth didn't delay in leaving the room. She discovered Philip awaiting her in the hall below. He looked up the instant he detected the light footfall on the stairs, and smiled that endearingly wicked smile of his up at her.

'Would I be correct in supposing you have been taken roundly to task for your peerless display on the dance floor last night?'

'My aunt may retain some antiquated notions, Philip, but she's certainly no dragon,' she told him, as she tried desperately to ignore the warmth in his eyes, knowing as she did that it was a look borne of affection and friendship, not love. 'Furthermore, I think age must surely be mellowing me. I'm beginning to understand her a deal better. My aunt is ambitious, not malicious. Although sometimes, like your own dear sister, she's not altogether wise.'

Philip caught the considering look she cast up at him

as they headed towards the side entrance. 'What's troubling you?'

She began to gnaw at her bottom lip, a clear indication to one who knew her well that she was mulling something over very carefully. Then she surprised him by asking, 'Did you happen to see young Napier earlier?'

'Naturally I was informed he'd been here, but he didn't ask to see me,' he answered, opening the door so that she could precede him into the stable-yard. 'Why do you ask?'

Surprising him somewhat, Beth stopped dead in her tracks, her mind having turned in an instant to the conundrum that had been puzzling her increasingly since her arrival that morning. 'Who else have you invited out riding?'

'No one, why?' His eyes suddenly glowed with that same wickedly provocative gleam that had brightened them so frequently the evening before. 'Unless you feel nervous in my company all of a sudden, that is, then I suppose I'll be obliged to endure the company of that rogue of a groom of yours.'

Ignoring the teasing, she pointed her finger, while demanding to know, 'Who, then, is to ride that filly, may I ask?'

'You, I sincerely trust. She's the reason I was absent from home recently. Went to Gloucestershire to look her over. Intend to breed with her at some point. For the time being, though, I'd like you to put her through her paces as often as you feel able.' He slanted a further provocative look. 'Think you're up to the task?'

'You just try to stop me!' Eager to be off though she was, Beth wasn't blind to the slightly troubled look her groom cast her as he assisted her to mount. 'No need for you to hang about here, Rudge, if you'd prefer to return to the Grange,' she told him, assuming that a disinclination to await her return must be behind the odd expression. 'Sir Philip will see me home safely.'

He opened his mouth, as though to say something. Then evidently thought better of it, and merely said that he'd be happy to remain at the Court and ride home with her later.

Philip had not been blind to the groom's worried look either, and put it down to the fact that he was concerned over his young mistress riding an unknown horse for the very first time. He, on the other hand, experienced no such qualms. He knew well enough that she was a superb horsewoman, and wasn't in the least surprised when, after a short period of careful assessment, she set off across the park at a gallop.

Easily matching the pace, Philip rode alongside as they traversed the park. The filly, after an initial high-spirited display, had behaved quite beautifully, so he was a little surprised when Beth moderated her speed without warning, finally drawing to a halt close to the western perimeter of the home wood, her gaze fixed.

Interested to discover just what had captured her attention so dramatically, Philip turned his head in time to see a cloaked figure disappear between the trees. 'Was that young Napier, by any chance? he asked, after assessing the figure's stature and mode of attire.

Beth nodded, her face wearing that same troubled look Philip had observed a short time earlier. 'He was at the Court to see Phoebe, but was denied the pleasure, so I understand. Let's go over by the stream and sit for a while.'

Philip was only too happy to oblige. After securely tethering both mounts, he joined her by the trout stream, where she had quickly settled herself on a conveniently fallen tree, yet another casualty of a particularly vicious storm the previous winter.

He chose not to sit beside her. Instead, he placed one booted foot on the wide trunk and rested his elbow on his knee, perfectly relaxed. 'What's troubling you?' he finally asked, when she continued to stare silently at the rippling waters of the stream.

The protracted sigh was clearly audible before she said, 'Tell me to mind my own business if you wish, Philip, and I shouldn't blame you if you did. But might I be permitted to know what your intentions are with regard to my cousin Phoebe?'

In truth, Philip was more surprised than anything else by the question. He shouldn't have been, though, he reminded himself, after recalling that, in bygone years, she'd never been afraid to quiz him over almost anything, no matter how personal. Why, on one particular occasion she'd even had the temerity to ask him outright if he'd ever taken a mistress! He'd had no intention of satisfying her curiosity on that occasion, and even though he experienced no such qualms now, he couldn't resist asking, 'What makes you suppose I have any interest at all?'

As this drew her head round sharply, he experienced no difficulty in recognising the hint of wariness behind the speculative look she cast up at him.

'Constance, of course! Really, I'm surprised at you, Beth!' He paused to slant her a look of mock reproach. 'I thought you'd more sense than to pay heed to my sister's flights of fancy. She's been trying to marry me off for the best part of three years to various suitable females. Which reminds me,' he added, a further more recent memory stirring. 'I cannot thank you enough for not aiding her on this occasion by inviting your aunt and cousin to prolong their stay in the West Country.'

Beth had the grace to look a little shamefaced at this. 'Truth to tell that was for my benefit, not yours.'

Although puzzled by the response, Philip didn't attempt to satisfy his curiosity. Instead he asked softly, little realising the very same question had been put to her by another quite recently, 'Would it have concerned you so very much had my interests been fixed?'

Behind them the mounts whinnied as though slightly disturbed by something. Philip, however, was too intent on studying a facial expression that had suddenly closed, becoming totally unreadable, to pay much heed to the horses.

Stepping over the log, he settled himself down beside her at last. Although she didn't attempt to move away from him, her gaze remained fixed on the area of park beyond the stream, just as though he wasn't there.

'You haven't answered my question,' he reminded her, and thought he could detect a slight tremor at the corner of her mouth. Whether the involuntary movement was the result of suppressed laughter or something quite different, he couldn't have said with any degree of certainty.

'You wouldn't have suited,' she responded at length, and in a level voice devoid of emotion. 'Phoebe isn't like…like any of her sisters.'

'No, indeed, she lacks confidence for a start. That's one reason why I took pity on her during the Season. An error of judgement on my part, perhaps, as it has resulted in needless and foolish speculation in some quarters,' he readily conceded. 'But my intentions were honourable, I assure you.'

This time when the same muscle twitched at the corner of her mouth it was the prelude to a rueful smile. 'I for one do not doubt that for a moment. But if you wish to avoid conjecture in the future, you must do your utmost to guard against it. And I include our own relationship in that warning. No doubt our departure from the Court this morning was observed by certain persons, so we'd best not tarry, otherwise before you know it some foolish gossipmonger will be romantically linking your name with mine.'

With a tinkling laugh that sounded distinctly false, even to her own ears, Beth rose to her feet and hurriedly made her way back across the grass to the horses, thereby denying him the opportunity to linger further. Her thoughts in turmoil, and feeling all at once emotionally drained, she wanted nothing more than to return to the Grange to recover those reserves of self-control that had been sorely depleted that morning.

Managing to mount the filly without assistance, she was eager to be gone, but even so she was not blind to the deeply pensive look in Philip's eyes as he drew ever nearer. 'I'll race you,' she challenged, desperately striving to maintain the pretence of bonhomie.

Without awaiting a response, she turned the filly and set off at the gallop. Even with the advantage she had given herself by unsportingly not granting him time to mount, she never supposed for a moment she'd stand the remotest chance of winning the race. Philip was a fine horseman, and the bay gelding was no slug. Consequently she expected to find him edging alongside well before she had reached the slight rise leading up to the Court. When she failed to detect the sound of thundering hooves approaching, curiosity got the better of her. Then it was as much as she could do to remain seated herself when she saw Philip sprawled on the ground and his saddleless mount trotting about aimlessly some distance away.

She swiftly turned the filly and was heading back in

a trice. Even though her one thought was to discover how badly Philip was hurt, she first concentrated her efforts on recapturing his mount, which had clearly become unsettled by what had occurred.

But what had happened? Keeping a firm grasp on the gelding's reins, she slipped to the ground, and took a few moments to soothe the horse enough so that when she finally released him he merely walked a few paces away and began to graze beside the filly. Then, heart pounding, she walked those few yards to where Philip lay, still motionless. A short distance away was his saddle, the strap clearly broken.

Dropping to her knees, Beth turned him carefully over on his back, and lifted his head gently on to her thighs, all the time silently praying that he would come round. His eyelids, however, didn't so much as flicker, even when she gently brushed the tussled brown hair from his forehead.

Desperately worried though she was she took much comfort from the fact that his breathing was regular, and that the only visible injury was a small gash near the temple, from which blood was slowly oozing. All the same, it was imperative that he was conveyed back to the Court as quickly as possible. And there was no way in the world she'd achieve that without help!

Once again placing his head gently on the ground, she scrambled to her feet. Uneasy in her mind about how the accident had occurred, she didn't want to leave him if she could possibly avoid it. She quickly realised her one ally might prove to be none other than the gelding which, she fervently hoped, would return to the stables if offered sufficient encouragement. Blessedly recapturing him with ease, she applied her crop to his flanks and, fulfilling her every hope, he set off at a canter up the gentle slope towards the house, finally disappearing from view as he trotted into the stable-yard.

The filly had begun to follow, but had abandoned the chase after a short distance only, and as she seemed content to graze on the lush grass again, Beth concentrated her attention on the unconscious man, once more cradling his head in her lap. Removing his right glove, she held his hand in her own. It was comforting to feel the warmth in his fingers, but only when she knew the full extent of his injuries could she be completely easy in her mind.

Taking out her handkerchief she placed it against the gash on his forehead, and watched the red stain slowly spreading over the fine lawn. 'Don't you dare be badly hurt... Life would be meaningless without you,' she murmured softly, a moment before she detected slight movement in the fingers she held.

By the time Rudge came cantering out of the stable-yard to investigate, Philip had blessedly regained consciousness. Apart from the throbbing ache in his temple, his only other main injury was to his right ankle, which Beth strongly suspected was sprained only.

With Rudge's assistance, and a deal of cursing on Sir Philip's part, the boot was finally removed, confirming Beth's suspicions. 'You'll be thanking me tomorrow for saving a decent pair of boots,' she told him, showing not a ha'p'orth of sympathy for the extra pain she'd inflicted. 'Had we left it on any longer, it would have needed to be cut off.'

Understandably enough Philip was hardly in a receptive mood, and merely scowled up at her before she turned her attention to her groom, requesting he return to the house in order to summon the doctor and have the carriage made ready to collect the master of the house.

'But first, Rudge,' she added in a low tone, and moving out of earshot of the injured man, 'I want you to take that saddle back to the stables, and conceal it somewhere until I've had a chance to examine it more closely.'

With a nod of assent, the groom collected the saddle and the filly, and returned with them both to the stable-yard. Then it was a matter of minutes only before Beth and Sir Philip were being conveyed back to the house in the carriage.

As she was now firmly convinced none of the injuries would prove in the least life-threatening, Beth didn't accompany Philip into the house to await the doctor's prognosis. Instead, she went round to the stable-yard in search of her faithful Rudge.

'You were right, Miss Beth,' he said, removing the saddle from the pile of straw where it had been adequately concealed. 'That there strap were cut almost through. With a knife, I reckon. Done deliberate, without a doubt.'

'I know it looks suspicious, Rudge. But we cannot be one hundred per cent certain it wasn't simply an accident, that it didn't come into contact with some sharp object here in the stables, and was overlooked.'

'I can,' he astounded her by responding.

She regarded him keenly. 'How can you be so sure?'

'Because I checked both saddles before you and the master 'ere set out. Force of 'abit, I s'pose. The saddle on the filly were fine. Nowt wrong wi' it at all. But the saddle on the bay were loose. Anyone trying to mount would 'ave fallen flat on 'is—' Rudge checked just in time. 'Well, you knows what I mean, miss. I called the young stable-lad 'ere all the names under the sun for 'is tardiness, and threatened to tell the 'ead groom. But the lad swore he'd done the job proper. And you know something, Miss Beth, I don't reckon he were spinning no yarn!'

'And you noticed no damage to the girth strap, then, yourself?'

'There weren't no damage, Miss Beth. I'd stake m'life on it. That took place when you were out riding. So seems to me you'd know best when that might 'ave 'appened.' He took a moment to run his fingers over the bristles on his chin. 'The mischief that went on 'ere in the stable-yard be another thing altogether. From what the stable-lad were saying, I reckon, apart from thee and me, there's been only one visitor to this 'ere yard this day, and you be knowing 'ee, Miss Beth, as you spoke to the young sprig yourself.'

Beth's mind's eye had already conjured up a vision of Crispin Napier standing by the horses, and appearing decidedly sheepish. She also clearly recalled seeing him disappear into the home wood. And, of course, it could only have been at the home wood, when she and Philip had sat by the trout stream, that someone had had the opportunity to damage the saddle strap.

Well, Crispin Napier certainly wasn't one of Sir Philip's most ardent admirers at the present time, Beth reminded herself. But did his dislike go so deep that he might wish the Baronet real harm? There was only one way she was going to find out!

She was lucky enough to find Mr Napier at the vicarage, and alone, as the Reverend Mr Chadwick and his wife were out and about in the gig, paying visits on one or two ill parishioners.

'Why, what a pleasant surprise, seeing you twice in one day!' he graciously announced, rising at once to his feet, though whether the sentiment had been genuine Beth wasn't altogether sure.

'Your pleasure might be short-lived when you discover why I'm here,' she informed him bluntly, the instant the housekeeper had departed.

All at once his smile faded and his expression became decidedly guarded. 'Yes, well may you look like that, Crispin Napier. What on earth possessed you to play such a foolish prank? And don't you dare try to deny it!' she ordered, cutting him off mid-sentence when he attempted to do just that. 'Apart from my groom, we two were the only visitors to the stable-yard.'

Seemingly realising it would be futile to lie, he had the grace to look shamefaced. 'I didn't mean any real harm,' he assured her, running a hand through his blond, curling locks, and appearing every inch the erring schoolboy. 'I felt hurt and angry because Sir Philip's servants wouldn't even allow me to see Phoebe. So in the end I had to leave a note.'

'Undoubtedly they were only obeying orders. More than likely my aunt's, not Sir Philip's,' she wasn't slow to point out.

'I know that,' he responded sombrely. 'The instant I loosened the girth I regretted it. But there was nothing I could do, because you came riding into the yard at that point. All I wanted was to make Sir Philip look foolish in front of Phoebe. I thought if he took a tumble when trying to mount, she wouldn't think so highly of him, think him so dashed perfect!' His expression grew suddenly mutinous. 'If you'd heard her singing his praises last night, saying what an elegant dancer he was and what an accomplished host. It was enough to turn a fellow queasy, so it was!'

Beth regarded him in silence, and drew her own conclusions. Clearly a slight tiff had taken place between the young couple at some point during the ball, which had undoubtedly been at the root of the mischievous act.

Mr Napier at last returned her gaze. 'You cannot imagine how guilty I felt when I saw it was you, not Phoebe, riding with him.' Unexpectedly, he brightened. 'He looked fine to me, so there was no harm done, was there?'

'Not then, no, Crispin,' she enlightened him. 'But it was a different story after we'd sat by the trout stream and then set off back to the Court. Someone deliberately cut the girth-strap on his saddle, and Philip did sustain a fall. Nothing serious, as things turned out, but even so the intent was there.'

He looked genuinely shocked. 'But that wasn't me, I swear it!'

She didn't doubt the truth of this for a moment, and was quick to assure him of the fact, before asking, 'But did you happen to see anyone in the home wood when you took a short cut through there this morning?'

He shook his head. 'No, wait a minute,' he corrected a moment later. 'There was someone. Assumed he must have been an estate worker.'

'In which direction was he heading?' Beth asked, eager for any information.

'The opposite direction to me. Roughly eastwards, I should say.'

'Towards the trout stream,' Beth muttered, before asking for a description of the man.

Mr Napier shook his head. 'Truth to tell, I didn't take

much notice. I was still thinking about Phoebe, and not in the best of moods.'

Beth wasn't prepared to concede defeat so easily. 'Come on, Crispin,' she urged him, 'there must have been something you noticed about the man. You said you thought he was a labourer. Evidently he wasn't well dressed.'

'No, not in the least. Quite shabby, in fact. That much I did notice. Always notice what people are wearing.' He raised one finger triumphantly. 'And he wasn't wearing a hat, now I come to think about it. Long, black hair, he had—matted, as though it hadn't seen a comb in a month of Sundays. Swarthy complexion, unshaven, the sort of cove you'd take for a footpad, though I have to say he made no attempt to interfere with me. If anything, he hurried past, looking the other way, as though he didn't wish to be seen. He was tall, too, now I come to think about it, several inches taller than me, at any rate, and lean.'

'Well done, Crispin!' Beth acknowledged, getting to her feet. 'At least you've given us something to go on. In all probability he'll turn out to be an estate worker. But one never knows. I'll see what I can discover in the next day or so.'

Chapter Seven

Philip raised his head from between the pages of the *Morning Post*, and almost found himself sighing with relief at sight of his portly uncle entering the library. Having been obliged to contend with the ministrations of a pack of well-meaning but annoyingly overprotective females for a period of almost twenty-four hours had been enough to try the patience of a saint. And he had never aimed so high!

'Thank heaven it's you, Waldo! For one heart-stopping moment I thought my sister had changed her mind and had decided not to join the party going to Wells Cathedral today, after all.'

'Don't worry, dear boy. I made my farewells whilst seeing Connie safely into the carriage personally. I must say young Joyce has done you proud. He managed to persuade all your remaining guests to join the party. Most of 'em will be leaving tomorrow,' he reminded his nephew, as he lowered his well-padded frame into the chair on the opposite side of the hearth. 'And I shall be gone from under your feet the instant the post-chaise arrives this morning.'

The latter reminder didn't precisely lift Philip's spirits. 'Yes, you're deserting me today and Simon Joyce is doing the very same thing tomorrow, leaving me with only guests of the fair sex in the house.' He tossed the paper aside irritably. 'I never thought I'd hear myself saying this…but I believe I'm turning into something of a misogynist. I'm becoming increasingly tired of female company.'

Waldo checked in the act of raising a pinch of snuff to one nostril for a second or two, and then sneezed violently, spilling a little of the silver box's contents down the front of his waistcoat.

'With one possible exception,' he countered sagely, while attempting to mop up the spillage with his handkerchief, with little effect as he continued to stare fixedly at his nephew, almost daring him to deny the assertion, or to pretend to misunderstand.

Philip didn't attempt either. All the same, Beth wasn't precisely basking in the sunshine of his approval at the present time, so he wasn't prepared to sing her praises quite yet.

'Little minx! Not satisfied with causing me the most excruciating pain by removing my boot, she then deserts me the instant we arrive back here, leaving me to suffer my sister's endless fussing.'

Waldo's large frame shook in silent, appreciative laughter. 'Sensible little filly. Always thought so. Instinctively knows when to make herself scarce. Never *de trop*, as it were.'

All at once his usual amiable expression began to fade and he looked distinctly thoughtful. 'Remember that time when she took herself off, without informing a soul, hardly, and joined old Augustus out in the Peninsula. Always wondered what really lay behind all that.'

He was quiet for a moment, clearly contemplating the enigma. 'Of course, she and her father were wondrous close. Touchingly so, I seem to recall. Very understandable, therefore, that she would want to be with him. Even so, I've always thought there was more to it than that. Always wondered, too, whether deep down she also thought you and that cousin of hers weren't so perfectly suited.'

As he was unable to supply the answer, Philip merely shrugged before revealing, 'All I can tell you is she's certainly not in favour of me forming an alliance with her youngest Barfield cousin. Of course, there's no question of any such thing,' he readily confirmed. 'That's all been in Connie's head. Notwithstanding, I gained the distinct impression that more lay at the root of Beth's objections than a belief that we wouldn't suit. And in that she's perfectly right, of course!' He shrugged again. 'Who knows, maybe you too are right, and she did have reservations about my proposed union with Eugenie. All I do know is that I've never regretted taking your sound advice all those years ago and delaying the union.'

Waldo returned to his pocket the handkerchief that had proven so ineffective at removing the yellow stain from his waistcoat. 'I knew eventually you'd come to your senses and realise you required something rather more than just beauty in a wife. I deeply regret matters between you went quite so far, and the engagement became official. Knowing you as I do, I truly believe you would have gone through with the marriage. Naturally I'm glad you were never honour-bound to do so. But not for the world would I have wished things to end so tragically.'

As his nephew offered no comment, Waldo added,

'A good many people have remarked in recent years on your resemblance to your father. And it's true to say in many ways you are similar, in looks, at any rate. But in temperament I rather fancy you favour your mother a good deal more, thank the Lord! She was no beauty, bless her! But in my humble opinion she had qualities far more worthy of note. Unlike your father, she always kept a remarkable cool head in times of stress, and always considered carefully before taking important decisions.'

'I learned the hard way the wisdom of doing precisely that,' Philip acknowledged, before belatedly coming to his late father's defence. 'There's no denying my father could be unbending on occasions, set in his ways. But no one could ever have accused him of being deliberately cruel or intolerant.'

'Perhaps not,' Waldo conceded. 'But he was wont to act on impulse, and rarely reconsidered. Whereas you, as you've said yourself, have learned the wisdom of deliberation before action. And that's no bad thing.'

The conversation was brought to an end by the butler who entered to announce Beth's arrival, and also to inform his master that the hired carriage had at last arrived at the Court.

'Splendid!' Waldo announced, rising slowly to his feet in order to place an avuncular kiss on one of Beth's soft cheeks the instant she entered the room. 'I can safely leave with a clear conscience now, knowing my nephew will be admirably entertained.'

One glance at Philip, clad in dressing gown and Turkish slippers, with his right leg resting on a foot-stool, gave Beth a pretty shrewd idea of what had been taking place at the Court since her departure the previous day. 'How can you be so cruel as to desert the poor fellow in his hour of need?' she teased, twinkling up at the big man who had always held a place in her affections.

'He'll do well enough now,' Waldo responded, taking a hurried leave of them both, with a smile of satisfaction lingering on his plump face.

'I didn't realise he was intending to leave the Court quite so soon,' Beth declared, the instant they were alone. 'Had I known, I would have tried to spend a little more time with him. He's always been a firm favourite of mine, as you well know.'

'Believe me the sentiment is entirely reciprocated,' Philip enlightened her, before revealing that his uncle had never intended making it a long stay. 'He's combining the visit with a short interlude in Bath, where he intends to look up some old friends.'

'He should consider taking the waters whilst he's there,' Beth suggested in her no-nonsense fashion. 'He's becoming increasingly portly, Philip. He's clearly become far too fond of the finer things in life. And speaking of which…' Beth went over to the decanters placed on the table in the corner. 'Do you mind if I help myself? I'm absolutely parched. Been out and about since early morning.'

'Not at all. And you may pour me a Madeira whilst you're about it.'

After doing as bidden, Beth made herself comfortable in the chair recently vacated by Philip's uncle. It was only then that it occurred to her that the place seemed surprisingly quiet. 'Where is everyone?'

'Visiting Wells. Between you and me, Beth, with the exception of Simon, who's leaving on the morrow, I shan't be sorry to see the back of my guests. And that includes my sister. I've already told her she's deserted her husband and children quite long enough. And I shan't permit her to use yesterday's trifling accident to me as an excuse to remain.'

Beth slanted a mocking glance. 'Philip, you're speaking with me, remember? That was no accident, as you're probably very well aware yourself by now.'

He didn't attempt to deny it. 'But there's a possibility, surely, the strap was damaged. Apparently some fault was discovered with the saddle before we set out, though my head groom didn't seem to know precisely what was amiss with it.'

'He might not, but I do know,' Beth returned, before divulging part of what she had discovered the day before. 'Crispin's actions were mischievous, not malicious. And there was no harm done. Rudge tightened the strap.'

'And I'm grateful to him for so doing,' Philip acknowledged, though puzzled. 'But why should young Napier wish to play such a childish prank? What have I ever done to him? I've always made a point of inviting him to join the various activities taking place here at the Court whenever he's stayed at the vicarage.'

Beth cast him a look of amused exasperation. 'That crack on the head yesterday must have been more serious than I'd supposed!' she declared, raising her eyes ceiling-wards. 'He's sweet on Phoebe, of course! She's the only reason he's down here at all. From what I can gather, he was denied the pleasure of even seeing her when he called here yesterday and, quite naturally, felt hurt and annoyed,' she continued. 'He wished to make you look foolish in Phoebe's eyes because...well, from what I can gather...she'd been singing your praises slightly too frequently for his liking at the ball the evening before. He regretted the impulse almost immediately, poor boy.'

'I'll poor boy him when next we meet!' Philip threatened, experiencing no such understanding.

'You'd do well to reconsider,' Beth advised, amused by the distinct lack of sympathy on his part. 'In view of Simon Joyce's departure on the morrow, Crispin might yet prove very useful to you. For a start, he could deputise for you and squire the ladies about for the remainder of their stay. Which would serve to get them from under your feet.'

All at once she was serious. 'As I've already revealed, Napier loosened the girth. He didn't cut the strap. That could only have happened when we were sat by the trout stream, don't you agree?'

Philip didn't immediately comment, even though he clearly recalled the horses whinnying, as though disturbed by something. Eventually he said, 'And you're sure it wasn't young Napier's handiwork? We saw him enter the wood, remember?'

'He swore he didn't do it, and I believe him,' Beth responded without having to give the matter a moment's thought. 'He did, however, see someone in the wood— a tall man with long, unkempt black hair. Remind you of anyone? Not your gamekeeper, is it?'

'No, he's quite the opposite build—short and stocky.' Philip shrugged. 'Can't say the description reminds me of anyone…at least no one immediately springs to mind. I'll maybe have a word with my steward and discover if he's hired any casual labour recently, though at this time of year I cannot imagine for what purpose.'

Although gratified that Philip had no intention of forgetting about the whole business, Beth wasn't prepared to abandon her own efforts to unearth the culprit. Consequently when she left the Court half an hour later she surprised her groom somewhat by setting out across the park in the opposite direction to the Grange.

'Where we bound for now, Miss Beth?' Rudge asked. 'Not going back to Markham, surely?'

Beth couldn't forbear a smile at the disgruntled tone. They had spent the better part of the morning walking about the local town in what had turned out to be a totally fruitless attempt to locate anyone who matched Mr Napier's description of the man in the wood. Silently she was obliged to own that it hadn't been the most sensible course of action she'd ever taken in her life. She would have done better to discover, first of all, if the man was indeed an estate worker. Unlike Philip, however, who was bent on approaching his steward, Beth suspected that a certain other employee would be more likely to provide her with what she wished to know.

'No, we're only going as far as the east gate to have a word with the keeper there.' She smiled wickedly as she cast her groom a sideways glance. 'You and he should rub along together famously. You're both prickly devils.'

Catching sight of George Dodd seated in the doorway of his cottage, contentedly pulling on his pipe, Beth quickly dismounted, and didn't delay in discovering what she wished to know.

The old man shook his head. 'No one like that working on the estate, that I do know. All master's people been 'ere for years. Knows when they're well off, see. Besides, no one 'ere 'ud do master 'arm. Well thought of by everyone, 'ee be.'

Removing the pipe from his mouth again, he used the end to scratch the side of his nose. 'Now 'is father were not so well liked. 'Ee did rub some up the wrong way. Got rid o' one or two of 'is tenants, I seem to recall. Caused some bad feeling at the time. Some thought 'ee were a bit 'arsh.'

Dodd favoured her with a searching look. 'Why be you wanting to know, Miss Beth, if you don't mind me asking, like?'

Knowing she could trust him implicitly, Beth didn't hesitate to satisfy his curiosity, and saw at once an arresting look flicker in the short-sighted eyes. 'What it is, Dodd? Have you suddenly thought of someone who might fit the description?'

'No, nowt like that, miss. Just thinking about that time when young master were out shooting in the wood with friends, back along, early in the summer. Gamekeeper said as 'ow a shot or two went awry. One came close to taking the master's hat clean off, seemingly. No one owned up to it, as I can recall. Didn't surprise me none, though, as some of those shooting were neighbours' young sons. So there were bound to be some high larks going on. But it do make 'ee wonder, now, if t'were just an accident.'

Although this was the first time she'd heard mention of any shooting incidents, Beth recalled quite clearly Crispin Napier mentioning being invited to a shooting party at the Court early in the summer, more than likely the very same one. In the next moment she dismissed the likelihood that he had been in any way responsible from her mind. He might well indulge in a prank where someone ended with a bruised ego, but he would never deliberately endanger someone's life. All the same she made a mental note to tax Philip about the incident at the earliest opportunity, and learn his views.

Discovering nothing further of real interest, Beth

didn't delay her departure. Throughout the journey back
to the Grange she mulled over what she had discovered
that day and, more importantly, what she had failed to
unearth. Try as she might, she couldn't rid herself of the
feeling that, since her return to her West Country home,
she had seen someone, somewhere local, who had fitted
young Crispin's description, if not exactly, then closely
enough to warrant further investigation. She was almost
sure, too, that the sighting had occurred during one of
her visits to the town. So there was nothing for it but to
keep searching in the more likely locations.

'Rudge,' she said, having come to a decision, 'after
you've taken Mrs Stride to the vicarage this evening, I
want you to return here at once. We're going back to
Markham.'

Quite naturally he was surprised, and didn't attempt
to hide the fact. 'But ain't you going to dine at the
vicarage too?'

'No, sadly I fear I must cry off, having succumbed
to one of my rare sick heads.' Smiling wickedly, she
placed a hand against her forehead. 'Tragic, isn't it?'

All at once the groom's expression changed dramatically, and he regarded her with evident suspicion. 'Now,
what be you about, Miss Beth? You ain't never given
way to trifling ills, not since I've known you, at any
rate.'

'True,' Beth was forced to acknowledge, as she dismounted and handed him the reins. 'I know it, you know
it, and Sir Philip knows that I'm disgustingly healthy as
a rule. All I need to do is convince darling Mrs Stride,
whose friendship with the vicar and his good lady wife
has proved so advantageous in more ways than one, that
I've succumbed to one of my oh, so very rare megrims.
Then we shall be free to scour the town again tonight.'

Whipping off his hat, Rudge scratched his head, clearly perplexed. 'That's all very well, miss. But do you think it'll do any good? We searched and searched this morning. And a fine lot of good it did us,' he reminded her.

'True,' she said again. 'But that I fancy was because we neglected to look in…quite the right places.'

All at once his suspicious look returned. 'And what would you be thinking be the right places, may I ask?'

'Well, you'd know best, of course. But I thought patronising a lowly tavern or two might prove worthwhile.'

'One or two…?' He appeared lost for words, but only for a moment. 'If you think I'm squiring a lady like you into such places, you can think again, Miss Beth, 'cause I tell you plainly, I ain't!'

'Of course you won't be escorting me,' she returned, smiling agreeably. 'You'll be taking your nephew Martin.'

After gaping open-mouthed at her for almost a full half-minute, the groom managed to exclaim, 'But I ain't got no nephew, as well you knows!'

'Come, come, you cannot have forgotten!' Beth coaxed, enjoying herself hugely at her bemused servant's expense. 'He's paying a brief visit to the area and he'll be eagerly awaiting your return this evening. And we'll not be taking the carriage. I'll have the horses ready saddled for you both, when you return from the vicarage.'

Later, when Beth joined her companion in the front parlour, and repeated her intention of not dining at the vicarage that evening, Ann betrayed no less astonishment than Rudge had done.

'It really is most annoying,' she went on, wondering when she had learned to be so devious. 'I was only remarking to you not so very long ago that I haven't succumbed to any trifling ailments for simply ages—years, in fact. Clearly it's a judgement on me! I woke this morning and knew at once I would suffer one of my rare bad heads.'

'You never mentioned anything at the breakfast table, dear,' Ann reminded her, not appearing wholly convinced it had to be said.

Not in the least discomposed, Beth shrugged. 'You know I cannot abide those who make a deal of fuss about trifling ills. I thought a ride into Markham might surely effect a cure. Sadly it hasn't. There's nothing for it but to retire early and have a good night's sleep.'

'The Chadwicks will be so disappointed,' Ann remarked, after seemingly accepting that Beth wasn't likely to change her mind. 'It's such a pity. I was so looking forward to it. It's the first time I've been invited to dine at the vicarage.'

Alarm bells instantly began to ring in Beth's head. 'Of course, I still expect you to go,' she declared. 'No, Ann,' she went on, holding up her hand against the protest that was about to be made. 'You being here will serve no useful purpose whatsoever. There's no reason why you shouldn't enjoy the evening. Rudge will take you and collect you in the carriage as arranged.'

Surprisingly Ann put up no further argument, and after a moment said, lowering her gaze, 'I should be grateful for the use of the carriage so that I do not have to walk to the vicarage. The light fails so early nowadays. But I might be able to beg a lift in Mr Bathurst's carriage on the homeward journey. He, so I understand, is collecting his friends the Frobishers en route, so there'll be room in the chaise for me on the homeward journey.

'And speaking of Mr Bathurst,' Ann went on, when Beth, smiling faintly, merely stared absently down at the hearth, 'he called here earlier. Seemed very disappointed not to find you at home, and said he would return the day after tomorrow. Said something about bringing a mutual friend along, if that was agreeable.'

This drew Beth's immediate attention. 'Yes, yes, I shall be at home. Perhaps you'll be kind enough to convey that message to him this evening?'

Receiving a nod and a slight smile in response, Beth studied her companion through narrowed, assessing eyes, as once again Ann gave her full attention to the fire screen she was embroidering.

'I must confess I've revised my opinion of your friendship with the Chadwicks,' she admitted. 'At the beginning I thought they were merely taking advantage of your good nature. Now I'm not so sure. Through their introduction, and others, of course, you've become well acquainted with a great many in the locale, the Frobishers included. Am I right in thinking it was none other than Mrs Frobisher who brought you that parcel of clothes the other day to distribute among the poor?'

'Yes, dear. Mrs Frobisher saw to it that all were laundered, and repaired where necessary. I shall take them along with me when I go to the vicarage this evening.'

'No, don't do that,' Beth countered. 'I'd like to take a look through them myself first, if I may? I seem to recall mention of a jacket, shirt and trousers. I know of someone who might be grateful for the—er—use of those.'

'Of course, dear. There's no hurry. I can always take them round another day, if they should prove un-

suitable,' Ann obligingly responded, thereby drawing a
further brief smile of satisfaction to curl her young
employer's shapely mouth.

Unfortunately that evening Beth experienced no
similar satisfaction. Her second visit to Markham was
turning out to be as unprofitable as the first that day. The
rough material of her borrowed masculine garb chafed
against her skin, the workman's boots she'd managed
to find were too large and too heavy, making walking
difficult. Moreover, the evening was by far the coldest
experienced that autumn. And if that was not bad
enough, her companion had not stopped cursing and
muttering under his breath since they had left the
Grange!

'Oh, for heaven's sake, Rudge, will you stop complaining!' she ordered, fast losing her patience. 'It's as
bad for me, as you. In fact, a good deal worse, if
anything! At least your clothes are your own, and your
shoes fit. I'm not precisely enjoying the experience of
being out on a bitterly cold night, either. Nor entering
these hostelries, where I swear I've collected unwanted
livestock,' she added, once again scratching beneath her
jacket.

She gazed with misgivings at the inn before her. Set
on the outskirts of the town, it appeared without doubt
the worst she'd visited thus far. Even in the dim light,
she could detect what appeared suspiciously like several
areas of tiles missing from the roof, cracked outer walls
and peeling paintwork, all of which gave her a strong
suspicion of what the interior must be like. At least,
though, there was the smell of smoke lingering in the
air, which suggested the landlord had a good fire going.

'No matter how successful we are, or otherwise,

we'll make this the last place we visit,' she promised, dismounting and leaving the horses tethered in a rundown outbuilding, which supposedly served as a stable.

The declaration did absolutely nothing to lessen the servant's troubled expression. 'Aye, that's all very well. But will it be the last 'un you'll ever visit? That's what's troubling me.'

'Now, that I couldn't say,' she was honest enough to admit. 'All depends on what, if anything, we discover. We might need to make return visits to several taverns in the not too distant future.'

Rudge groaned. 'He'll murder me, so 'ee will, when he finds out. And find out 'ee will, you may be sure o' that, Miss Beth!'

'What the deuce are you muttering about now?' she demanded to know, her patience rapidly waning once more. 'You're answerable to no one, except me. And don't call me Miss Beth! I'm your nephew, remember?'

The instant Beth entered the dimly lit room, her worst fears were realised. She was assailed by the smell of unwashed bodies, and general mustiness. So offensive were the combined odours that she was on the point of swinging round on her heels and marching straight back out again, only to check at the last moment, when she caught sight of a figure slouched over a rickety table close to the fire.

Making her way over to the counter in order to purchase two tankards of ale, she alerted Rudge's attention to the man who had captured her interest. 'Do you know him? Have you ever seen him before?'

'Can't say as I 'ave,' he admitted, after a quick, surreptitious glance. He waited a moment or two before repeating the action, and then frowned. 'Seem to recollect one of those other two seated at the same table, though. It'll come to me, no doubt, if you give me time to think on it.'

As the seats dotted about the room were all occupied, Beth and Rudge had no alternative but to prop themselves against a wall, and try to appear as inconspicuous as possible. It was only to be expected that two complete strangers would arouse some interest among the hostelry's regular patrons, and so it proved to be. After a few minutes, though, curiosity lessened, and murmured exchanges became more frequent, as the patrons turned their attention once more to their tankards of ale and nearest companions, with one noticeable exception.

'That one I reckons I know keeps looking over,' Rudge disclosed. 'Seems to know me, too. Now all three of 'em be staring this way. Whatever you do, miss, don't turn round,' he warned, 'cause if it's the cove I think it is, he'll mayhap recognise you, even dressed as you are.'

'Who do you think it is?' Beth asked, heeding the advice by keeping her back turned, and also pulling the misshapen hat, which she'd managed to find in a trunk in the attic, lower down about her ears.

'I ain't positive, but I reckon 'ee be that private whose leg you saved...can't rightly remember whether it was...San Marcial, or mayhap after the battle at Vera. You remember, Miss Beth,' Rudge prompted. 'That young surgeon—ha, butcher more like!—were all for taking it off above the knee, but you stopped 'im. Said as 'ow it might be saved if the ball was removed. You did it an' all, remember? Mind, it left the leg a bit stiff, as I recall, couldn't bend it. Sent 'ome soon afterwards. Looks as if it's still giving 'im trouble, stuck out straight like that.' He frowned heavily. 'What was 'is name now...Clegg, or summat like.'

'Yes, that's right,' Beth agreed, having by this time recalled the incident. She risked the briefest of glances over her shoulder. 'Private Tom Clegg. I remember seeing him, now, in Markham on one of my visits. I couldn't place him then. Didn't realise he came from round these parts. Seem to recall him telling me he had a wife and child…a boy, I think. I wonder what he's doing here?'

This was a circumstance she could not have foreseen, and Beth was sensible enough to acknowledge it silently at once. She had spent a deal of time with Private Tom Clegg in an attempt to save his leg, not to mention his life, and there was every chance he would succeed in penetrating her disguise if curiosity got the better of him, and he decided to come over. Yet, although it might prove dangerous to remain, she couldn't resist asking Rudge to study the tall man with the matted, long black hair, sitting at the same table.

He shook his head. 'May 'ave been out there with us in Spain, but I don't remember 'im. Nor t'other one, neither.'

All at once he tossed what was left in his tankard down his throat. 'Come on, miss, we'd best not tarry. Looks as though Clegg's about to get up, and 'ee might take it into 'is 'ead to come over if 'ee 'as recognised me.'

Once again Beth heeded the advice, and hurriedly followed Rudge from the inn without so much as a backward glance. All the same, she couldn't resist looking over her shoulder as they rode off down the road, and could clearly see someone silhouetted in the doorway, though whether it was Tom Clegg or not was impossible to judge.

'I cannot make up my mind whether coming across Clegg is a good or a bad thing,' Beth declared, after riding along in silence for some distance. 'What's his connection with that dark-haired man? If a friend, would he be willing to reveal things that might shed light on why Sir Philip was harmed?'

'We don't even know yet, miss, whether t'other one be the man seen in the wood, let alone if it were 'ee that cut the saddle strap.'

'True enough,' Beth acknowledged. 'Young Mr Napier might be able to recognise him, but it's far from certain. Added to which it might prove difficult persuading such a pernickety young man to enter a tavern of that low order. He'd stand out a mile, and very likely arouse suspicion.' She refused to be too downcast. 'If it is our man, and it cannot be denied he does fit the description very nicely, then at least we know he visits that particular inn, and so it shouldn't be too difficult a matter to discover something about him. '

Even in the darkness it was possible to see the expression of acute dismay on the servant's face. It was easily discernible in his voice too as he said, 'You're never thinking of going back there, miss, surely…? Why, 'tis madness! Sooner or later Clegg'll be bound to realise who you are.'

'That's a risk I might be forced to take if I want to get to the truth.'

Chapter Eight

Although far too sensible to ignore the well-respected local practitioner's sound advice, Sir Philip wasn't accustomed to idling his time away. Consequently, the following day he resumed, at least in part, overseeing estate matters.

Except for his right ankle, which remained painful and swollen, and which necessitated the continued wearing of soft slippers, he felt none the worse for his ordeal. Nor had he allowed what had surely been nothing more than an asinine attempt to hurt him prey on his mind.

He was very well aware that there was a deal of bitterness towards his class at the present time—understandable when one considered the plight of the vast majority of the poor. All the same, until convinced otherwise, he was inclined to believe the perpetrator, prompted by searing resentment, had acted on impulse rather than out of any deep-seated grievance against him personally. He and Beth had just happened to be in the wrong place at the wrong time, and he had become the innocent victim of someone's pent-up frustrations at life's injustices. Thank the Lord the perpetrator had not taken it into his head to damage both saddles!

As the door opened Philip raised his eyes from the papers in his hand to see his butler entering the room. One glance was sufficient to warn him that all was not well with this punctilious major-domo. There was about the servant the air of a man who was acting counter to doctrine, prompted by obligation rather than inclination.

'Yes, what is it, Stebbings?'

'There is a person without wishful to have a word in private with you, sir, if convenient.'

The loud sniff that preceded the disclosure gave Philip every reason to suppose that the visitor very likely belonged to the lower orders. 'And does this person have a name?'

'It is Miss Ashworth's manservant, sir.' It was at this point the butler appeared to be having some difficulty in forming his words. 'Given that you are unable to walk any great distance, I was obliged to invite the person to take a step into the hall, as I was assured the matter which he wishes to discuss is of real importance.'

Philip didn't doubt it for a moment. Master Amos Rudge might be an unorthodox servant, and an extremely impertinent one to boot, but he was not in the least ingratiating, and would never have sought an interview for his own benefit. Consequently Philip didn't hesitate to have him shown in immediately.

'Come in, man! Come in and take a seat,' he invited, when Rudge remained by the door, turning his floppy, misshapen hat in his hands, and showing none of his usual swaggering self-confidence.

'Begging your pardon, sir, but I won't sit. It wouldn't be fitting, not with me in m'working clothes,' he responded, taking a further tentative step or two into the book-lined room. 'And the truth of the matter is, sir, I'm not 'appy about being 'ere at all.'

That was patently obvious. It seemed as though all the servant's natural bravado had been left at the side entrance. Philip, suspecting that the interview had been sought only after a deal of soul searching, attempted to make Rudge feel a little more at ease by thanking him for the service he'd rendered in the stable-yard a couple of days before.

'No, need to thank me, sir. Force of 'abit, as yer might say,' Rudge responded, before appearing troubled again. 'And that's really why I'm 'ere.'

'You wish to tell me something more about the incident involving the saddle?' Philip prompted, when the groom merely stared intently down at the logs burning in the hearth.

'It's Miss Beth, sir. She's only gone and taken it into 'er 'ead to look for the blighter 'erself. Scoured Markham yesterday, both morning and evening, so we did. Mistress seems to s'ppose we may 'ave found 'im, too. And that's what's got me worried. Now she's got the bit between 'er teeth, there'll be no stopping 'er. Like as not she'll go back there. And she won't listen to me, sir.'

Alarm bells were well and truly chiming in Philip's head, as he instinctively suspected the worst. He had believed Beth had outgrown her childish, headstrong ways. Seemingly he had been wrong.

'Where, precisely, did you eventually run the supposed miscreant to earth?'

His expression giving absolutely nothing away, Rudge continued to focus on some spot a foot or two above the Baronet's head. 'In a tavern, sir, on the outskirts of the town.'

A moment's silence, then, 'Do you mean to tell me your mistress walked willy-nilly into a hostelry of that low order, without even considering the consequences of her actions?' Philip clapped a hand over his eyes. 'God in heaven! It was a wonder she managed to leave with her virtue intact!'

'She were in disguise, as yer might say,' Rudge assured him. 'She were pretending to be my...nephew, like.'

This information did absolutely nothing to ease Philip's troubled state. 'Kindly pull the bell-cord over there, and then hand me my stick!' he ordered, in the ominously quiet tone that would have instantly alerted anyone who knew him well to the fact that he wasn't in the best of moods. 'I shall deal with the matter from here on.'

'I was trusting you would, sir,' Rudge responded, clearly well pleased with the outcome of the visit.

Beth managed to conceal her surprise rather better than did her companion when Sir Philip hobbled into the front parlour at the Grange later that same morning. One glance at the almost rigid set of his aristocratic features was sufficient warning that all was not well with him. Had she needed further proof that he was far from his usual calm, collected self then she only needed to consider his slightly bizarre attire. Highly praised for his sartorial elegance, he appeared a trifle absurd sporting one highly polished top-boot, and one gold-and-crimson curly-toed slipper.

Having a fairly shrewd notion about precisely what had given rise to this totally unexpected visit, she turned to her companion. 'I am of the considered opinion, Ann, that Sir Philip would much prefer, in this instance, to speak with me in private.'

Although she had managed to maintain quite beautifully a steady control over her voice, she was nowhere near as successful in preventing the sparkle of wicked enjoyment glinting in her eyes. 'As I have no desire to be held responsible for him suffering an apoplexy, I am on this occasion prepared to dispense with convention and allow him to vent his spleen in private,' she added, moving across the room in order to open the door for her somewhat bemused companion. 'So, if you wouldn't mind…?'

Philip, who had maintained remarkable control over his temper thus far, waited only until Mrs Stride had left the room, before voicing his feelings. 'If you were a dozen or so years younger, my girl, I'd know exactly how to deal with you!'

Far from chastened, Beth gurgled appreciatively. 'It's possibly as well for you I'm no longer a child. In your present condition you'd suffer a deal more than I would in an attempt to catch me.

'Oh, sit down do, Philip,' she added when he continued to glower at her like an irate father fast approaching the end of his tether. 'I can guess what has brought you here. And quite frankly I could throttle Rudge for his tale-bearing! In fact, I'm strongly tempted to turn him off at the twelvemonth for such disloyalty!'

'Do so,' Philip invited, even though he was certain the threat had been a totally empty one, 'and I shall instantly offer him employment up at the Court. I need a replacement for my head groom, who'll be retiring shortly.'

Beth raised her brows at this as she considerately positioned a footstool in order for him to rest his injured ankle. 'You've changed your tune,' she reminded him, as she went across to the decanters to pour him a glass of a particularly fine burgundy she'd discovered in the cellar a couple of days before. 'I thought you considered him an impudent rogue.'

'And so he is!' Philip acknowledged. 'But it's plain to see he's good with horses,' he added fair-mindedly, after sampling the wine and nodding approval. 'He's also conscientious. And I should imagine intensely loyal to those for whom he works.'

'But not to me, it would seem. As he's proved by going to see you today.'

Although the response had been swiftly delivered, Philip could detect no trace of resentment in either voice or expression. All the same, he felt obliged to justify what had been tantamount to a breach of trust on Rudge's part.

'Deep concern over your welfare forced him to seek an interview with me, Beth, nothing more.'

'I'm fully aware of it,' she responded, maintaining quite beautifully a matter-of-fact tone. 'I just wish he'd waited a while before playing the tale-bearer, that's all. It just so happens I went looking for him earlier this morning in order to tell him I'd experienced a change of heart. I wondered where he was hiding himself.'

Over the rim of his glass, Philip studied her intently. She appeared so serenely self-possessed that it was hard to imagine she would ever embark on any such madcap escapade. His curiosity got the better of him and he found himself asking, 'What on earth possessed you to behave so rashly?'

'The truth…?' Beth lifted her gaze from the rich, red liquid in her glass to meet his. 'A combination of rampant curiosity, conviction and sheer devilment.'

Although it wasn't quite the answer he had expected, he didn't for an instance doubt the truth of it, and couldn't forbear a smile, even though he remained deeply disturbed by her actions of the evening before. 'Would you care to elucidate a trifle?'

Without giving the matter too much consideration she decided to oblige him. 'I was curious to discover whether someone I'd once spotted in Markham and the stranger young Napier saw in the home wood were one and the same person. I do not know what your views may be on the matter. However, I am inclined to believe that whoever cut your saddle strap did so with malice aforethought. He intends you harm, personally, otherwise he would have cut the strap on the filly as well. Furthermore, I'm not at all convinced that it is his first malicious act against you. I have learned of a certain shooting incident in the home wood. Whether that was purely an accident must surely be called into question now in light of recent events, though I do not suppose for a moment that young Napier was behind it. And although I'm prepared to admit my actions last night might have been foolhardy, they were not totally fruitless. It might be possible now to discover more about that black-haired man as, seemingly, one of his associates is known to Rudge and me.'

After considering carefully everything she had disclosed, Philip said, 'And you believe this associate might be persuaded to pass on information about the man you suppose has some personal grievance against me?'

'He might be, yes,' Beth responded, though there was a clear note of doubt in her voice. 'Private Tom Clegg was wounded in Spain, quite late in the campaign. I managed to persuade an army surgeon not to cut off his leg, and allow me to attempt to remove the lead ball from the knee myself.

'Yes, Philip, quite shocking, is it not,' she went on,

after detecting the look of disapproval that he was unable to suppress. 'Here in England I would have been called to account for such actions, but out there in Spain...' She shrugged. 'Overworked army surgeons were grateful for what help they could get. And, on balance, I believe I did more good than harm. At least I managed to save Master Clegg's leg. And perhaps because of this he may feel he owes me a debt of gratitude, though whether it will be sufficient to induce him to betray confidences is quite another matter.'

'But certainly worth a try.' Although still not wholly convinced that someone, living not too far away, had a hatred of him personally, Philip thought it couldn't do any harm to discover something about the dark-haired patron of that certain wayside inn. All at once something was lurking in the back of his mind, a memory he just didn't seem able to capture.

'I should like Rudge to return to the inn. As he's acquainted with this man Clegg, he's most likely to achieve results. And I'd like George Dodd to go along too. He's worked on the estate for over forty years, so he knows what went on in the past. Besides which, there aren't too many people in these parts with whom he isn't acquainted, so he'll be able to ferret around closer to home as well, hopefully without arousing suspicion.'

Philip took a moment to finish off his wine and set the glass aside before adding, 'I'll work out some details later so that the pair of them will be able to call at the inn without arousing suspicions. Would you be agreeable to such a scheme, and doing without your manservant for some lengthy periods in the near future?'

The smile he received in response was both spontaneous and disarming. 'What you're really asking is will

I refrain from involving myself in the matter further. The answer to which is yes,' she assured him. 'After due reflection, I realised that I couldn't return to the inn without risking being unmasked as an impostor. A girl of ten dressing in breeches might give rise to general disapproval; a woman of my years behaving in a similar manner would be considered scandalous if it should ever become common knowledge. And I have no real desire to become an object of ridicule.'

Philip rose to take his leave, highly satisfied with the outcome of the visit. He waited for her to rise also. Then, without taking a moment even to consider, he reached out an arm, and placed his hand gently against her left cheek. 'You cannot know how relieved I am by that assurance. Malicious gossip about you is one thing…but I couldn't bear it if harm ever came to you. You are very…precious to me, Beth.'

All at once every vestige of colour faded from her face, and it became totally expressionless. Taking a hurried step away, so that his outstretched hand was left in mid-air, she turned her back on him and walked across to the window.

'I need no reminders of how you feel about me, Philip,' she assured him in a voice devoid of any trace of emotion. 'I have known for some considerable time precisely what I mean to you.'

The following morning Beth received a visit from her aunt, during which Lady Henrietta apprised her niece of her intention to leave the following day. The visit, though brief, was cordial enough, ending with each of them voicing the hope that there would be a reunion between them in the spring.

'That should please Philip, at any rate,' Beth remarked wryly as she returned to the front parlour, after seeing her aunt and cousin safely into their carriage. 'And Phoebe, too, I do not doubt. I detected a suppressed excitement about her—well concealed, it is true, but there none the less. No doubt she's very much looking forward to returning to Surrey and resuming a—er—normal routine.'

Ann did not misunderstand, and smiled as she continued with her sewing. 'Do you suppose Lady Henrietta might be brought to look favourably on a match between her youngest daughter and her neighbours' son?'

'I think it's more than likely she'll hold out for one more Season,' Beth answered after due consideration. 'Ideally she would like Phoebe to ape her elder sisters, of course, by achieving a good match.'

'But Mr Napier doesn't exactly come from a family of paupers,' Ann pointed out.'

'Far from it,' Beth concurred. 'But no title, remember. However, as I believe I've mentioned before, my aunt might be ambitious, but she isn't cruel. And she's certainly no fool. Her leaving Staveley Court earlier than planned is proof of that. She would have realised by now that the invitation was issued by Lady Chalford, and that Philip's show of interest in Phoebe during the Season stemmed from altruism, not a desire to make her his wife.'

'And of course your cousin and Mr Napier are still very young, little more than children, both. It wouldn't hurt them to wait a year or two longer before making any real commitment.'

'I couldn't agree more,' Beth responded, before bending to throw the last of the logs on to the fire.

After absently watching the actions of her employer, Ann frowned. 'It isn't like Rudge to let the basket run so low.' Her frown deepened. 'Now I come to consider it I haven't seen him at all this morning. Where is he, do you suppose?'

'He's over at the Court,' Beth willingly enlightened her. Although she trusted Ann implicitly, she had neither confided her fears over the matter of the damaged saddle, nor divulged the steps that were currently being taken in an attempt to identify the malefactor, and so merely added, 'Philip has a task he wishes him to undertake. No doubt Rudge will be back before long.'

Either she was satisfied with the response, or the clear sounds of further visitors being shown into the house channelled her thoughts in a new direction. The next moment she was on her feet, her expression testament to her absolute delight when Charles Bathurst led the way into the room.

Conversely, Beth's attention was firmly fixed on the tall gentleman entering the room in their amiable neighbour's wake. She moved forward, hands outstretched, and instantly had them captured and held fast in strong fingers.

His smile, warm and spontaneous, instantly softened the harsh lines of a face that had once undoubtedly been handsome. Sadly this was no longer the case. A misspent youth coupled with years of hardship had etched deep crevices into the olive-coloured skin. A paling scar, the outcome of an altercation with a French hussar, ran down the length of one slightly sunken cheek to a mouth that frequently betrayed a cynical twist. His hair, overlong and as black as midnight, almost reached his shoulders, and seemed to accentuate the ice-blue coldness of perfectly almond-shaped eyes.

Yet, for all that, Beth had never feared him. Nor had she ever found him in the least unapproachable. In fact, the opposite was true. He was one of the few people she'd known in her life whom she had truly respected and trusted. Furthermore, she owed him a debt of gratitude she knew she could never hope to repay.

'Why, if it isn't Major Black!' Ann exclaimed, catching sight of him at last. 'I never thought to have the pleasure of renewing my acquaintance with you, sir.'

'Nor I you, ma'am,' he responded, releasing his hold on Beth's hands in order to take one of the widow's briefly in his own. 'It is a pleasure to see you both again. And looking so well, I might add.'

With the initial exchange of pleasantries over, Beth invited her gentlemen visitors to seat themselves, and furnished them both with a glass of wine from her late father's excellent cellar, whilst they began to catch up on each other's news. After a short time only, however, Charles Bathurst engineered it so that Beth and his friend could be alone for a while by the simple expedient of inviting Ann to take a turn round the garden with him, an invitation that was accepted with alacrity.

'Would I be correct in assuming there's a faint whiff of romance in the air?' the Major remarked, thereby breaking the brief silence that had ensued since the couple's departure.'

Beth didn't pretend to misunderstand. 'There's certainly a mutual attraction there. That's plain to see! But whether it will lead to a more lasting attachment is anybody's guess. I try not to pry, or get involved. And being several years younger than Ann, I'm hardly in a position to offer advice, though I did once advocate caution. Since then, of course, I've come to know Mr Bathurst a little better.'

The Major regarded her through half-closed lids. 'And your advice now?'

'Would be precisely the same,' she told him in all

honesty. 'Mr Bathurst strikes me as an honourable gentleman who'd never dream of playing fast and loose with a lady's emotions. That said, his own feelings might never stretch beyond respect and friendship, and Ann might be forced to settle for that with a good grace.'

That sardonic twist she remembered so well curled his lips. 'Like, I strongly suspect, you have done.'

Her hand shook ever so slightly. Then she was mistress of herself once more and returned his steady gaze without so much as a blink. 'And why should you suppose that, Major? Have I ever given you any reason to suppose I'm nursing a broken heart?'

For a moment it seemed he would not answer, then, his eyes never wavering from hers for a second, he said, 'I would be the first to acknowledge we are more acquaintances than friends. That said, we have been in each other's company on numerous occasions in the past years. You are a fine-looking young woman, Miss Ashworth, and quite naturally attracted the attention of many young officers during your time in Spain. Yet not once did I see you cast out so much as a lure, or offer the least encouragement to any man, myself included.'

Beth, not so foolish as to attempt a denial, smiled wryly as she said, 'Life, I suspect, hasn't been totally kind to either of us, Major. Our experiences, though un-doubtedly vastly contrasting, have left us bruised and cynical for the most part.'

'Maybe,' he conceded. 'But you have a heart, Miss Ashworth.'

'And you have not…?' Beth challenged. 'You'll never persuade me to believe that. So pray do not waste your breath in attempting to try.'

'You may have seen the best in me, ma'am,' he responded. 'But you have yet to see the worst.'

Even that blunt response did not give her pause for thought. 'And I doubt I ever shall, Major. And if that was a veiled reference to you being accused of murdering two very close members of your family, I tell you plainly I don't believe it for a moment.'

Once again he smiled, only this time it was softer, and contained an element of warmth. 'Well, I thank you for that, Miss Ashworth, at least. But the truth of the matter is I cannot be sure that I didn't commit the act.'

'Yes, I've already had it on the best authority that you were blind drunk at the time.'

His lips twitched again at this fine example of plain speaking on her part. 'I'm sorry if that offends your sensibilities, ma'am.'

'It doesn't. I've seen men in their cups before.' Her matter-of-fact response produced a rich rumble of masculine laughter, spontaneous and warm. 'I'm very well aware that you're capable of killing people, Major. But you're not a fool. Had you murdered your father and brother, you'd hardly have returned to your bedchamber to await being taken into custody.'

'Now that, I must acknowledge, is very true,' he agreed.

'I assume that, once you've been cleared of any wrongdoing, you'll attempt to discover who is responsible for the death of your relatives?'

Once again his teeth flashed in a sardonic smile. 'That is not high on my list of priorities at the present time, Miss Ashworth,' he surprisingly divulged. 'If the truth be known, I returned to the land of my birth primarily to honour a debt of gratitude to a friend by taking care of his offspring.' His blue eyes travelled to a spot somewhere above their heads. 'Though why my late friend should have entrusted the welfare of his two children into the hands of such a ne'er-do-well the Lord only knows!'

'Yes, perhaps He does indeed know,' Beth agreed softly, before the sounds of a further caller arriving at the house reached her ears. Moments later the door opened, and she was astonished to see Philip enter the room.

Dressed in riding garb, top boots and all, he was obviously attempting to resume a normal routine. It was clear, though, by the continued slight limp that his right ankle was still causing him some discomfort.

'Are you sure you should be jaunting about on horseback so soon after the accident?' she asked, betraying her concern as she rose in one smoothly effortless movement to her feet in order to furnish him with a glass of wine.

The Major had risen also, and by so doing had instantly captured Philip's attention. Beth watched as the Major extended his right hand; noticed too the slight hesitation before Philip clasped it in his own as she made the introductions.

'Black?' Philip echoed, his voice containing a distinct thread of uncertainty. He released his hold, but continued to scrutinise the army officer's physiognomy. 'We've met before, have we not?'

Beth began to feel distinctly uneasy. She knew next to nothing about Major Black's early life, save what she had discovered from Charles Bathurst. Everything about him, of course, had suggested that he hadn't sprung from the lower orders. But never until that moment had it crossed her mind to suppose that the paths of the two men, still eyeing each other in a distinctly wary fashion, like a couple of pugilists about to

indulge in a bout of fisticuffs, had crossed at some point
in the dim and distant past.

Beth was at a loss to know what to do for the best.
Although she trusted Philip implicitly, she had pledged
not to reveal what she had been told about the Major's
unfortunate predicament, and she had no intention of
breaking her word to Charles Bathurst. Yet she knew her
childhood friend was remarkably astute. Blessed with
a memory that rarely failed him, it was only a matter of
time, surely, before Philip recalled where he and the
Major had met before? Her only course of action was
to attempt to delay that recall for as long as possible.

'You may possibly be correct in that assumption,
Philip. But it certainly wasn't in recent years. Major
Black has been out in the Peninsula, almost from the
start of the campaign.'

A valiant attempt on her part to divert him it might
have been, but it had been singularly unsuccessful as his
gaze had never wavered even for an instant in order to
glance in her direction.

His mind too had clearly remained focused, a fact
that became frighteningly apparent a second or two
later when he said, 'Black, I wonder, now? Or is
it…perhaps…Blackwood? If my memory serves me
correctly, the Honourable Sebastian Blackwood.' There
was a noticeable curl to his top lip now that distinctly
resembled the one frequently worn by the Major. 'Now
Viscount Blackwood, unless I much mistake the matter.'

This news was so startling that Beth was momentarily lost for words. Never had she considered for a
moment that the Major's position on the social ladder
had been quite so high! His slightly ironic bow in
response merely confirmed what Philip had disclosed
was true, leaving her desperately wondering what she

should say next in an attempt to dispel the faintly antagonistic ambience between the two men.

Fortunately help came in the solid form of Charles Bathurst, escorting Ann back into the room. Sir Philip's unexpected presence in the parlour caused him to check momentarily on the threshold. Thankfully, though, he recovered his poise almost at once, offering Beth the golden opportunity to recover hers whilst he greeted his neighbour in a jovial fashion. His swift glance in her direction betrayed his obvious concern, however. Consequently she wasn't unduly surprised when he quickly made an excuse to leave.

'Would you be good enough to show the gentlemen to their carriage, Ann, whilst I remain to entertain Sir Philip? There is a matter we need to discuss in private,' Beth said, and then, after a final farewell to her visitors, and a look that revealed clearly enough to them both that she would deal with the situation from here on, she went across to the window in order to witness their departure.

'I could have wished you had not come today, Philip,' she admitted with total sincerity, knowing full well that she could say exactly what she felt without fear of being disturbed. Even if Ann had sensed the atmosphere in the room, she was far too well bred to interrupt what she very well knew was a private conversation in order to satisfy her curiosity.

'I'm not surprised,' he returned, helping himself to the glass of wine she had quite failed to pour him. 'Are you in the habit of hobnobbing with murderers?'

This won him her full attention, as he knew it would. She swung round and there was no mistaking the scornful expression on her face. 'You don't honestly believe that, surely?'

'He was accused of it, I know that much. I didn't know that he was acquainted with Bathurst. Though, perhaps I should have done. Blackwood Manor, his ancestral home, is in Northamptonshire, if my memory serves me correctly. And, as you probably recall my mentioning, Bathurst lived in that part of the country for a time as well.'

Belatedly remembering her manners, Beth invited him to sit down, before divulging that she hadn't realised the Major held a title. As she now realised that Philip knew as much, if not a deal more, about Lord Blackwood's somewhat chequered past, she saw little reason in not revealing what had passed between herself and Charles Bathurst on the evening of his dinner- party, whilst they had been closeted in the library, and why the Viscount was now in the area.

'I can perfectly understand Bathurst's involvement in this affair, Beth,' he said, after listening to everything she had to say, 'and his wanting to help a friend. But how can you be so sure of Blackwood's innocence? Are you so well acquainted with him?'

'Not well, no,' she freely admitted. 'But I know Wellington thought highly of him, as did my own father. I know he's quite capable of killing people. He might even be capable of cold-blooded murder. But one thing he is not, and that's a fool. If he had murdered his father and brother, he wouldn't have remained after committing the acts, tamely waiting for the authorities to arrive and take him into custody.'

'Possibly not,' Philip felt obliged to acknowledge, before revealing, 'I'll admit I never knew Blackwood well. He's a couple of years my senior, and has never numbered among my circle of friends. All the same, what I do know of him does not redound to his credit.

He was wild in his youth, shocking society with his exploits. He considered it an honour to be thought one of the most notorious rakes in Georgian England.'

Beth's initial response to this was to gurgle with laughter. 'Though heaven only knows why I should find it so amusing,' she declared, after a moment's consideration. 'What I should feel is offended, I suppose, as he's never attempted to seduce me, not once! I can only assume he's either a reformed character, or I'm not to his taste.'

She was suddenly serious. 'You won't betray his whereabouts, will you, Philip?' It had sounded more like a statement of fact than an entreaty. 'Bathurst is only striving to prevent his friend from committing any kind of folly whilst his name is being cleared. Charles considered his lordship would be safer in the country than in London.'

'Had I been a local Justice of the Peace, which I might add I'm likely to become in a year or two, I might have been obliged to take a different view, but as it is…' His shrug was proof enough that he was indifferent to the Viscount's fate. 'I bear him no ill will, personally. As I mentioned before, I'm not well acquainted with him. Added to which, I cannot imagine Bathurst risking his reputation if he wasn't totally convinced of Blackwood's innocence.'

More than satisfied with the response, Beth changed the subject by belatedly asking him why she had been honoured by his unexpected visit that day.

His expressive brows rose in faint hauteur. 'Do I need an excuse to call?'

'Not at all,' she assured him, secretly amused by this unusual show of pique on his part. 'Nevertheless, I know you well enough to be sure you rarely do things without good reason. You're still favouring that right ankle of yours, so I cannot imagine you rode over here just for the pleasure of seeing me.'

His expression suddenly was impossible to read, and, like her enigmatic earlier visitor, he considered her from beneath half-hooded lids. 'Can you not? he responded smoothly, before adding in a much more businesslike tone, 'As a matter of fact I did have a reason. I wished to inform you that Rudge will be away for much of the day, and the evening too, I strongly suspect. I've arranged for him and Dodd to deliver one or two items in the cart to a place several miles south of Markham. Calling in at that inn on the return journey to refresh themselves will not be considered odd.' When her only response was to frown, he added, 'I hope Rudge's long absence will not inconvenience you too much.'

'No, I suppose not,' she eventually conceded. 'Although I could have done with him here to take a note over to Charles Bathurst to assure him you have no intention of betraying his friend's whereabouts.'

'Fear not, my precious one, I shall ride over and assure him of that, personally, if it will ease your mind,' and so saying he rose to his feet, and grasped both her hands in order to draw her to hers. 'As I've already told you, I bear Blackwood no ill will.'

Although she made no attempt to withdraw them from his, she did stare down at her captured hands for several moments. Nevertheless, when she finally raised her head, her expression was as different as it could have been from the one he had seen when he had touched her the day before.

'You may not bear him a grudge. But are you so very sure Viscount Blackwood doesn't bear you one?' There was no mistaking the wicked amusement dancing in her eyes. 'I've just realised that being tall and dark, with a slightly swarthy complexion, he bears an uncanny resemblance to the person young Napier saw in your home wood!'

Chapter Nine

Philip's arrival at Charles Bathurst's home later that same day produced vastly contrasting reactions in the two gentlemen sitting comfortably in the drawing room. Viscount Blackwood, evidently having become a master at controlling emotion, merely favoured the unexpected visitor with a brief, quizzical glance and an equally brief nod of welcome, whilst the owner of the handsome country property almost leapt to his feet, and appeared all at once decidedly ill at ease.

'Good gad! Never expected to see you again today, Staveley. Can I get you a glass of wine?'

'I didn't plan to see you, either,' he admitted. 'And a glass of burgundy would be most welcome.'

Once a servant had positioned a further easy chair nearer the hearth and had departed, Philip didn't waste time in making himself comfortable or coming to the point of his visit. 'I'm here, ostensibly, at Miss Ashworth's behest. She wished me to assure you both that I've no intention of divulging Blackwood's presence under this roof.'

The Viscount's expression didn't alter. Charles

Bathurst, on the other hand, appeared instantly relieved, and didn't hesitate to voice his heartfelt appreciation. 'That's dashed good of you, Staveley!'

All at once he appeared a little shamefaced. 'The truth of the matter is I was hoping, as Blackwood here assured me you were only ever acquaintances, that maybe you wouldn't recognise my friend should your paths happen to cross whilst he was here. Felt I oughtn't to confide in you by coming straight out and asking a man in your position not to reveal that I'm harbouring a known felon under my roof. Not at all the thing, as you're a close friend of the local Justice of the Peace, not to mention hotly favoured as the next in line for the position.'

'True,' Philip was obliged to acknowledge with wry amusement. 'But as it's only a matter of time, so I understand, before Blackwood's name is cleared, no good would come of revealing the presence of a suspected murderer within our midst. It would only lead to needless gossip and foolish hysteria. Furthermore I have no grievance against Blackwood personally. And I trust,' Philip added, for the first time addressing the Viscount directly, 'you have none against me?'

'Nothing immediately springs to mind,' he acknowledged, the cynical curl to his lip very much in evidence.

'In that case I can safely assume it wasn't you who made that recent attempt on my life,' Philip responded, which once again caused his neighbour to start visibly.

'Good gad, Staveley! Are you in earnest?' Charles Bathurst was clearly having trouble coming to terms with such a thing. 'But who in the world would wish you harm? You're one of the most well-respected, not to mention well-liked, persons hereabouts.'

'Yes, I too find it hard to credit,' the Viscount put in, when Philip failed to respond to the fulsome praise. 'My

recollection is that you were always considered a ve-
ritable pillar of the community, never having had so
much as a breath of scandal attached to your name.' His
smile grew more twisted. 'Now, an attempt on my own
life would come as no surprise to anyone, least of all to
me. I can think of at least half-a-dozen cuckolded
husbands who'd relish putting a period to my existence.'

'That is nothing of which to be proud, Blackwood!'
his good friend quickly pointed out, like some disapproving elder brother.

'I wasn't for an instant suggesting it was,' the
Viscount returned, not visibly chastened. 'The fact
remains, though, that one cannot alter one's past, no
matter how much one might wish to do so. And it is to
the past, surely, that Staveley must look, recent or more
distant, if he wishes to unearth one with grievance
enough against him to wish him harm.'

'When was the attempt made?' Charles Bathurst
asked, appearing slightly bewildered, as though still
having difficulty in accepting such a thing might have
happened.

'My riding accident was, in fact, no accident.
Someone deliberately cut the girth strap on my saddle
so that it was only a matter of time before it snapped.
As things turned out, I wasn't badly hurt. But it might
easily have been quite otherwise. If I'd fallen awkwardly, I might have broken my neck.'

'Yes, indeed,' Charles agreed. 'But why on earth
should you suppose Blackwood might be responsible?
He didn't arrive here until the day before yesterday.'

'I didn't seriously imagine he was to blame,' Philip
assured them both, smiling crookedly himself now. 'I'm
afraid my darling Beth has a rather perverse sense of

humour. She derived no little amusement in pointing out that Lord Blackwood bears an uncanny resemblance to the man seen loitering in the home wood just prior to the incident taking place.'

All at once Philip was serious. 'Except for my servants, few knew I intended riding out on that particular morning. No one could possibly have known which direction I intended to take. Truth to tell, I'd no very fixed idea myself, so the act couldn't possibly have been premeditated. All the same, Beth happened to be with me at the time. And I will not have her life placed in jeopardy through thoughtless acts. The miscreant must be found and at the very least investigated, even if I should decide not to bring charges against him.'

Charles Bathurst nodded in agreement. 'And if there's anything we can do you only have to ask, though as I'm sure you can appreciate I'm trying to keep my good friend here out of the public gaze as much as possible.'

Philip experienced a degree of sympathy towards the Viscount. For a man who had spent most of his adult life thus far doing more or less as he pleased, the enforced incarceration would be doubly irksome.

'If you feel like a change of scenery, Blackwood, come dine with me at the Court one evening. My sister is leaving in the morning, so your anonymity will be assured.'

Bathurst saw his visitor to the door, personally, and then returned to the library to find his friend helping himself to more wine. 'I must say that was dashed hospitable of Staveley to invite you over to his place, particularly as you've never been a friend of his.'

The Viscount's teeth flashed in one of his sardonic smiles. 'I'm forced to agree, and do appreciate the kindness of the gesture. All the same, I cannot help feeling I would be a deal safer away from this wretched county.'

'Good gad, man! You cannot be judging the place by that isolated incident involving Staveley?'

'Naturally not,' Blackwood assured him, appearing genuinely amused as he stared down at the liquid in his glass. 'None the less, there's undeniably a dangerous condition lurking hereabouts that appears to be afflicting the unattached males of the species.'

It was with decidedly mixed feelings that Sir Philip handed his sister into her travelling carriage the following morning. She had been at the Court almost two months, her longest ever visit since her marriage to the easygoing Lord Chalford. In one way it would be a relief to have the house to himself again, and not need to trouble about playing the genial host when he would much prefer to be alone. Yet he would miss her. Lacking a deeply penetrating wit, she was perhaps not the most stimulating companion. All the same, her quaint views on life could be highly diverting on occasions.

No sooner had the carriage moved out of the yard than he mounted his favourite hack and set off across the park to keep an appointment with his steward, after which he went directly to the eastern lodge gate in order to consult with the gatekeeper.

As it was a damp and dreary morning Philip wasn't unduly surprised to find his oldest estate worker keeping warm inside the single-storey thatched dwelling, which had been his home for more than forty years. Having already turned sixty, Dodd now had few duties. He helped out from time to time doing the occasional odd job about the estate, and of course he remained in sole charge of the east gate. Although his duties could hardly be described as taxing, they kept him reasonably well occupied. Which was perhaps just as well, for, apart from work, there was precious little else in his life. He had never married, a fact borne out by the lack of those little feminine touches that turned a dwelling into a home.

Seating himself on the only other chair, Philip joined him by the hearth, and didn't waste time in attempting to discover if his faithful elderly retainer had discovered anything worthy of note.

'Some,' Dodd revealed, removing the clay pipe from between his lips. 'The three men Rudge saw at that there inn were there again last night. The one young Rudge knows, Tom Clegg be 'is name, ain't from round these parts, so I can't tell you owt about 'ee. But I knows the other two. The short, weasel-faced 'un be a Markham man, born and bred, and works for local chandler. T'other one, one Rudge were interested in, be Murslow…Rolf Murslow.'

Philip waited patiently for more details, but when the old man began pulling on his pipe again, he found himself asking, 'Should I know him?'

Dodd seemed to consider for a moment. 'No, mayhap, you don't remember. You'd 'ave been n' more than a boy when it 'appened.'

'When what happened?'

'The Murslows were tenants o' yourn in yer father's day. Idle loafers, the lot of 'em. Seemingly never paid rents on time, and didn't look after the land proper. Anyway, yer father 'ad 'ad enough and turned 'em out, and gave the living to others, more deserving, like. Now I ain't saying yer father weren't within 'is rights to do what 'ee did. But the fact remains Murslow's wife and three of 'is young 'uns were ill at the time. They all died soon afterwards while Murslow and the oldest lad, Rolf, were about looking for work. Seemingly the pair of 'em took up the tinker's trade and went peddling their wares all over the county. Must 'ave made money somewhere, 'cause the old man returned to these parts some few years back and bought 'imself a place a couple o' mile or so t'other side o' Markham. Where young Rolf were at the time, I couldn't say. Might 'ave taken the King's shilling for all I know, or he might 'ave continued to peddle 'is wares in another part of the county. Anyhow, 'ee moved back into these parts 'imself a year or so back, just afore 'is father died, and found 'imself an old cottage not far distant from that tavern 'ee favours. Far as I know, 'ee be still doing the tinker's trade. As well as other things, I don't doubt.'

After considering carefully what he had been told, Philip shook his head. 'If he does harbour a grievance, and I could quite understand if he did so, he's waited a damned long time to get even with my family. Of course, he hasn't been back in the area that long, I suppose...but even so...'

'It ain't a mite o' good, sir, you trying to think like a cove of Murslow's stamp,' Dodd advised, with a wisdom borne of an extensive knowledge of human nature. 'You be an educated gent. And an honest one to boot! Murslow don't think like you, sir. Nor like me, neither, come to that. 'Ee and 'is kind don't believe in 'onest toil. They be out for what they can get. Only 'ee knows why 'ee were prowling the 'ome wood that day. But I'll lay odds 'ee weren't lying in wait for you. I ain't saying 'ee didn't cut the saddle strap. Chances are, sir, 'ee did. You just 'appened to be in the wrong place at the wrong time, and 'ee took 'is chance. But you should be asking yourself what took 'im to the 'ome wood in the first place.'

Philip repeated these pearls of wisdom at the Grange a short time later, where he was lucky enough to find

Beth quite alone in the parlour, her companion having once again offered her services in an attempt to ease the plight of the poor in the parish.

'It's what you thought all along,' Beth remarked, after mulling things over. 'And you're most probably right, now I come to reconsider the matter. Yes, it is more than likely that Murslow just happened to be in that spot at the right time, as far as he was concerned, and extracted an impromptu and petty revenge for what your father did to his family.'

'Unless he admits to it, though, it can never be proved, of course,' Philip pointed out, totally without rancour. He was striving to keep a clear head, not allow personal feelings towards the man who had attempted to harm him cloud his judgement. 'Something brought Murslow on to my land. He could have been considering a spot of poaching, and was deciding where best to lay traps later, under cover of darkness, when he just happened to catch sight of us riding in the park.'

'A distinct possibility,' Beth agreed. 'He could also have been watching the house. Don't forget that from the western perimeter of the home wood there's an unrestricted view up the rise to the Court. He could spend as long as he wished surveying the comings and goings without being observed himself.'

Philip was quick to follow her line of thinking. 'There's been no attempt at a break in yet,' he assured her.

'Hardly surprising, as there have been so many folk putting up at the house recently. Too many people about the place, their comings and goings too unpredictable. No, he'd be prepared to bide his time and wait for things to return to normal, as they have done now. Rich pickings at your place, Philip. The richest round these parts, by a long chalk,' she reminded him. 'That knowledge, coupled with his grievance against the Staveley family, just might tempt him to take the risk one night.'

In one way Beth was relieved to think that her first assumption concerning the affair of the saddle strap had been wide of the mark, and that it hadn't been a pre-meditated attack. Which also prompted her to take the view that the shooting incident in the home wood at the beginning of the summer had been purely and simply an accident, a shot that had gone sadly awry. After all, it was highly improbable that Murslow would get to hear about a shooting party being arranged, and even if he had, it was unlikely he'd risk venturing into the wood with so many people about.

Consequently she no longer held the view that Philip was in danger of losing his life. All the same, he would need to remain on his guard whenever he ventured forth. There was every chance that Murslow, if granted the opportunity, would attempt a further assault, even if his intention was not to murder.

'More than likely he's an opportunist who acts on impulse,' she said, after echoing her fears aloud. 'But even so, there's no saying what he might do next, or when. Whilst he remains in the area, you'd do well not to venture forth alone.'

'If you expect me to drag a groom along every time I go out, you can think again, my girl!' he told her in no uncertain terms.

'But you expect me to do just that,' she countered, slightly miffed.

'Certainly.' He held up his hand against the protest she was about to make, silencing her in an instant. 'Yes, I know you think you can look after yourself very well, that you can shoot as well as any man. But the fact is you're not a man, and you don't possess a man's strength.'

He had spoken out of loving concern for her well-being, never supposing for a moment that she was in any danger personally, or that his slight fears for her welfare would one day soon spiral to become a heartbreaking reality, almost too great for him to bear.

The slight disquiet was thrust aside almost at once by a sudden thought. 'By the by, you may rest easy in the knowledge that I did ride over to see Bathurst and assured him I'd no intention of revealing to anyone his guest's true identity. I even went so far as to invite the guest himself to dine at the Court one evening.'

'That was kind of you,' Beth responded, her feeling of pique having been quickly forgotten.

Philip shrugged, unwilling to take credit where none was due. 'It was no skin off my nose. As I've mentioned before, we've never been friends, and I cannot imagine that state of affairs ever changing to any significant degree. But I've nothing against the fellow personally.'

He regarded her in silence for a moment, his expression difficult to read. 'Unlike you, Beth, I am more discerning when it comes to choosing friends.'

Although she realised it was undoubtedly a criticism of her closer association with the Viscount, it never occurred to her to consider from where his disapproval had sprung.

'Yes, I do think highly of him,' she freely admitted. 'I know nothing of his doings in his early life. I know him to be only a very brave man. Furthermore, I personally owe him a debt of gratitude I could never hope to repay.'

'Why so?'

Beth saw no reason not to satisfy his evident curiosity. 'He put his own life at risk by ensuring my critically injured father was brought back to camp, even though he must have been very well aware himself that there was very little chance of Papa surviving.'

As she had clearly gained his full attention, Beth wasn't reticent to reveal more. 'It happened before the Crossing of the Bidassoa,' she began. 'Wellington needed to be kept informed about Soult's movements, and so my father and the man I knew then as Major Black were away from camp much of the time. On their final mission together they were attacked by four French cavalrymen out scouting the area. My father was badly wounded in the first exchange of fire, though he did bring down one of the French. Instead of riding away and saving himself, Major Black remained with my father. He reloaded his pistol and shot another of the Frenchmen and overcame the fourth by bringing him down off his horse, and beating him in hand-to-hand combat. That is how he acquired the scar on his cheek.' She held his gaze levelly. 'Don't ever ask me to despise a man who could do that.'

'No, indeed,' he answered softly, rising to his feet in order to take his leave. 'And fear not. I don't suppose I shall be in his company so frequently that I'll be in any danger of allowing my less charitable feelings towards him show.'

No one could have been more surprised than Philip to find a note from none other than the Viscount himself awaiting him on his return, proposing he dine at the Court that very evening. As he had no prior engagement, Philip saw no reason to refuse, and dashed off a quick reply to be delivered by hand.

He was even more surprised to discover that the seventh Viscount Blackwood proved to be remarkably genial company. He was clearly an intelligent man whose slightly cynical view on life wasn't without its amusing side. He remained doubtful that he could ever come to look upon him as a personal friend; perhaps only time would reveal that. Furthermore, he would certainly consider very seriously before trusting any young female member of his family into his care; and even though Beth had given the impression that her feelings towards the Viscount didn't go beyond that of deep gratitude, there was no escaping the fact that the man exuded an easy charm that the majority of the fair sex would undoubtedly find fascinating.

After dinner Philip invited his guest to repair to the library, where he set up the chessboard between them. The Viscount proved to be a skilful player and a worthy opponent. Eventually, though, both men were content to abandon the game for the more relaxing pastime of a fireside chat.

'Are you any closer to discovering precisely who is responsible for cutting your saddle strap?' the Viscount asked, after revealing a few of his own plans for the future.

'I've a fairly shrewd idea now of who it might have been, yes. Proving it might be difficult, however,' Philip conceded. 'The most likely candidate is the son of a tenant my father evicted some years ago.'

'Ah, yes! The sins of the father...' The Viscount's teeth flashed in one of his saturnine smiles. 'I know all about that.'

Philip regarded his guest in silence for a moment. He had refrained thus far from prying into certain aspects of the Viscount's reprehensible past. Given the opening, however, he couldn't resist saying,

'I cared very much for my father. He was no saint.

All the same, on balance, I believe he was a good man, worthy of respect. You could not say the same about yours, I fear.'

'Assuredly not,' the Viscount responded, reaching for the decanter that the butler had positioned conveniently to hand. 'I still hold him responsible for my dear mother's early demise. I never made any secret of the fact I detested him, along with my half-brother. It was little wonder I was accused of their murders.'

The tone had been so impersonal that they might have been discussing nothing of more importance than the weather. Yet Philip had already decided that the Viscount was a far more complex man than one might at first suppose, that beneath the outward show of indifference and cynicism was a deeply thoughtful and sensitive man who rarely allowed his inmost thoughts, his inmost feelings, to surface.

True, he did not know him well; perhaps he never would. Notwithstanding, Philip was able to say with conviction, 'But you didn't murder them.'

The Viscount raised ice-blue eyes to meet those of his host across the chessboard. 'I'm reliably informed I did not. But, in truth, I recall little of what took place that night.'

There was a distinct edge of finality in the deep, throaty voice that revealed clearly enough that the subject was no longer open for discussion. Consequently Philip didn't attempt to probe further, and parted from his guest a short time later, each having acquired a certain knowledge and respect for the other.

The following morning, Beth paid her first visit to Markham since her tour of the town's less reputable taverns. She was quite properly accompanied by her

companion this time, so no fault could have been found
with her behaviour. All the same, she was beginning to
feel increasingly that this visit would turn out to be a
devilish dull venture compared to her last; until, that is,
Ann happened to catch sight of a familiar, tall figure
standing in the town's main street.

'Wasn't that Major Black we just passed, peering in
the milliner's window?'

'Surely not! What on earth could possibly be of
interest to him in a milliner's?' Although doubtful, Beth
took the trouble to draw down the window and poke her
head out. Then almost immediately afterwards she
shouted up to Rudge to turn into the forecourt of the
White Hart Inn, which was so very conveniently
situated just ahead.

Hardly waiting for the carriage to draw to a halt, she
sprang down and raced back along the street. 'Are you
mad?' she demanded, the instant she reached the
Viscount's side. 'What on earth are you doing here, in
the centre of Markham in broad daylight?' She began
to tug at his arm with some urgency. 'Oh, come away,
do, before you draw attention to yourself!'

'Nothing out of the way in a fellow staring in a shop
window,' he pointed out, after politely doffing his broad-
rimmed hat and obliging her by accompanying her back
along the street. 'I might have been considering buying
a new bonnet for my wife, after all.'

Beth glanced up at him in some exasperation, all at
once appreciating that poor Charles Bathurst would
have his hands full in trying to keep his friend out of
trouble until such time as all charges against the
Viscount were dropped.

'One glance at you, my lord… I mean, Major,' she
hastily corrected, 'and no one would suppose for a

moment you were married. The instant you open your mouth it's clear you're an educated man. But what woman of your class would happily tie herself to someone who resembles nothing so much as a Spanish guerrillero? A milliner would be much more likely to suspect you of buying a hat for a…a ladybird!'

It was at this point that Beth surprisingly discovered that the Viscount's eyes, although unnervingly penetrating on occasions, could suddenly develop a most disarming twinkle, not unlike Philip's.

'I really must remember to have a word with Staveley when next we meet. He must attempt to do something about your immodest train of thought. That a young lady of your genteel upbringing should know anything about birds of paradise, let alone bring them up in conversation, quite shocks me!'

Ignoring the teasing, Beth demanded to know why he imagined her neighbour had any influence over her behaviour. His lordship, however, wisely declined to answer. Instead, as they arrived at the inn's forecourt, he hailed Beth's groom, who happened to be conversing with a man whose limp suggested he, too, might possibly have been yet another participant of the Peninsular War.

'Why, 'tis Major Black, sir!' Rudge grasped the Viscount's hand warmly. 'Miss Beth said as 'ow you were staying in these parts. 'Tis good to see you again after all this time. You be the second old campaigner I've met up with today.'

The Viscount transferred his gaze to the servant's companion, and then frowned. 'Do I know you?'

'No, sir. But I saw you once or twice, I fancy, before I stopped a lead ball at Vera. If it hadn't been for Miss Ashworth, 'ere, they would 'ave had m'leg.'

Seeing this as a golden opportunity to discover a

little more about the dark-haired man whom she had seen supping ale at that wayside inn, Beth steered the conversation away from the past by saying, 'It's Private Clegg, isn't it?'

'Aye, ma'am, Tom Clegg,' he responded, politely touching his forelock with a grimy finger.

'I don't recall you mentioning you came from around these parts,' she remarked, in an attempt to maintain the conversation for a while.

'Come from south of the county, miss. Came up this way looking for work. Thought to try my luck in Bristol, but didn't get that far, and ended up 'ere. Landlord always needs extra 'elp on market days. Manage to find the odd day's work 'ere and there at other places in town as well. So I gets by, as yer might say.'

All at once he seemed unable to meet her gaze, and eager to be about his duties too. Beth, however, managed to foil his efforts by enquiring after his family. 'I'm sure I'm right in thinking you've a wife and young son. Are they staying in Markham with you?'

She swiftly discovered that it was entirely the wrong tactic to adopt when the eyes that finally met hers were cold and distinctly hostile. 'No, they ain't wi' me no more. They be with their maker.'

Unfortunately the landlord chose that moment to emerge from his inn, and Tom Clegg, evidently not wanting to be found gossiping, promptly limped away to help the drayman who had just pulled up in the fore-court to unload his cart.

Although disappointed that her attempt to discover more about the dark-haired man had come to nought, Beth quickly decided she could at least attempt to curtail the imprudent behaviour of the tall man standing beside her, and invited him to take an early luncheon with them at the inn.

His prompt acceptance was all that was needed for her to steer him hurriedly towards the entrance. It was only when she took a step inside that she recalled she had no means of paying for the meal.

'Oh, my reticule!' she exclaimed, glancing quickly at Ann, only to discover that her companion was carrying just her own. 'I must have left it in the carriage.'

'I'm at your service, ma'am,' the Viscount responded, and before she could reach out a hand in an attempt to stay him, he had swung round on his heels and was heading across the forecourt to the spot where Rudge had left the carriage.

The main street was a throng. Passing vehicles, hawkers selling their wares, local farmers driving their stock, not to mention the crowds of revellers enjoying the festivities a market day provided, all added to the general hubbub. Consequently it wasn't surprising that the Viscount quite failed to hear the warning cry as he made his way back over to the inn, swinging the reticule round and round his finger as he did so. It was only when something solid cannoned into him, momentarily knocking the breath out of his body as it thrust him hard against the inn wall, that he realised a large barrel had toppled off the back of the dray cart and had been rolling speedily across the forecourt in his direction. It smashed against the inn wall a matter of a couple of feet only from where he stood, splintering as it did so and disgorging its contents, much to the delight of a couple of street urchins.

'All right, gov'ner?'

The Viscount stared down at his unlikely rescuer. Several inches shorter than himself, not to mention several stones lighter as well, the lame inn worker had moved with surprising agility, and had betrayed remarkable reserves of strength in someone who had been clearly surviving on a meagre diet for some little time.

'It's Clegg, isn't it?'

'Aye, sir, Tom Clegg.' He limped a step or two away. 'As long as you be all right, I'd best get on with m'work.'

'Not so fast,' his lordship countered, holding the smaller man captive, as much by the strength of his penetrating gaze as by the hand he rested on one thin shoulder. 'I assumed from what you were saying earlier that you have no permanent employment.'

The bitterness the man felt was evident in his twisted smile. 'Ain't likely to get none, neither. Who'd take on a man with a gammy leg when 'ee can easily find one sound of limb?'

'It seems to me you can move quickly enough when you have a mind to do so,' the Viscount returned. 'You served me a good turn. Not even my severest critics could ever accuse me of not repaying a debt. And I owe you a debt of gratitude, Clegg, that in a few weeks from now I shall possibly be in a position to repay. Keep out of trouble, and we'll discuss a permanent position for you at a later date…if, that is, you are willing to accompany me to my home when I leave this county.'

'Do you truly mean it, Major, sir?' Clearly he was unwilling to believe this great piece of good fortune. 'You could find me a position somewhere?'

'When you know me better, Clegg, you will discover that I never make false promises,' his lordship assured him. 'I am at present putting up with a friend of mine, Charles Bathurst. I shall return here to Markham on the first market day held next month. Be at this inn, and we

shall discuss the matter further…providing you keep
out of trouble in the meantime.'

With that he disappeared into the inn, once again
swinging the reticule in a carefree attitude as he did so,
and leaving the bewildered Clegg to stare after him,
scratching his head, clearly not knowing quite what to
think.

Chapter Ten

'Poor Charles Bathurst has certainly got his hands full with his lordship as a house-guest,' Beth remarked, when she and Philip, taking advantage of the first reasonably fine November morning, set out for a ride together.

This was the first occasion she had seen him since her chance meeting with Lord Blackwood in the local town the previous week, so she wasn't short of things about which to converse. Yet time and again her thoughts returned to the Viscount and his imprudent behaviour, a fact that was not overlooked by her companion.

'Clearly you're very concerned about him, Beth.' Although he had spoken in a level tone, there was a certain hardness in the look he cast her. 'Save for locking him in the cellar, I don't see there's much Charles can do, however.'

She was forced to agree, but couldn't resist adding, 'Had his lordship been a simple soul, one could have made allowances for such folly on his part. The fact is, though, he's quite the opposite.' She shook her head, at a loss to understand. 'It's almost as if he deliberately goes out of his way to court trouble.'

'Whether justified or not, he was stigmatised by many for his devil-may-care attitude in his youth,' Philip reminded her, after a few moments' quiet deliberation. 'I've never known him well enough to form an opinion of his character. But, as you've said yourself, he's certainly no fool. And he's more than capable of taking care of himself. The day may dawn, of course, when the feelings of another become of paramount importance to him. And who knows—hat special someone might well come to influence his behaviour to a certain extent. But until that day dawns, I very much fear Viscount Blackwood will continue to do very much as he pleases.'

'Yes, you're probably right,' Beth acknowledged, as she stared between her horse's ears at a distant spot on the road ahead. 'So the sooner he forms a lasting and meaningful attachment, the better it will be for all those who are concerned about his welfare. As you've said yourself, he gives the impression of being a care-for-nobody. But I believe, as I strongly suspect you do too, that there's much beneath the surface that he successfully conceals from the world at large. I think also that if he ever should be fortunate to find that special someone, he would guard her well.'

At this Philip looked at her more keenly than before, his gaze openly assessing. Beth, however, was oblivious to the intensity of his regard. She continued staring at the road ahead, frowning heavily as she revealed what had taken place in the forecourt of the White Hart Inn.

'I can perfectly understand why he should feel grateful to the man Clegg,' she continued, striving to be fair. 'Those particular ale barrels being unloaded that morning were large, and he might well have suffered real hurt had the thing hit him.' She raised one hand in a helpless little gesture. 'But to go and offer a complete stranger employment is the height of folly. He knows next to nothing about Tom Clegg, save that he served in the army for a while.' She shook her head, all at once looking guilt-stricken. 'It might have been grossly inter- fering on my part, but I did feel obliged to mention— how shall I phrase it—the undesirable company Tom's been keeping since his arrival in Markham.'

Philip managed to suppress a smile. 'I take it from your tone that you were not wholly successful in influ- encing my lord's decision.'

'Ha! A complete waste of breath,' she freely admitted. 'He merely brushed my concerns aside, saying he had frequently been guilty of mixing with undesirables, and that Clegg, clearly down on his luck, deserved a chance.'

Philip refrained from pointing out that the Viscount had spoken no less than the truth, that Blackwood had not always fraternised with those from the more privi- leged classes, and was perhaps a sounder judge of char- acter because of it.

'Perhaps only time will tell whether Blackwood is being sensible or not to offer employment to a complete stranger. But I shall say this—according to what George Dodd told me only yesterday, there's been no sign of Clegg at that wayside tavern during the past few evenings. Seemingly he's staying well clear of Murslow and his cronies.'

This was news to Beth, and she was forced to ac- knowledge that it just might be that Clegg, with the prospect of full-time employment and a chance of a better life, was determined to mend his ways. All the same, she couldn't help thinking that Clegg might have proved useful if he'd remained close to Murslow and his cronies, especially if he could have been persuaded to reveal what he knew about Rolf Murslow's recent activities, and echoed her thoughts aloud.

Philip, however, was sceptical. 'I know nothing of Clegg, or what manner of man he may be. It's to his credit, of course, that he came to Blackwood's aid on that occasion. The act in itself was undoubtedly spontaneous, and therefore done without thought of largesse. Which suggests, does it not, that the man possesses certain principles, even though he has evidently fallen on hard times. As yet we do not know just how close the bond between him and Murslow might have been. Not particularly strong, I wouldn't have thought, as Clegg has chosen to distance himself.'

Beth was silent for a moment, mulling over what had been said, then released her breath in a tiny sigh borne of frustration. 'Even though I did help Clegg by removing a lead ball from his knee, we never came to know each other that well.' She smiled wryly. 'Being a colonel's daughter, I was discouraged from fraternising with those from the lower ranks. Consequently, as soon as he showed signs of recovery, Clegg was nursed by other soldiers' wives.

'You must surely be aware that Wellington referred to the majority of his army as the scum of the earth,' she continued, after a further rueful smile. 'And it must be said there were numerous thieves, rapists and drunkards, not to mention murderers, among the lower ranks. Even so, I gained the distinct impression that Clegg was a cut above the average recruit. He was always most respectful whenever he spoke to me. So it doesn't really surprise me that you suspect him of being a man of certain principles. Which, again, is a great pity in one way.'

'Why so?' he prompted when she once again fell silent.

'Because if he's received any kind of help since his arrival in Markham from Murslow, I cannot imagine he would betray any confidences they might share, even if the bond of friendship between them has never been particularly strong.'

'No, indeed,' Philip agreed. 'Nor could I imagine him betraying confidences to a complete stranger, such as myself.'

Beth turned to him with an arresting look in her eyes. 'But might he consider he owes allegiance to Lord Blackwood, his future employer?'

'He might, yes,' Philip conceded, appreciating at once where her thoughts were leading. 'But whether Blackwood would take advantage of his position is quite another matter.

'I'll see what, if anything, I can discover tonight,' he went on when Beth remained silent, once again mulling over what he had said. 'I'm dining with Bathurst at his home this evening, as it happens,' Philip revealed. 'I'd be surprised if his lordship wasn't present. I'll make a point of mentioning Clegg during the evening, and discover if I can whether Blackwood knows anything more than we do about the man he intends to employ, and, if so, whether he might be persuaded to reveal what he knows. The evening should prove... interesting.'

Although he felt he had concealed remarkably well the ever-increasing resentment he was experiencing over Beth's evident partiality for Viscount Blackwood, Philip was too honest a person not to acknowledge the truth of it himself. All the same, what lay at the root of the resentment continued to elude him.

But just how deep did this evident regard on her part go? he couldn't help wondering, as he sat opposite the Viscount at the dinner table that evening.

There was no getting away from the fact that Blackwood was a charismatic devil. Undeniably attractive, he did indeed possess more than his fair share of natural charm. Notwithstanding, Beth had a good head on her shoulders, and wouldn't be influenced by a surfeit of charm alone. Clearly Blackwood possessed traits she much admired—courage, to name but one. Added to which, she was very much beholden to him, still, for his unselfish behaviour towards her father.

Undoubtedly at great personal risk to himself, he had brought the fatally wounded Colonel Ashworth back to camp, and to his daughter, to receive at least a half-decent burial. Naturally Beth would feel respect for such a selfless act and, in consequence, would hold the Viscount in high regard. But did her feelings go rather deeper than a respectful fondness? Philip couldn't help wondering.

'Does the style in which I've tied my cravat this evening not match your high standards, Staveley?' the Viscount enquired suavely, after having endured the Baronet's continued frowning scrutiny for some little time. 'Clearly there is something about my person that does not meet with your full approval.'

Although he was not slow to acknowledge his lack of manners, his innate honesty refused to allow him to deny the assertion. 'Yes, there is something troubling me. Several things, as it happens. I went riding with

Miss Ashworth earlier today, and she happened to mention that you were well on the way to acquiring a new servant.'

A moment's silence, then, 'Well, what of it?'

Not only had his lordship's gaze been unwavering, there had been a suggestion of steeliness in his pleasantly mellow voice; a hint, maybe, that he wasn't the type of man to brook any interference in his personal concerns.

Philip could well appreciate this viewpoint, for he too wouldn't take kindly to a mere acquaintance—for he was little more than that to the Viscount, after all—meddling in his affairs. None the less, this didn't prevent him from remarking, 'I understand Beth has already warned you that the man you intend to employ has been mixing with some bad company of late. He's definitely acquainted with the man I strongly suspect of having been responsible for damaging my saddle that day.'

Philip could now well understand Beth's frustration. For all the reaction he got from the Viscount, he might as well have saved his breath. The host's response, however, could not have been more different.

'And having discovered this, you still offered the fellow employment...?' Bathurst demanded, still looking slightly dumbfounded. 'You must be all about in your head, Sebastian! You'll find yourself relieved of your purse, and more besides, at the first opportunity, I do not doubt.'

Betraying his sublime unconcern by the faintest of smiles, the Viscount reached for the port decanter in order to replenish his glass. 'I have no such fears, Charles,' he responded at length. 'I'm not such a poor judge of character.'

He then focused his attention on the man seated directly opposite. 'Your interest in Clegg is of a more private nature—understandably so. But if it is your intention to attempt to persuade me to interrogate him on your behalf about his activities in Markham prior to our paths crossing, I tell you plainly you will be wasting your breath, for I will not.'

Once again it was the host who betrayed his dissatisfaction with the response. 'Well, I consider that damnably disobliging of you, Blackwood!'

'Not at all,' Philip interjected calmly, before Bathurst could continue to voice his disapproval of his good friend's attitude. 'I perfectly understand his sentiments. Had I been in his position, I might possibly have felt the same. After all, we are not friends. He owes me nothing.'

'Maybe not, Staveley,' the Viscount responded, 'but that isn't my reason for not obliging you. The man Clegg did me a good turn. I repaid him by offering him the chance of employment within the next few weeks, even though I had already judged by his general demeanour, his reluctance to meet my gaze, that his activities might not have been all law-abiding since his return from the Peninsula.'

'And having already suspected this, you still go and offer the fellow employment!' Charles Bathurst cast an anguished look at the plasterwork ceiling above his head. 'I despair of you sometimes, Blackwood!'

Far from offended, the Viscount frankly laughed. 'I would be amazed if you did not. A gentleman who has, with perhaps one possible breach, always upheld the law, not to mention practised it for many years as well, is bound to feel as you do.' His smile faded, and he was suddenly serious. 'But I, on the other hand, Charles, am not a paragon of all the virtues. I've never made any secret of the fact that very many of my past activities could not withstand close scrutiny, most especially by a pillar of the community such as yourself. I'm not proud of myself. But neither am I such a hypocrite as to condemn a man for indulging in a little petty theft in order to put food into his belly, for I honestly believe Clegg's been involved in nothing more than that. And then only when he couldn't find work. However, I did issue the firm warning that, if he wishes to work for me, he must keep his nose clean from now on.'

'Which he appears to be doing,' Philip enlightened them, 'as he's staying well clear of a certain Rolf Murslow, the person I believe is responsible for damaging my saddle.'

'I'm not surprised to hear that,' the Viscount responded, after staring thoughtfully down into the contents of his glass. 'The incident at the White Hart that day was witnessed by a young doctor who's setting up a practice in town. He took it upon himself to discover if either of us was hurt. We fell into talking, and after discovering I'd offered Clegg a position, he asked if I'd object to him employing Clegg until such time as he came to work for me. Seemingly the house the doctor's recently purchased is in need of a few minor repairs, which he wishes to effect before his wife and children join him in a few weeks. It was arranged that Clegg should stay with the doctor in one of the attic rooms for the duration of his employment.'

'Do you suppose that this Clegg and Murslow might have been involved in criminal activities together?' Charles Bathurst asked, breaking the silence that had ensued since his friend had finished speaking.

'It's certainly a strong possibility,' Philip acknowledged. 'Although I have to say I do not think Clegg was in any way involved in the cutting of my saddle.' He shrugged. 'Why should he have been? After all, he's no grudge against me or my family.'

The Viscount raised his eyes from the liquid in his glass to stare directly at the Baronet once more. 'Which suggests to me that perhaps Rolf Murslow has. I distinctly recall, on the evening I dined with you at the Court, your mentioning that some action of your late father's just might be behind the incident. Would I be correct in supposing that this Murslow is none other than the son of the tenant your father evicted?'

Philip didn't attempt to suppress an appreciative smile at the astuteness, not to mention the acute memory, of the man seated opposite. Seemingly they had more in common than he had imagined, for he too was renowned for his sharp recall.

He readily confirmed his lordship's assumptions. 'Of course I can perfectly understand why the fellow should feel bitter towards my family, and wish to extract some form of petty revenge,' he continued, once again proving how fair-minded he could be. 'Truth to tell, even if I was able to obtain proof of his guilt, I wouldn't want to involve the magistrates. If that one incident is to be the end of it, I would settle for delivering a verbal warning to the rogue myself.' He frowned. 'But I cannot help feeling he was in the home wood that day for quite another purpose. I strongly suspect he was attempting to gauge how easy it would be to break in to the Court and relieve me of some of my possessions.'

'Good gad, man!' Charles Bathurst exclaimed. 'I hope you're not willing to overlook that too, should it occur?'

'Indeed not,' Philip assured him. 'In fact, I've already taken steps to increase security. If he should attempt to break into my home and is caught in the act, I shan't think twice about having him placed before a magistrate.'

'But an attempted break in at your home isn't what really troubles you, is it?' the Viscount prompted when Philip fell silent, staring frowningly down at some imaginary spot on the table.

He shook his head. 'No, it isn't,' he finally admitted. 'I don't know for certain what manner of man Murslow is. He may be nothing more than a rogue who's not above indulging in a spot of petty theft when the mood takes him, as I've been led to believe. If so, all well and good. Without proof of his wrongdoing, I cannot approach him, and must be prepared to do nothing for the present, and maybe run the risk of losing a few possessions. Even so, I'd like to be sure that a thirst for revenge wouldn't lead Murslow to more desperate measures. I have no desire, you see, to be for ever looking over my shoulder, just to be certain there is no one lurking behind some tree or hedgerow with a pistol levelled at my head.'

'I can appreciate how you feel, Staveley,' the Viscount responded, thereby revealing there was an understanding side to his nature too. 'That is the existence I endured during my years out there in the Peninsula, and I cannot say I'm sorry that part of my life is now over. The difference is, of course, that kind of existence was entirely of my own choosing; you would not choose to be for ever on your guard. And you shouldn't be obliged to live so through no fault of your own. I told Clegg I'd look him out again on the first market day held in December. The doctor might wish to retain his services, and Clegg might indeed choose to stay. If not, and his desire to come with me to Northamptonshire remains, then I shall see what, if anything, he is prepared to reveal about this man Murslow.'

* * *

Philip saw nothing of Viscount Blackwood during the following three weeks. Then, as good as his word, his lordship called at the Court early one afternoon, following his planned visit to Markham.

Receiving his lordship in the library, Philip soon had his visitor settled in a chair by the hearth. While enjoying a glass of Madeira, the Viscount revealed what he had discovered that very morning.

'I'm sorry I'm not able to tell you more. But as I made clear to you at the outset, I had no intention of resorting to coercion, or using my position as his future employer to prise information out of him.'

'I can appreciate your feelings in the matter,' Philip acknowledged, not wholly disappointed with what he had just learned. 'And because the information was freely given, we can assume, I think, that it is true.'

'I have no reason to doubt it,' the Viscount responded.

'No, indeed,' Philip concurred. 'And I assume that, because he was willing to reveal what he did, he does intend to go with you when you return to the ancestral home.'

'Yes, it would seem so. Apparently the good doctor did broach the subject of a permanent position within his household, but Clegg declined, though he will continue working at the practitioner's home for the next couple of weeks, while the doctor's away collecting his wife and family.' The Viscount's teeth flashed in a saturnine smile. 'I cannot quite make up my mind whether the decision stemmed from an earnest desire to work for me, or an earnest wish to remove from the locale as quickly as possible, and begin afresh. I suspect the latter, for as I've mentioned before I do not think all

Clegg's activities since his arrival in Markham could withstand close scrutiny.

'Without going into details, there is some justification for his fall from grace,' the Viscount continued, 'of which, he openly admits, he isn't proud. Unlike Murslow, Clegg's basically a decent sort, not afraid of hard graft. From what little he did tell me, I gained the impression that, although not a man to be trusted, to date Murslow hasn't been involved in anything other than petty theft, and general mischief. So even though he might bear you a grudge, it isn't likely he'll lie in wait in order to take a pot-shot at you. Judging by what I've learned about him, I don't think he's the type to resort to murder.'

'Well, that's something, at any rate,' Philip conceded, as he escorted the Viscount round to the stables personally.

There was a bitterly cold nip in the air; undoubtedly a foretaste of what was to come. December was now upon them, with the prospect of weeks of inclement weather and limited travel.

He glanced at his companion as a thought occurred to him. 'I assume it's still your intention to remain with Bathurst until your name has been cleared?'

The Viscount betrayed surprise. 'Ah! Evidently Bathurst failed to mention it when last you saw him. I learned last week that I've been completely vindicated, and can once again wander freely about the realm without fear of being taken into custody.'

'I assume, then, that your departure will not be long delayed?' Philip ventured, after offering his sincerest congratulations.

A suspicion of a smile once again clung to the Viscount's lips. 'For the present I'm making no plans.

I have a strong suspicion, you see, that a certain—er—someone in the locale, to whom I am sincerely attached for obvious reasons, would very much appreciate my continued presence.'

And with that he mounted his horse and rode away, leaving Philip to follow his progress along the driveway, feeling as if stark reality had just dealt him the severest blow in the region of his solar plexus.

Having increasingly in recent years tended to consider carefully before taking action, Philip behaved quite out of character by not taking time to mull over what the Viscount had said. Instead he ordered his favourite hack saddled, and was soon heading across the park in a westerly direction.

After discovering Beth was not at home, he headed for the market town, where her housekeeper had assured him her young mistress had gone to purchase material in order to increase her winter wardrobe. Sure enough, on his arrival in Markham, he quickly ran her to earth in the well-patronised haberdashery on the main street, where she was in the process of making up her mind between two different coloured materials.

It was Meg, the young maid, who first drew her mistress's attention to the shop's newest arrival. After greeting him in her casually friendly fashion, Beth bade him come and help her make her choice. It was only when she won no response whatsoever that she turned to look at him more closely.

'Why, whatever is the matter? You're staring at me as if I were a complete stranger.'

This at least produced a response. He joined her at the counter, but continued to concentrate his gaze on the delicate features framed in yet another fetching bonnet.

'Well…?' Beth prompted. 'Would you choose the blue or the amber?'

'Er…' Philip at last managed to drag his eyes away from the beloved face and stared down briefly at the display on the counter. 'Why not have both?' he suggested, betraying at least a token interest.

'Why not, indeed!' Beth agreed. 'And it isn't an extravagance. My winter wardrobe is woefully inadequate, as is poor Ann's. I'd best purchase two lengths for her as well.'

This alerted Philip to a fact that had escaped him entirely up until then. 'And where is the excellent Mrs Stride hiding herself today? Not indisposed, I trust?'

'As it happens, yes. She's contracted a chill and has taken to her bed. Which isn't really surprising. She's been spending a deal of time of late walking in the most inclement weather for—er—differing reasons.'

It was at this point that Beth's attention was claimed by the proprietress of the shop, and for the following five minutes or so she concentrated on making several purchases.

'Once the materials have been packaged up, Meg, bring them along to the carriage, will you? Sir Philip, I'm sure, will kindly stand my escort.'

Beth didn't wait for him to acquiesce, but wasn't unduly surprised to find him at her heels as she left the premises. She was surprised, however, to discover his favourite hack, in the hands of a grubby urchin, directly outside the shop, for as a rule he tended to stable his horses at the White Hart whenever he visited Markham.

A thought occurred to her. 'You didn't come to town for the sole purpose of seeking me out, by any chance, did you?'

'As it happens, I did,' he freely admitted, after tossing

the boy a coin and once more taking charge of the bay himself. He didn't attempt to mount. Instead, he walked alongside Beth in the direction of her carriage, awaiting her return further along the main street.

'I received a visit from Blackwood earlier today,' he revealed, while all the time studying her intently for the slightest reaction. There was none, save for a look of mild interest.

Slightly relieved, he pressed on, recounting almost verbatim what the Viscount had told him. 'I'm not unduly concerned about Murslow now. As long as he doesn't attempt any other mischief, I shan't take matters further. I'd get no satisfaction out of persecuting the fellow.'

When all she did was to nod in agreement with this sentiment, he broached the one subject that had preyed on his mind to the exclusion of all else for the past hour or so.

'While he was with me, Blackwood also mentioned he intends to delay his return to his ancestral home and remain in the locale for a while.'

The instant raising of finely arched brows was proof enough that she had been quite ignorant of this fact, even before she said, 'Really? I wonder what's brought about that resolve? Of course, now he's free to go about without fear of being taken into custody, he can come and go as he pleases.'

Philip was instantly alert. 'Oh, so you'd already been informed about that, had you?'

'Oh, yes,' she readily confirmed. 'Both he and Bathurst paid a visit the other day and told us the good news.' Her spontaneous smile was full of gentle affection. 'I'm so very pleased for him, Philip! To a man of his stamp any degree of confinement, no matter how small, is tantamount to a prison sentence. Even if he does stay in the area, I don't imagine we'll see so much of him from now on. There are plenty of places of interest to visit in these parts, are there not?'

'True,' he agreed, before pointing out something she'd seemingly overlooked. 'But December's hardly the month to indulge in a spot of sightseeing. And I do not for a moment suppose it's for that reason he has chosen to remain, especially as he's not exactly kept himself confined to Bathurst's home during his stay in the county.'

They had by this time arrived at the waiting carriage and, after a brief acknowledgement of Amos Rudge's presence up on the box, Philip once again scrutinised Beth's features. 'After all,' he continued, 'I suspect he's called upon you a dozen or more times since he's been in the locale.'

'Certainly a fair few,' she freely admitted, showing him the perfection of her profile as she turned her head to stare down the road. 'He's accompanied Bathurst every time he's paid a call in recent weeks, at any rate.' She frowned suddenly. 'Are you sure he didn't offer any explanation for his choosing to remain? It really is most odd.'

Once again Philip experienced that unpleasant feeling in the pit of his stomach. 'He merely said something about staying because someone to whom he is sincerely attached would undoubtedly appreciate his remaining in the locale.'

Although she continued to stare down the main street and, in consequence, offered him only a partial view of her face, he thought he detected what appeared to be an arresting look flicker over her profile.

'I wonder now,' she murmured, before nodding and smiling enigmatically. 'Of course, he must have realised! He's such a clever, clever devil!'

Then all at once her expression changed and her brows clearly snapped together. 'I don't know, though... Unless I much mistake the matter that's the new doctor's house down the road, there. And isn't that none other than Murslow leaning on the fence, conversing with Tom Clegg?'

Philip, of course, didn't know Clegg by sight. In truth, he had some difficulty in recognising Murslow as the man he had seen idly leaning against the wall all those many weeks ago, staring at him in a distinctly unfriendly fashion. All the same, from descriptions he'd been given by various people recently, including Beth herself, he didn't doubt the identity of either man.

'Evidently Viscount Blackwood is far less perceptive than I had thought,' Beth surprisingly remarked as she turned her full attention to Philip once more. 'Correct me if I'm wrong, but didn't he seem to suppose that Clegg had severed all ties with his former life here?'

Philip considered for a moment. In Clegg's defence it had to be said that he appeared more interested in continuing with his repair of the garden gate than conversing with Murslow. Nevertheless, he considered it might be worthwhile just mentioning the fact to the Viscount when next they happened to meet.

He might not have been so quick to dismiss the episode from his mind had he happened to notice the intense and prolonged look Rolf Murslow cast in their direction a moment or two later, when he at last caught sight of the Baronet. Philip might have been more concerned, still, had he observed the quick verbal exchange that then took place between the two men, after Clegg had been roused to focus his attention on the lady who was at that moment being gently assisted to enter the carriage.

Chapter Eleven

On her arrival back at the Grange, later that same afternoon, Beth discovered that Ann had decided not to venture from the warm comfort of her bed, and so went along to her friend's chamber to see how she fared. She discovered her, thankfully, awake, and propped against a mound of pillows, though she did look particularly sorry for herself.

'Oh, you poor dear, aren't you feeling any better?' she asked while approaching the bed.

'I am feeling a little more the thing, as it happens. I'm just so bored,' the invalid declared mournfully. 'I know I shouldn't ask it of you, because I should hate for you to contract the wretched thing, but would you bear me company for just a little while? You could sit in the chair, over there, not too close to me.'

'Nonsense! If I'm going to catch a chill, I'll catch one,' Beth responded matter-of-factly. Then, promptly plumping herself down on the edge of the bed, she revealed how successful her shopping trip to Markham had been. 'I ended by purchasing four different coloured lengths, so you'll be fully occupied in making your dresses when you're up and about again.'

'That was kind of you to choose material for me too. I know I shall like them, because you always know what suits me,' Ann responded, smiling fondly before memory stirred. 'By the by, you had a visitor whilst you were out. I understand Sir Philip called. Naturally I couldn't receive him, so I honestly don't know whether the matter was urgent or not.'

'We met up in town, as it happens,' Beth revealed. 'He admitted he came for the sole purpose of searching me out. But for the life of me I cannot imagine why. He had absolutely nothing of real import to discuss. Well, at least nothing that couldn't have kept for another time.' She frowned as she recalled details of the encounter. 'He was in an unusual mood—didn't seem quite himself. He did reveal something, though,' she added, her frown disappearing as she smiled wickedly down at the invalid. 'Told me that Viscount Blackwood had decided to remain with Charles for a while longer. Now what, do you suppose, could have prompted that decision?'

Ann's gaze darted everywhere except in Beth's direction, and the heightened colour in her cheeks had absolutely nothing to do with a suddenly worsening fever.

'I really c-cannot imagine,' she responded lamely, much to Beth's further amusement.

'Oh, can't you, indeed! she scoffed. 'Well, I jolly well can! You cannot go about smelling of April and May at this season of the year and not expect people to draw their own conclusions.'

Taking pity on her delightfully flustered companion, Beth grew serious. 'I'd be the first to admit I had reservations about Charles Bathurst when he first began to pay you particular attention. But during these past weeks, after his numerous visits here, I've come to know him a deal better, and no longer doubt the sincerity of his intentions towards you. He's an honourable gentleman, one who would never play fast and loose with a lady's feelings. I suspect the only reason he's delayed in declaring himself is simply because of his worry over his friend the Viscount. Now that -er- little problem has been very satisfactorily resolved, Charles, I'm sure, will start to focus more on his own personal concerns.'

'Perhaps,' Ann allowed, all at once sounding uncertain. 'I own that we rub along together remarkably well, have from the very first. But he has never once broached the subject of matrimony, never so much as even hinted at it.'

Beth herself had no misgivings. 'Well, when he does I hope you'll have sense enough to accept him. No one who knows you could doubt the affection in which you held your late husband. But you've been a widow now for over five years. You deserve another chance of happiness. And I for one do not doubt for a moment you'll achieve just that with Charles.'

'I've been happy with you, dear,' Ann declared, reaching out to clasp one of Beth's hands fondly.

'I know you have. But you'll be happier, still, married to Mr Bathurst, with your numerous progeny about you.'

Evidently the pleasurable image her mind's eye had instantly conjured up of herself surrounded by several offspring was short-lived, for Ann's smile faded and she looked earnestly up at the young woman who, almost from the first, had meant so very much more to her than just an employer.

'But what will you do if…if my situation should happen to change in the foreseeable future.'

'Do…?' Beth was nonplussed for a moment or two.

'Why, wish you every happiness, of course, and visit you often.'

'But, Beth, dear, you can hardly remain here, alone, without any suitable female to bear you company. Should you attempt to do so,' Ann warned, 'it would give rise to a deal of gossip.'

In truth, Beth had never given the matter of employing another companion much thought, and betrayed her lack of interest by a slight shrug. 'Time enough to consider that. I might even enlist my Aunt Hetta's help when I spend some time in London with her in the spring. That should please her. She loves to have her advice sought. She's bound to know of someone suitable, a distant relative, maybe.'

'Yes, she may well,' Ann agreed, though still looking troubled. 'But it won't please her if she discovers you've lived here alone for any length of time. And what Sir Philip will have to say on the—'

'He will have no say in the matter!' Beth snapped, her expression as harsh as her voice. 'I'm my own mistress, and shall brook no interference from anyone, not even from such a good friend as Sir Philip.'

'Oh, Beth,' Ann murmured, clearly concerned. 'I've known almost from the first time I saw you two together.' The slender hand beneath her own was hastily withdrawn. 'When you told me all those years ago that you would never marry,' she continued, undeterred by the very negative reaction, 'I sincerely believed it was simply because you had yet to meet a man you could love. How wrong I was! You've known him all your life, haven't you?'

Very slowly Beth rose from the bed and went across to the door. 'My long-standing relationship with Sir Philip is not open for discussion…now or ever,' she declared in a clear, carrying voice, and then left the room, without so much as a backward glance.

The following day Ann felt sufficiently recovered to venture down to the front parlour, where she spent the entire morning lying with a rug over her knees on the sofa, receiving visits from several friends and neighbours, one of whom left without her package containing old clothes, intended for the vicarage.

'I fear Mrs Frobisher is becoming quite feather-brained!' Ann declared, after she had discovered from the housekeeper that a package had been left in the hall. 'That's the second time she's left things behind.'

Their less than cordial parting of the previous day having been completely forgotten, Beth slanted her companion a mocking glance. 'Haven't you got that woman's measure yet, Ann…? I'm surprised at you! You aren't usually so obtuse. There's absolutely nothing wrong with Mrs Frobisher, except she's the most shocking gossipmonger who ever drew breath. She leaves those things here quite deliberately, simply because she knows you'll eventually pass them on to the vicarage. Having become such a close friend of the Chadwicks, you are far more likely to discover all the latest village scandal, or at least a deal more than she would if she visited the vicarage herself. You mark my words, she'll conveniently remember the package in a day or two's time and return here, fervently hoping, of course, that you've taken it along to the vicarage for her by then.

'Well, she's going to be disappointed,' Beth went on, rising to her feet, her pointed little chin set in dogged determination, 'because I'm going to take it round to the vicarage myself, as you're nowhere near well enough to venture forth.'

'Do you think you should, dear?' Ann responded, after casting a worried glance in the direction of the window. 'It doesn't look at all pleasant out there today. It's been quite dull and overcast all morning. And I swear there was a flurry of snow earlier.'

Undeterred, Beth went across to the door. 'Don't worry, I'll wrap up warmly. I shouldn't be gone too long. Should be back in good time for luncheon. But if for any reason I'm late you have your broth in here on a tray, and I'll have mine when I return. I heard the other day that a springer spaniel bitch had given birth to a litter of pups. If I'm not too long at the vicarage, I just might take a look at them. Mrs Chadwick will know who the owner is, I'm sure.'

Delaying only for the time it took to collect her fur-lined cloak and pick up the parcel of clothes, Beth set off on the fifteen-minute walk to the vicarage.

By the time she had reached her destination, she was thankful she'd had sense enough to collect her warmest cloak before leaving the house. A biting east wind had blown up some time during the morning, and the sky did indeed look leaden and threatening. None the less, after discovering from Mrs Chadwick the name and direction of the owner of the pups, Beth decided to risk the weather deteriorating to pay a call on the elderly widowed lady who lived down a narrow lane in a cottage almost directly opposite the smithy.

Save for a covered wagon standing on the side of the road, the main village street was virtually deserted. Those inhabitants who were not hard at work were, seemingly, not straying too far away from their firesides on such a bitterly cold day; a sensible decision wholly embraced by the elderly woman who promptly invited

Beth to step inside her modest yet well-maintained dwelling to view the pups.

Discovering that none of the dogs had been promised, Beth had the pick of the litter. Three were near-miniatures of their sweet-faced mother, all equally gorgeous. The fourth, however, was a somewhat odd-looking shaggy grey ball of fur, which suggested strongly that the father in all likelihood was of indeterminate breed. Yet it was undeniably this one that instantly took a liking to Beth as soon as she sat herself near to the range in the comfortably warm kitchen. Frisking round the hem of her skirts, it demanded attention, which she eventually gave by picking it up and placing it in her lap.

'Well, the little scamp certainly seems to have taken quite a shine to you, miss,' the old lady beamed. 'He's the only dog in the litter.'

Beth was not quite so enthusiastic about the preference she was being shown by the odd-looking pup. In truth, she would have much preferred one of the bitches, and yet she just hadn't the heart to shun the little ball of grey fur that was showing her such affection. She stared down at the dark little eyes staring adoringly back up at her and wondered if she were mad even to consider taking him.

'I think we can safely assume the father is not another spaniel?'

'No, dear,' the old lady responded, staring less charitably at the odd one of the litter. 'Had it not been for that little fellow, I might have hoped that old Major Webster's spaniel had been responsible. But I very much fear the blacksmith's great hairy thing got there first.'

Beth managed to stifle a groan. She'd had reason to

engage the blacksmith's services on three separate occasions since her return to the village, and had seen the
dog that was left to roam free about the smithy. It wasn't
that it was vicious, merely large and definitely not what
one would describe as appealing.

Something in her expression must have betrayed
Beth's reluctance to commit herself, for the old lady
suggested taking a little time to think it over. 'And if
you'd really prefer one of the bitches, I'd be happy to
keep one back for you, miss, though of course they're
not ready to leave their mother quite yet.'

With a suspicion of creaking joints she rose to her
feet. 'Now, can I tempt you to take a drop of something warm to help keep out the cold on the
homeward journey?'

Having lived among country folk for much of her
life, Beth would never have dreamt of hurting the
elderly lady's feelings by spurning her hospitality, and
happily accepted the offer of mulled wine.

Having become something of a connoisseur in recent
years, Beth couldn't forbear a slight shudder as she took
her first sip of the very generous measure of the home-
made elderberry concoction. None the less, she persevered and was soon finding the spicy, aromatic brew very
warming. It was only when she at last placed the little dog
on the floor and got to her feet, ready to leave, that she
realised the tipple was far stronger than she had imagined.

'Oh dear,' she said, feeling the need to steady herself
momentarily by grasping the back of the chair. 'You're
very hospitable with your measures, ma'am.'

'Yes, it can be somewhat powerful to those not used
to it,' the widow agreed, before slowly bending to pick
up the little dog that seemed determined not to let Beth
out of his sight. 'No, you can't go with her, you silly

boy,' she said, addressing him directly. 'The lady's not
decided to have you yet.'

'True. But seemingly he's chosen me,' Beth
declared. 'You may consider you've found that one a
home. I'll be back to collect him when he's ready to
leave his mother.'

It wasn't until she stepped out into the narrow lane
that Beth experienced the full effects of the beverage she
had consumed. To say she felt light headed and irre-
sponsible would have been a gross exaggeration. All the
same, much later, she was shamefully forced to own that
she couldn't possibly have been perfectly sober, otherwise why hadn't she taken more notice of the covered
wagon, which she had observed earlier in the main street,
stood at the entrance to the lane? Had she had her full
wits about her surely she would have considered by the
number of pots and pans hanging on various hooks at the
back that it was in all likelihood a tinker's conveyance?

Sadly though at the time she didn't consider it
strange that a vehicle was almost blocking the narrow
lane, forcing her to squeeze past on the uneven and
muddy grass verge. It wasn't until she drew level with
the poorly nourished animal between the shafts, and
glanced up into the thin face of the unkempt owner, that
a *frisson* of uneasiness ran down the length of her spine.

Unfortunately, by then, it was already too late. In the
next moment something hard made painful contact with
the back of her neck, resulting in her retaining no
memory whatsoever of the following few hours.

No one observing Sir Philip Staveley, resting in his
favourite chair in his library, close to a roaring fire,
would have supposed for a moment that he had spent
one of the most frustratingly profitless days of his entire

life, for, except for a slight meditative look, his expression was quite impassive.

Renowned for his cool deliberation and sound judgement, he had spent a considerable amount of time ruminating over what was very likely to be the most important course of action he'd ever take in his life. To fail was unthinkable, too heartrending even to contemplate.

Yet after hours of careful consideration he was no nearer knowing which stratagem to adopt: should he declare himself openly, admit just how much she meant to him, and sweep her off her feet by the sheer depth of his own passion; or be more circumspect, and attempt to win her by degrees, using gentle persuasion, just like any other gentleman of the least sensibility would be inclined to do on finally deciding on the very special lady with whom he wished to spend the rest of his life?

Unable to suppress a bark of self-deprecating laughter, he went over to find solace in the contents of the decanter containing a fine old claret. Just why it had taken him so long to realise what should have been apparent almost from the day they had been reunited would always remain a mystery. Yet, it was true none the less. It had taken Viscount Blackwood's arrival on the scene to bring him to his senses. If he had found the mere thought of Beth married to another man unbearable, how would he go on if it became a reality?

His hand shook involuntarily, spilling some of the contents of his glass. So preoccupied was he by that one unendurable thought that he was oblivious to the red stain spreading over his waistcoat.

Eventually, though, cool reason took command, forcing him to accept that Beth's affections might truly be engaged. It was not so difficult to comprehend, either. Undeniably Beth had blossomed into a well-favoured young woman in both face and figure, and there was no refuting Blackwood's devilish charm. They were bound to be attracted to each other. He took a moment to consider this more fully. Was that all it was, though—mere attraction based on mutual respect? Or had it already gone much deeper than that? But even if it remained just a genuine friendship between them, did that make his own position any more favourable?

Returning to his chair, Philip attempted to recall each and every one of their encounters since her return from abroad in the late summer. True, at first her treatment of him had been slightly on the cool side. But that was only to be expected, after all, he reasoned. Beth had left Somerset little more than a girl, and had returned a woman. She had far too much self-respect to wish to be accused of casting out lures in order to entrap one of the most eligible bachelors in the county...and yet...

His eyes narrowed speculatively as he focused on an imaginary spot on the wall opposite. No, there was more to it than that; he felt certain of it. Whenever he had offered her a helping hand to alight from her carriage or dismount from her horse, she had shown her appreciation with a gracious smile. When he had swirled her about the room, his hand resting lightly on her trim waist, on that memorable occasion they had first waltzed together, she had been dazzlingly animated, seeming totally impervious to the more intimate contact.

Yet there had been other times, he reminded himself, when this had been far from the case. There had been several occasions when he had instinctively reached for her, and she had—yes—almost recoiled at his touch. But why...? Did she find him so abhorrent that she had to steel herself in order to accept any form of contact?

He shook his head in the next moment as the answer flashed into his head. No, he couldn't believe that was so. Yet, there had to be some reason for those occasionally negative reactions towards him, surely?

The rigorous application of the door-knocker echoing in the hall succeeded in interrupting his train of thought, and a moment or two later Charles Bathurst surprisingly swept into the room, breathless, his expression grim.

'I called, Staveley, to see if Miss Ashworth was with you, but your butler has already confirmed that she has not been at the Court this day.'

Although Philip maintained quite beautifully an air of calm, his every sense was instantly alerted. 'How long has she been missing?'

'Seemingly she left the house shortly after midday. I called mid-afternoon to see how Mrs Stride went on. Naturally she was somewhat concerned at Miss Ashworth's non-return, but only became genuinely worried when the light began to fade. I've already sent that manservant at the Grange into the village to see what he can discover. I thought to try here in the meantime.' He sighed. 'Sadly, to no avail, however.'

Philip glanced up at the mantel-clock. It wanted only a few minutes to five. Already it was dark outside, and the wind, which had been gradually increasing in strength throughout the afternoon, was gusting threateningly about the eaves.

'Beth is one of the few females of my acquaintance who has a healthy respect for time. She is rarely tardy without good reason.' Although he rose abruptly to his feet, he remained remarkably composed. 'Perhaps if you'll allow me a few minutes, Bathurst, I shall accompany you back to the Grange.'

Before Philip had reached the door, he heard the

sounds of another arrival, and wasn't unduly surprised to discover Amos Rudge being admitted to the house. The butler, who had evidently already grasped the fact that something was sadly amiss, for once did not betray even so much as a flicker of disdain as he moved to one side, holding the door wide.

'Come in, man! Come in, and tell us what you've found out!' Philip beckoned Rudge into the library, eager to learn what had been discovered, whilst already sensing, by the servant's doleful expression, that the news about to be shared was not good.

Rudge wasn't slow in confirming this. 'She called at the vicarage, right enough, but stayed only to 'and over a parcel of clothing, and pass the time of day. Then, seemingly, Miss Beth took it into her 'ead to look over a litter of curs. The old lady that owns the dogs said she'd been there right enough, and left, mayhap, a few minutes after two.'

Philip easily detected the puzzled expression lurking behind the servant's concerned look. 'Do you doubt what the woman told you?'

'Well, no, sir, not exactly. It's just…' Rudge scratched his head, now looking genuinely perplexed. 'It's just that I don't see as 'ow Miss Beth could 'ave been quite 'erself, as yer might say, not if she chose that particular cur. But the old woman said it were so, and I've no reason to disbelieve 'er. Said she stood at the front door and watched Miss Beth walk towards the main village street, until she were lost from sight behind a tinker's cart blocking the lane.'

'Then, she certainly must have been heading homewards, surely?' Charles Bathurst suggested. 'Ann has already told me she expected to see her back soon after luncheon.'

'I didn't even know she'd left the 'ouse, sir,' Rudge disclosed, addressing Mr Bathurst. 'Until you sent for me, that is. Why didn't she ask me to go with 'er, or one of the maids?'

'No one's blaming you, Rudge,' Philip put in, resting his hand briefly on the older man's coat sleeve. 'No one knows your mistress better than I do. She was ever that way. You cannot believe the effort it took me years ago to persuade her to take a groom along whenever she went out riding. Because she didn't intend being out for very long, she wouldn't think to take a servant with her, not merely to walk about the village where she grew up.'

Charles brightened. 'Perhaps that's the answer, then! As she knows most everyone in the place, she possibly went to visit someone else, and has merely lost track of time.'

Philip, however, knew better. 'Beth might be head-strong, still, on occasions. But one thing she has never been and that's insensitive to the feelings of others. She has far too much regard for Mrs Stride to cause her un-necessary anxiety.' He shook his head, looking grave himself now. 'No, something happened to Beth after she had left that old lady's cottage, something over which she had absolutely no control.'

He looked searchingly at Rudge, as a thought occurred to him. 'A tinker's wagon, you say, blocking the lane?'

Before the servant could confirm this, there was a further loud thundering on the front door, quickly followed by a slight commotion in the hall. Then Viscount Blackwood strode in, supporting his own recently engaged manservant, who was deathly pale and not altogether steady on his feet.

'Sit him down here,' Philip suggested, showing his usual presence of mind, not to mention consideration for the servant who was clearly injured. 'What happened to him?'

'He was hit over the head, hurled down a series of steps, and then locked in a cellar, from where he managed to escape by prising the lock with a metal bar. Then, borrowing the young doctor's horse, he was riding out of Markham to see me, when I happened to pass him on the road. As soon as I discovered what had happened, I didn't hesitate to bring him here.' The Viscount then addressed Philip directly. 'Am I right in thinking you have a doctor, here, in the local village?'

Philip nodded as he glanced across at his butler, still hovering by the door awaiting instructions. 'See to it, Stebbings,' he ordered before once again going across to his array of sparkling crystal decanters. 'Undoubtedly it's entirely the wrong thing to give him, but I expect your servant would appreciate a brandy.'

'You might appreciate a stiff one yourself, Staveley, when you hear what Clegg has to say,' the Viscount suggested sardonically.

'I think I can already guess,' Philip responded, ignoring the advice. He had the feeling he would need all his wits about him before this day drew to a close.

'All the same, I should appreciate hearing it from your own lips, Clegg. If you're up to it, that is?' he added, handing the injured man the filled glass, and gaining some satisfaction in seeing a semblance of colour returning to the servant's face as he sampled the very generous measure of amber liquid gratefully. 'Would your visit here have anything to do with Miss Ashworth's disappearance earlier today, and your friend Murslow's involvement?'

Although clearly startled, Clegg confirmed Philip's suspicions at once, 'But 'ee be no friend o' mine.' He lowered his head, clearly remorseful. 'Oh, I admit I stood on watch a time or two while he robbed a place. And I ain't proud of it, neither. But I felt I owed 'im, see? 'Ee were the only one to offer me 'elp when I first came 'ere. Gave me a place to stay and shared 'is food wi' me.'

He gazed across at Sir Philip, who now stood by the hearth, his right arm resting on the mantel-shelf, looking for all the world as though he hadn't a single care. 'But I 'ad nowt to do wi' that business wi' your saddle, sir. That I swear!'

'Ahh, so you know all about that, do you,' Philip returned in a trice, although not doubting the man's word.

'Murslow came into the inn one evening bragging about it, so 'ee did. Said as 'ow you deserved it on account of your pa throwing 'is family out of their 'ome. Were quite put out later, so 'ee were, when he found out you weren't that badly 'urt. At the very least 'ee'd 'oped you'd break a leg.' Clegg shrugged. ''Ad nowt to do wi' me, though, sir. I 'ad no part in it.'

'But that wasn't his real reason for coming to the Court that day, was it?'

'No, it weren't,' Clegg readily confirmed. 'Came to look the place over, so 'ee did. See 'ow easy it would be to break in, like. 'Ee thinks you owe 'im, see. 'Ee wants money from you, not yer life.'

Only the whitening of the knuckles on his right hand as he gripped the mantel-shelf betrayed his innermost feelings, for his voice was as controlled as ever as he said, 'And is that the reason why he abducted Miss Ashworth earlier today? Is it his intention to hold her up for ransom?'

'I think you must repeat what you told me earlier,' the Viscount suggested when all Clegg did was nod.

'It were about mid-afternoon, or there abouts, when 'ee came knocking on the doctor's kitchen door. Said as 'ow 'ee'd something to show me in the cart. I thought 'ee'd been out poaching, or such like.' The colour once again left his face, as he added, 'Can't tell you 'ow I felt when I saw Miss Ashworth lying there under that cover.'

'She…she…wasn't…?'

Charles Bathurst didn't seem able to bring himself to finish the question at the forefront of his mind. Clegg, however, was swift to reassure him. 'She were breathing, sir. Bound, gagged, and unconscious, but she were alive. I'd stake my life on it.'

'What happened then?' Philip prompted, relieved certainly, but wanting to learn everything, no matter how harrowing.

'Knowing the doctor be away from 'ome, Murslow wanted me to 'ide Miss Ashworth in the 'ouse, and scribble a note to you, asking for money for 'er safe return. You see, sir, I 'appened to say to Murslow once that my—my wife Mary taught me some book learning. I can read better than I can write. But I can scribble well enough for folk to understand. Anyhow, I told 'im I'd 'ave nowt to do wi' it, that I'd done enough for 'im already. Besides…' he shrugged '…don't 'old with 'urting women, especially not ladies like Miss Ashworth. She were good to me. And I don't forget it, neither! Told 'im I'd tell 'is lordship, 'ere, what were going on, if he didn't leave the lady wi' me. Told 'im I'd make up some tale about 'ow I'd found 'er, and wouldn't mention 'im. But 'ee were 'aving none of it, and we argued summat terrible. But after a bit I thought he were starting to see sense. Then the next thing I knew I came to in the cellar.'

'And you've no idea where he might have taken

her?' Philip asked, as soon as he'd considered everything he'd learned.

''Could be keeping her in 'alf-a-dozen different places, sir, that I know to. And that's the truth of it,' Clegg responded, not sounding too hopeful. 'There's 'is own place and outbuildings on the edge of Markham. Then there's that there inn he favours. Him and the landlord be as thick as thieves. It were that there landlord 'elped get rid of the goods he stole. Do anything for money, so 'ee would. Mayhap 'ee'd even 'ide the lady, sir.'

Clegg thought for a moment. 'Then there's that real crony of 'is, one that works for local chandler.' He looked across at Rudge. 'You know 'ee, weasel-faced cove, with a squint. Always 'anging round wi' Murslow. 'Ee might 'ave helped 'ide her somewhere. Then there's 'is father's old place, out Little Crompton way, some three or four mile t'other side of Markham. Overheard Murslow talking about it once. The cottage, seemingly, be n'more than a neglected, tumbledown old ruin now. But the large outbuilding, so I'm told, be sturdy enough. Local farmer been renting it this past year or so to shelter stock, I seem to remember someone saying.'

Eyes narrowing, the Viscount looked thoughtfully down at his injured servant. 'I believe I've seen that place on my travels abroad in recent weeks. Little Crompton, unless I'm very much mistaken, is the place where the local landlord's hospitality is equalled by his comely daughter's warm and very generous disposition.'

Although his lordship's amorous liaisons in recent weeks didn't precisely raise a chuckle, his remarks certainly lightened the mood, if only briefly.

'In that case, Blackwood, can I rely on you to search out the place, which will leave Rudge and myself free to scour Markham,' Philip suggested as he reached for the bell-pull.

'I'll come wi' 'ee, sir.' Tom Clegg made a valiant attempt to rise from the chair, only to be prevented from so doing by the Viscount's firm hand on his shoulder.

'No, you won't,' his lordship countered, his voice soft, though determined. 'You have done more than enough already this day. You'll stay here so that the doctor can take a look at you. And don't you dare to leave until my return!'

'Yes, but what about me?' Bathurst announced. 'Surely you've no objection to me accompanying you?'

'He might not, but I have,' Philip put in unequivocally, before raising one hand against further protest. 'No, Charles, I want you to return to the Grange. My Beth is a resourceful girl,' he went on to explain, his voice noticeably softer. 'She'll do her utmost to effect an escape. If she does succeed she'll head for home, and I want you to be there to guard her with your life until I arrive.'

Charles exchanged a brief, knowing look with his friend the Viscount before finally nodding his head in agreement.

Chapter Twelve

The first thing that began to occur to Beth during that slow return to consciousness was that she was cold; the second, as she forced her eyes open, was to wonder why her highly efficient housekeeper hadn't bothered to light the candles in the parlour. Finally, as the last remaining layers of grey mist cleared, she realised she wasn't at the Grange at all, and that for some reason she was incapable of moving either hands or feet. Then her head began to throb painfully, obliging her to abandon further attempts at coherent thought.

For several minutes she lay there, eyes closed, just listening to the howling wind rattling the tiles above her head. It seemed echoey, not like a house at all, more like some sort of outbuilding. And the reason she couldn't move her arms or legs was obvious—for some reason they had been tightly bound.

Memory then returned with a vengeance: the early afternoon walk in the village; the litter of pups; the tinker's cart…and Murslow! She'd been abducted! But why…? Dear God! Best not think about that right now, she told herself.

It took some little time to overcome the throbbing ache in her head and to attempt to sit up. Eventually her great determination was rewarded, and she succeeded in propping herself against the conveniently positioned wooden pillar directly behind her. Having already detected other sounds apart from the wind, she had subconsciously realised she was not alone in the makeshift prison, and once her eyes had grown moderately accustomed to the gloom she could see she was sharing her accommodation with a sturdy horse, and some other, smaller creature that she couldn't so easily recognise from where she sat. The hay beneath and surrounding her only went to confirm that she was in some sort of animal shelter. Just why she had been brought here, and left, was a conundrum she'd still prefer to contemplate only if she could find no means of escape.

Surely the barn must contain some sharp object, somewhere, on which she might attempt to sever her bonds? Beth reasoned, and was once again attempting to pierce the structure's gloomy interior, when she clearly detected between the gusts of wind the unmistakable clip-clopping of a horse's hooves close by.

Hard on the heels of her first thought, that it must surely be her abductor returning, was whether to topple on to her side again and feign unconsciousness. It took a moment only to decide against this. Sooner or later she would be forced to confront Murslow. What could possibly be gained by delaying the encounter?

A creaking sound off to her right was a clear indication of the precise location of the entrance. She turned her head in time to detect a slight increase in light; not much, it was true, though sufficient for her to see the clear outline of the figure that crept stealthily into the barn. Instinctively she knew something wasn't quite right. Murslow was tall; the figure standing in the aperture was tall. Yet she doubted it was the tinker standing there. Did Murslow own a voluminous cloak boasting many capes…? Possibly, if he'd stolen it, she quickly reasoned. But was he also the proud owner of a perfectly shaped beaver hat worn at such a stylish, jaunty angle…? Surely not!

'Beth…Miss Ashworth, are you in here?' the wearer of the fashionable attire enquired in a deep and clearly refined voice.

For several seconds it was as much as Beth could do to gape in astonishment. She was sure she recognised that huskily attractive masculine timbre. 'Major Black…I mean, my lord, is that you?'

The bark of triumphant laughter was answer enough, as was the muttered oath that quickly followed. 'Confound it! I've just stubbed my toe! I can't see a blighted thing in here. Where are you, girl?'

'Over here,' she called. Quickly realising she would need to guide him by the sound of her voice, she added, 'It does take a little time for your eyes to adjust, but I can see you clearly enough. Yes, that's right, this way. But whatever you do, don't trip over my legs.'

For several moments, after having located her exact whereabouts, and having knelt down beside her, his lordship stared at her in silence, before asking the question that had evidently been in the forefront of his mind.

Beth didn't pretend to misunderstand his concerns. 'Apart from hitting me over the head, and binding my hands and feet, I don't think Murslow's touched me. I would imagine I'd know about it, wouldn't I?'

In the following moments Beth was to appreciate for the first time just how much of an innate gentleman

Viscount Blackwood truly was when he replied with a touch of respectful hesitancy, 'Er—yes, I expect you would.' Then, with a swift return to his normally self-assured tone, he added, 'Well, let's get you released from these bonds, and return you to civilisation.'

Beth obligingly inched away from the post so that he could more easily reach her wrists, but not before she had looked him over a second time, just to assure herself that it was indeed Viscount Blackwood, for in truth he looked so different.

At some point since their last encounter he'd taken the trouble to visit a barber, and had had his long mane of black hair shorn to a more acceptable length. Furthermore, from somewhere he had acquired some new and fashionable attire, so that, just like Philip, he appeared now every inch a gentleman of means.

Resisting the temptation to tease him over his vastly improved appearance, she channelled her thoughts on her present predicament by asking the question at the forefront of her own mind. 'How on earth did you know where to find me? Even I haven't a clue where I am.'

'You're in a large outbuilding on the outskirts of the village of Little Crompton on the Markham road. The building now belongs to Murslow, but is leased to a local farmer.'

Beth was suddenly struck by an astounding thought. 'So you knew Murslow was my abductor before I told you so! How on earth did you discover that?'

'I'll tell you when I've managed to release you from these bonds,' his lordship responded, struggling with a particularly stubborn knot. 'I don't believe we have much time. The weather is—'

'A deal less time than yer think, m'fine lord,' a voice hissed from directly behind his lordship. The next moment the Viscount grunted and slumped forward, just as Beth slew round to find a smugly satisfied look on her abductor's unprepossessing face.

'So 'ee came to look fer yer 'imself, did 'ee. Well, it don't surprise me none. Knew 'ee were sweet on yer on account o' the way he looks at yer. And it's saved me the bother of finding someone able to scribble good enough to get word to 'im.'

That Murslow had managed to arrive totally undetected by either the Viscount or herself didn't surprise Beth unduly. While the gusts of wind were howling about the barn it was virtually impossible to detect any other sounds. His reaction to her rescuer, however, she did find most puzzling.

'Who do you imagine this to be?' she asked, gesturing with her head to the prostrate form at her side.

'Staveley, o' course,' he growled.

'Well, I hate to be the bearer of bad tidings, but it is not he.'

'Eh?' Seemingly her abductor strongly suspected he wasn't being told the truth. Using his foot, he instantly turned the Viscount over none too gently so as to study his face more closely. Evidently still unsure, he cursed, swung round on his heels and left the building.

Between the gusts of howling wind, Beth once again managed to detect the unmistakable sounds of a horse-drawn vehicle coming to a halt directly outside the barn. A minute or so later Murslow was back, holding a lighted lantern aloft in one hand, and some lengths of rope in his other, his hat and coat clearly glistening with flecks of snow.

'Who be 'ee?' he demanded of Beth, after staring down in astonished silence at his lordship's face.

'Viscount Blackwood,' she obliged him, seeing no

reason to lie. 'A gentleman who isn't likely to forgive or forget that you rendered him unconscious,' she added, with a degree of satisfaction, while praying his lordship wasn't badly hurt.

Murslow's reaction surprised her somewhat, however. He merely scowled for several moments, then muttered, ''Ee be the one Tom Clegg'll be working for, once young doctor returns to town… So t'was my old friend Cleggy told 'im.'

Beth too frowned, as she watched the tinker tightly binding his lordship's wrists and ankles, not quite knowing what to make of the latter disclosure. Was Clegg party to the abduction…? If so, why had he then gone on to confide in his lordship? It didn't make any sense at all! Only one thing was certain.

'So Tom Clegg knew you'd kidnapped me?'

His expression turned surly. 'Took you to the doctor's 'ouse, didn't I, more fool me! Thought Clegg 'ud 'elp by keeping you 'idden there, and scribble a note to Staveley. But he wouldn't. Must 'ave broke out the cellar, curse 'im!'

Beth at last began to see the light. 'Were you, per- chance, intending to hold me for ransom in the hope of extracting a substantial sum of money from Sir Philip?'

'Why not?' he snarled. ''Ee owes me.'

'He owes you nothing!' Beth countered, all at once more angry than afraid. 'You've no notion of what manner of man he is. He already knows it was you who tampered with his saddle strap that day. He chose to do nothing about that. But let me assure you he will not take such a lenient view of my abduction.'

As she could see at a glance that Murslow was con- sidering what she had said, and appeared instantly less self-assured, Beth didn't hesitate to thrust home her advantage. 'You don't imagine, surely, that his lordship here is the only person out searching for me, do you? There may be others on their way here already. And if one of them happens to be Sir Philip, be sure he'll not rest until he finds me. Forget any idea you may have had of returning to Markham. You'll be taken into custody as soon as you show your face in the town. Your only hope is to put as much distance as you can between yourself and this place… And time is not on your side,' she added for good measure. 'It has begun to snow heavily already, has it not?'

Beth could almost see the glimmer of uncertainty turning to fear in Murslow's eyes. So it came as no very real surprise when he didn't delay too long in leaving her to her own devices. What she hadn't considered was that he would rifle through his lordship's pockets, relieving him of his valuables, not to mention his pistol, or that he would also, in order to aid his departure, purloin the horse that had brought his lordship to such an isolated spot.

Being a pragmatic sort of female, Beth didn't dwell on the rogue's insufferable behaviour for very long. Instead, she concentrated her thoughts on how best to make herself and the Viscount more comfortable until they were able to leave themselves, or help arrived.

Thankfully, in his own haste to leave, Murslow hadn't troubled himself to recheck her bonds. Although nowhere near free of her wrist restraint, the Viscount had loosened several knots sufficiently for her to work one hand loose after a few minutes' concentrated effort. Then it was an easy matter to free her ankles and also to release his lordship. His low moan as she did so was a relief to hear, for it gave her every reason to hope that he wasn't too badly hurt, and would soon regain consciousness enabling them to depart also.

Unfortunately, just one look outside the barn was sufficient to dash instantly the latter hope of an immediate return to civilisation. It was nothing short of a blizzard. Snowflakes the size of pennies had already covered the landscape so thoroughly that it was impossible to determine in which direction Murslow had ridden. The wind had begun to whip the snow into drifts, as much as a foot high in some places. What appalled Beth more even than this was the fact that Murslow had left his poor undernourished horse still harnessed to the shafts of his battered wagon, at the mercy of the elements.

By the time she had the beast settled into the stall beside the farmer's sturdy cob and what she could clearly now see was a donkey, had catered for its needs as best she could, and had also rifled through Murslow's wagon for a variety of articles that might help make the enforced confinement a little more comfortable, his lordship was already sitting up on his straw bed, rubbing the back of his neck.

Seemingly he had already come to the conclusion that Murslow must have departed, because he was cursing under his breath over the purloining of his valuables.

'Yes, I'm sorry I couldn't do anything to stop him,' Beth apologised, once more joining him on the hay, bringing with her some tallow candles, yet another carriage lamp, and a length of rough sheeting, 'though I must confess at the time I considered it a small price to pay to be rid of him.'

'It's not the money, my pistol or even my fob watch I resent so much as my silver flask. It contained rum. I could do with a drop right now, I don't mind admitting!'

She tried to appear suitably sympathetic, but failed quite miserably, and laughingly suggested he might like to take a drink from the horse's bucket if he felt that thirsty. He satisfied himself with casting her a darkling look before asking if she was sure Murslow didn't intend to return.

'I shouldn't imagine he will,' Beth answered, betraying her indifference. 'The fellow is little more than an avaricious fool. Nevertheless, I don't doubt he has a strong sense of self-preservation. By the by, he's departed on your horse. Or should I say, rather, poor Charles Bathurst's mount,' she went on to reveal, in the same matter-of-fact tone. 'In which direction is impossible now to ascertain because of the depth of snow now lying out there. But I cannot imagine he would have made for Markham.'

'You're an amazing girl!' his lordship surprised her by announcing, his appreciative smile also betraying admiration. 'You've been assaulted, abducted, and now find yourself with little choice but to stay possibly overnight in accommodation that offers few creature comforts, and you take it all in your stride. The vast majority of your sex would have succumbed to a fit of the vapours long before now.'

'Some would, certainly,' Beth was obliged to agree. 'And to very little purpose, I might add.' She shrugged. 'I suppose to some I might betray a sad lack of sensibility, but the truth is I feel more annoyed than anything else. It was such an ill-judged escapade! I don't for a moment think he'd planned to abduct me. Like Philip that day, I just happened to be in the wrong place at the wrong time and Murslow took advantage of the fact that there were few people about.'

Her angry scowl faded as she bethought herself of something Murslow had disclosed. 'I understand that it was none other than Tom Clegg who raised the alarm. I hope he isn't badly hurt.'

'That I couldn't say with any conviction. Like us, he suffered a blow to the head. But he was thrown down a series of cellar steps, which didn't do that injured knee of his any good at all. But a doctor's been summoned, and I'm sure Staveley's people will look after him.'

Even in the dim light thrown out by the two carriage lamps his lordship could clearly see a softer look just for a moment flicker over her features, before she said, 'So Philip does know.'

'Oh, he knows, right enough,' he assured her. 'I wouldn't be at all surprised if he and Rudge weren't still scouring Markham as we speak. As far as we were aware, Murslow might have taken you to any one of a dozen different places. It just so happens that I noticed this large outbuilding on my travels about your county, and was sure I could locate it again without too much trouble.' He smiled crookedly. 'I'm sorry you're having to put up with me. It might so easily have been your friend Staveley who found you. You'd no doubt have felt much more comfortable with him to bear you company.'

'No, I wouldn't,' she admitted hastily, and then immediately afterwards looked away in case her expression betrayed a deal more than she wished to reveal.

With only the occasional lapse she had managed wonderfully well to maintain control over her emotions whenever Philips was near. But, for heaven's sake, she was only human! Spending what might turn out to be several hours in such close proximity to the being she had adored throughout her life would have been too much even for her iron resolve.

'What I mean to say is that I consider you as good a protector as Philip,' she assured him, hoping he'd overlook her earlier *faux pas*.

Unfortunately his lordship stared at her in silence for so long that she felt sure she hadn't made good her blunder. Then he surprised her by saying, 'Well, I haven't made such a good job of protecting you thus far. I've evidently become sloppy since my return from Spain. I used to be much more alert.'

'No one could possibly have heard Murslow above this wind,' she pointed out, thankful that she was no longer being subjected to such piercing scrutiny. 'And don't forget he's possibly learnt to walk as stealthily as a cat whilst engaged in his less lawful pursuits.'

He nodded as he rose to his feet. 'True. But I think we'd be foolish to make any further assumptions by attempting to predict what he might do now. So I think I shall position myself a little nearer the door for the next hour or so. You, in the meantime, should try to get some sleep.'

'Oh, but surely, sir, there's no need,' Beth countered. 'You'd be much more comfortable here with me on the hay.'

'What a very tempting invitation, Miss Ashworth!' The Viscount's even, white teeth flashed in the darkness. 'My inclinations may be honourable on occasions. But, my dear girl, unlike Sir Philip, I do not always act upon them. I shall be a deal more comfortable nearer the door, believe me!'

Like most rumours, it was difficult to know precisely where it had started, or by whom, for that matter. It might have been any one of a couple of dozen people who first began to suspect that something untoward had taken place at some point during that bitterly cold day in December.

When Sir Philip first became aware of the tittle-tattle circulating, he was furious. His anger was soon replaced, however, by a searing sense of guilt, and he was obliged to own that he might well have been instrumental in starting the rumours in the first place.

In his anxiety over Beth's well-being, he had not been as circumspect as he might otherwise have been. When he had entered that particular tavern favoured by Murslow, he had made it abundantly clear to all present, most especially the landlord and his slatternly spouse, that the tinker was wanted by the authorities, and anyone harbouring the miscreant would be dealt with severely.

His visit to the chandler soon afterwards, and his fierce interrogation of the tinker's particular friend, had certainly raised several brows, as had Sir Philip's overnight stay at the White Hart, with none other than Miss Ashworth's manservant.

Beth's early morning arrival in Markham the following day in a tinker's cart, and accompanied by that rather handsome gentleman staying with Mr Bathurst, had only succeeded in encouraging the gossipmongers to ply their trade. Consequently within the space of forty-eight hours most all of Markham and its environs had heard the rumour that the late Colonel Ashworth's daughter had stayed away from home for an entire night, with only a gentleman to bear her company!

Surprisingly enough one of the few who remained oblivious to the salacious gossip was Beth herself. The day after her return to the Grange she was struck down by the same malady that had afflicted Mrs Stride during the previous days. Only in Beth's case it turned out to be a much severer case, which necessitated the services of the local practitioner, and an enforced stay in bed.

Consequently, she received no visitors for several days, and Ann was able to protect her friend from the malicious rumours circulating about her. Nevertheless, like Beth herself, Ann was nothing if not a realist. She knew she could not shield Beth forever, and all too quickly the day came when Beth insisted she was well enough to attempt to resume a normal life by going down to the parlour for at least part of the day.

'So it was Charles who called earlier this morning,' Beth remarked, after being presented with yet another token, a posy of flowers. 'Not easy to come by at this time of year, and expensive, I shouldn't wonder.' Beth's eyes instinctively strayed to the exotic blooms that had arrived for her only the day before. 'Philip's so lucky to have that heated conservatory. He can maintain such a wonderful array of flowers throughout the year.'

'Indeed, he can,' Ann responded. 'Charles is seriously considering having one constructed against the south-facing wall at his home. Like Sir Philip, he's beginning to become interested in the more unusual species.'

Beth's eyes began to dance, a clear indication that she was well on the road to a full recovery. 'Oh, I think he's shown an interest in one rare specimen for some considerable time.'

Although there was a sudden increase in colour in Ann's cheeks, she refused to be drawn. So Beth decided on a more direct approach by asking, 'Well, are you any closer to forming an understanding?'

'He hasn't declared himself, no, if that's what you're asking me.'

'You know full well it is,' Beth returned in her normally blunt fashion, before she was struck by a sudden thought. 'But then the poor fellow has hardly been granted much opportunity to do so in recent weeks, now has he? First you were ill, then I go and contract that wretched chill. You've been playing the devoted nursemaid for the past seven days, hardly leaving my bedside at all during daylight hours.'

Beth's conscience began to prick her. 'Well, the very next time he calls, you are to spend time with him, understand? Go out for a walk...or something.'

'Oh, I couldn't possibly do that!' Ann countered in a trice. 'I couldn't possibly reconcile it with my conscience if I were to desert you before you are fully restored to health.'

Beth might have felt much moved by such an illustration of devotion had not Ann seemed unable to meet her eyes. All at once she sensed there was more to this recent cosseting on Ann's part than a desire to be the perfect companion. A moment later Beth was certain there was much more behind the overprotective display, when the door opened and the housekeeper informed Ann there was a visitor awaiting her in the hall.

Although she couldn't be absolutely sure, Beth strongly suspected the two women exchanged a conspiratorial look as they were about to leave the room. She listened and could just detect the quietly spoken words in the hall. Then Ann was back, cheerily informing her that it was only Mrs Frobisher making a brief visit, and that she would call again when the invalid was feeling more herself.

Beth regarded her companion with wry amusement, a look that Ann was evidently unwilling to meet. 'Yes, well may you look away, Mrs Stride!' she admonished softly. 'I'm quite well enough to receive visitors, even one of Mrs Frobisher's stamp, whose visits, I might remind you, are never normally brief. So what malicious gossip had she to impart that you were determined not to let me hear…? Or can I guess?'

Ann managed to withstand that piercingly assessing azure-eyed scrutiny for all of thirty seconds before admitting defeat. 'Oh, well, I suppose you're bound to find out sooner or later.' She raised one hand in a despairing gesture. 'Sir Philip…Charles…we've all been trying our best to quash the rumours, but you know what people are. You were seen, you see, Beth dear, returning in the tinker's cart with Lord Blackwood that morning.'

'Considering half the population of Markham were out at the time attempting to clear the snow off the roads, I'd be very surprised if we hadn't been seen,' Beth returned without so much as batting an eyelid.

'Yes, but, dear, rumours were already being put about that you were missing, and of course when you returned with his lordship, people weren't slow to suggest you spent the entire night together.'

'And so we did!' Beth pointed out. 'So they are speaking no less than the truth. And he behaved like a perfect gentleman throughout the whole time, keeping watch by the door, hardly ever coming anywhere near me, until first light, when we decided we'd attempt to leave.'

'I'm sure that's true, dear. No one doubts it, not even Sir Philip. But the fact remains rumours at present are rife, and people are saying the most outrageous things.'

'Oh, let them,' Beth said dismissively. 'If the worst comes to the worst, I'll have a word with the Reverend Mr Chadwick. He's known me all my life, and will stand my friend. His wife will follow his lead, and quash the rumours, at least those circulating in the village.' She was suddenly more concerned. 'I don't care so much for myself. I can always stay with Aunt Hetta, or dear Aunt

Matilda in Plymouth if things become too unpleasant. But the one thing I do not want is for Lord Blackwood to feel honour-bound to offer me the protection of his name.'

Beth's fears were realised two days later, when Mr Bathurst turned up with the Viscount on one of their regular visits. From the moment they arrived it was quite evident to Beth, at least, that Charles wished to offer his friend the opportunity to declare himself in private. Ann, ever loyal, ignored all the subtle hints to leave the room; until, that is, Beth herself persuaded her friend that a walk in the fresh air with Charles would do her the world of good, after being cooped up indoors for so many days, for Beth had sense enough to realise that if the Viscount was denied the opportunity of doing the honourable thing this time, then he would be back before too long to try again.

In one way she found it extremely gratifying to know that her assessment of his character had been so accurate; in another way, though, she felt deeply saddened to be obliged to decline what had been such a sincere declaration from a chivalrous man. But decline it she did, gracefully, yet absolutely.

Except for a wry smile, his expression betrayed neither relief nor disappointment. 'At the risk of seeming miffed, Beth, may I be permitted to know why you cannot bring yourself to accept my hand in marriage? I would do my utmost to make you happy.'

If her heart had not belonged so completely to another, Beth might have reconsidered the proposal from the man whom she respected so highly. Yet the moment of indecision was soon over. She cared for him too much to condemn him to a union that might never be truly fulfilled.

'I'm certain you would, my lord,' she responded softly. 'But I also know that you would not have made me an offer of marriage if you did not feel obliged to do so.'

He didn't attempt to deny it. 'I would not have chosen this precise time to marry, it is true,' he admitted. 'I would have preferred some time to set right certain matters in the eyes of the world. That said,' he added, after reaching for her hands, and holding them willing captives in his own, 'I have never met a woman I have wished to marry more.'

'Prettily said, my lord, and I believe you sincerely mean every word. But I also believe you have yet to meet the right lady for you. When you do, I think you will know, and will not accept a refusal so graciously.'

Withdrawing her hands, Beth went to stand by the window to look out on to a garden that was quietly resting until the sun's warmth began to return. 'You are far too gallant to admit it, but I sincerely believe you feel a sense of relief. You are no more in love with me than I am with you. Believe me when I tell you I care for you too deeply to marry you. I foolishly gave my heart at a very young age. I have yet to retrieve it.

'In truth, I cannot be certain I ever shall…'

Chapter Thirteen

Although she hadn't found the interview with Viscount Blackwood downright embarrassing, precisely, Beth hadn't felt altogether comfortable either, especially with herself, and the answer both her heart and conscience had dictated she must give.

Even now, after having mulled over the proposal for a full twenty-four hours, she was still questioning whether she would have made the same decision if Sir Philip Staveley had never played any part in her life. Or, worse, if Philip had already been married.

She shook her head, wondering at herself for considering either possibility. Of course she would! She would never accept a proposal from a gentleman simply because he felt honour-bound to offer the protection of his name. All the same, she couldn't ignore the tiny voice of honesty that reminded her that, had she still been heart-whole, Viscount Blackwood was just the type of man who might so very easily have claimed it.

But the fact remained that most tender of organs did belong irrevocably to another. It mattered not a whit whether Philip was married or not. How could she re-

concile it with her conscience to marry a man in order
to attain a semblance of contentment, and by so doing
ruin any chance he might have had of finding real happiness with someone else? Viscount Blackwood
deserved better, far more than she might ever be able to
give him. Yes, she had made the right decision!

The parlour door opening instantly broke her train
of thought, and she turned her head to discover the very
being responsible for her never having attempted to
find happiness with another man. Surprisingly enough
she experienced a moment's searing resentment towards
him. Then, as she rose to her feet to greet him, foremost
in her mind was that he deserved not censure, only
gratitude for doing his utmost to ensure her safe return,
after that ludicrous episode involving Rolf Murslow.

'So you've decided to pay me a visit at long last, be-
lieving, no doubt, there's little risk to your health now
by so doing,' she teased him, but for once received no
light-hearted response.

'On the contrary, I've called on several occasions.
Mrs Stride assured me, however, that you were not well
enough to receive visitors, and I had no reason to
question her judgement.'

The fact that she had yet to glimpse the warmth of
his smile only went to reinforce her suspicion that all
was not well with him at the present time. All the same,
she knew him well enough to be sure that to ply him
with questions would avail her nothing if he was determined to keep his own counsel. Consequently she
merely provided him with refreshment before discovering the answer to something that had occurred to her
only a couple of days before: namely, if the sturdy cob
had been returned to its rightful owner, after its valiant
pulling of the tinker's cart through the snowdrifts on that

unforgettable morning, enabling Viscount Blackwood and herself to return to Markham.

This did ignite a semblance of a smile, but it was fleeting indeed. 'And none too pleased the farmer was either,' he revealed. 'Oh, he didn't object so much to you making use of his horse. He appreciated you had little choice. The tinker's animal might not have had the strength to make the journey through the snow. But he very much resented the damage done to the padlock that he himself had fitted to the barn door. I explained I rather thought Murslow had been responsible for that piece of wanton damage, and suggested the use of the tinker's horse and cart as compensation. After all, Murslow's hardly likely to return to claim them. And the animal will be a deal better off with the farmer. He at least takes care of his stock.'

'True,' Beth agreed. 'Yet, for all that he's an idle rogue, not to mention a thief, strangely enough I bear Murslow no ill will. After all, he didn't intend me any lasting harm. In his eyes I was merely a means to an end. It was you he was intent on relieving of money.'

He appeared surprised by her forgiving attitude. 'Aren't you forgetting he assaulted you, rendering you unconscious, thereby forcing you to endure the most primitive conditions for an entire night?'

'No, I don't forget that,' she responded, smiling wryly. 'But if I'm honest, I would be obliged to admit I was to some extent to blame for what happened to me that day.'

One shapely masculine brow rose in a questioning arch. 'Why so?'

'Because, Philip, I'm ashamed to say I wasn't perfectly sober at the time of the abduction,' she revealed with total honesty. 'The widowed lady I called to see that day is rather generous with her measures of mulled wine.' She shrugged. 'Who knows, had I decided to risk hurting the old lady's feelings by refusing her hospitality, I might have been able to avoid the encounter with Murslow altogether, or, at the very least, have regained consciousness much quicker, and might then have succeeded in escaping long before the blizzard set in, or the search for me was instigated. And by so doing, of course, have avoided all the silliness that is taking place now.'

The hand raising the glass to his lips checked for an instant. 'Ahh, so you've heard about the rumours, have you?' he said, after finally sampling his wine. 'Well, I suppose it was only a matter of time before your own ears were sullied.'

'Of course it was,' she readily concurred. 'Ann was foolish to attempt to shield me for as long as she did. I was bound to find out sooner or later what was being said about me.'

His sigh was audible, betraying his concern. 'It quite amazed me to discover just how many spiteful tabbies there are among our neighbours.'

Beth, on the other hand, was determined not to become cast down by it all. 'Well, what do you expect, Philip? It's wintertime, after all, and little enough to occupy them, except sit round their firesides indulging in gossip. It will all have been forgotten by the spring. You wait and see.'

He favoured her with a considering look. 'You appear to be taking a very light view of the matter, Beth.'

'Well, what do you expect me to do? Run away to Aunt Hetta, or inflict myself on dear old Aunt Matilda in Plymouth until the rumours have run their course?' She glanced away, thereby successfully concealing the bitter regret that just for an instant was mirrored in her eyes. 'Briefly, I considered that might be just the solution, but then thought better of it. Running away solves nothing, as I once discovered for myself. Thank the Lord I'm not so poor spirited now! My friends, my true friends, will stand by me, I'm certain.'

'You may be sure of it,' he returned abruptly. 'And that, in part, is what has brought me here today.'

Having always considered his a most graceful masculine deportment, Beth was surprised to see him rise quite awkwardly to his feet, almost spilling what was left in his glass in the process, and then pace up and down fitfully, like some wild, tethered creature endeavouring to break free from its restraint. He was clearly very troubled about something.

All at once he came to an abrupt halt, and stared at her intently for quite some little time in silence, before finally saying, 'Beth, you and I have known each other a good many years. So I think it's safe to say that we have an extensive knowledge of each other's character.'

His voice, his mien, was really most peculiar, more like that of some unenthusiastic tutor presenting a lecture that he was reluctant to give than a self-assured gentleman whose ease of manner was legend. Consequently Beth concluded that whatever it was he wished to impart was not precisely coming to his lips with consummate ease.

'I think it's also true to say that for the most part we have always rubbed along together remarkably well,' he continued in the same studied manner. 'We are, not to put too fine a point on it, close friends. And as such I feel it gives me the right to say that I think you would do better to adopt a more serious attitude to what is presently being said about you. A reputation, once damaged, is not so easily repaired, especially a woman's.'

Swinging round on his heels, he went to stand by the window. 'Believe me when I tell you I have done my utmost to quash the rumours. But they persist in certain quarters.' He took a deep, steadying breath. 'Therefore I sincerely believe there is only one course of action left open to me if I am to successfully guard you against further calumny, and that is to offer you the protection of my name.'

Had he not still been standing with his back towards her, Philip would undoubtedly have detected the flicker of raw despair in her eyes before the delicate lids were lowered. Then Beth rose to her feet to grasp the mantelshelf tightly in an attempt to regain control over her emotions, the foremost of which was very quickly searing anger.

Yet when she spoke she sounded remarkably composed, if a touch mocking. 'Well, well, well! What a very lucky girl I am—two proposals of marriage in as many days!'

He swung round at this to face her again. 'Two?' he echoed, clearly startled.

'Why yes, Philip. Didn't you know? Viscount Blackwood also offered the protection of his name. And, I might add, he did so with a deal more eloquence and conviction.'

He took a step towards her, then checked. 'You didn't accept him, did you?'

Very slowly Beth turned her head to meet his gaze, her own faintly contemptuous. 'Why, if I didn't know better, I might almost suppose you wished to marry me.' Her shout of laughter held a distinctly derisive ring to it. 'No, I did not. But I will tell you this—he stood far more chance of persuading me than you ever could. I should never marry for such an absurd reason, least of all you.'

She turned away from him, only just managing to fight back the tears that she knew would inevitably overwhelm her. 'You have your answer. Now kindly behave like the gentleman I know you to be and leave me alone.'

Towards the end of the week Beth received the news she had been longing to hear, when her companion returned to the house, after an early afternoon stroll with Charles Bathurst. 'Oh, Ann, I'm so happy for you!' she declared, embracing her warmly. 'Have you set a date yet?'

'Charles is seeing Mr Chadwick as we speak, and hopes to fix on a date at the end of January.' Ann wasn't slow to detect a flicker of disappointment in the younger woman's eyes. 'What is it, dear? What's wrong?'

'I'm just being immensely selfish, that's all,' Beth admitted. 'I was hoping not to lose you quite so soon.' She rose to her feet and, chortling gaily, went over to the escritoire to consult her diary. 'I must say it won't give us much time to have new gowns made. We must visit the dressmaker in the morning without fail. We'll certainly be busy for the next few weeks. I'm quite looking forward to it.'

Ann, however, wasn't fooled by the display of cheerful enthusiasm. She hadn't forgotten those telltale signs of a severe bout of weeping she'd glimpsed when she had returned from doing the marketing a few days before. At first she had thought that Beth had learned some of the nastier snippets of gossip circulating about her. However, when she had discovered the identity of the only visitor to the house during her absence, she had felt sure this could not be so. Sir Philip was far too diplomatic to repeat anything he might have heard. Yet something had upset Beth deeply on that particular morning.

'It isn't you who is being selfish, it is I.' Ann settled herself in a chair by the hearth, and spread her fingers towards the blazing fire. 'Of course you'll need more time to find another companion. I'll speak to Charles tomorrow and ask him to delay the wedding until the spring. It's a much nicer time to hold such an event, after all.'

'You'll do no such thing!' Beth could not have sounded more determined had she tried. 'If the worst comes to the worst, I can always inflict myself on Aunt Hetta until a suitable replacement has been found. Not that I think I shall ever employ anyone I like half so well.'

'But, my dear, I couldn't reconcile it with my conscience if I were to abandon you now, especially while there's all this silly tittle-tattling persisting about you.'

'Oh, no, not you as well!' Beth glanced ceiling-wards. 'Why must everyone suppose I'm so poor-spirited that I need protecting from the gossipmongers' vicious tongues?'

Ann raised her head at this. 'Is that why Sir Philip called the other day?' She knew at once she had touched a very raw nerve indeed. 'Is that what upset you so much, Beth…? I could tell, you know. Sir Philip, like Lord Blackwood, offered you the protection of his name, didn't he?'

Undeterred by the total lack of response, Ann added, 'I can understand perfectly your reasons for declining his lordship's offer of marriage, even though I know you think highly of him… But Sir Philip is a different matter entirely, Yet you refused him too, didn't you? Why, Beth, why? I know it's what you've always—'

'You know nothing!' Beth cut in, looking far angrier than Ann had ever seen her appear before. 'I would never accept a proposal for such a reason! Never, do you understand, especially not from him!'

She began to pace the room, much as Philip himself had done days before, though her movements were a deal more graceful, and her expression betrayed a deal more determination too.

'I have been grossly at fault to allow this state of affairs to continue for as long as I have. I see that now,' she went on, her expression now more thoughtful than irate. 'It's high time I put a stop to all this gossip and rank stupidity!'

To say that Beth was wholly successful in her endeavours would have been an exaggeration. None the less, her visit to the vicarage and the Reverend Mr Chadwick's subsequent Sunday sermon on the evils of idle chatter certainly went some way to curbing the gossipmongers plying their trade.

Beth's hastily organised evening card-party for female neighbours only to celebrate Ann's betrothal to Mr Bathurst was not only a brilliant notion, but also a resounding success, and resulted in the more influential people in the locale dividing into two distinct factions: those, now the overwhelming majority, who decreed that Miss Bethany Ashworth had merely been the innocent victim of an unfortunate occurrence, and deserved support not censure; and those few, perhaps offended by Beth at some point in the distant past, who continued to fuel the gossip by nasty remarks, but to a much lesser extent.

In truth, though, neither Ann nor Beth were granted much time to consider local opinion. Both quickly became immersed in putting together a suitable trousseau for the future bride, and overseeing the removal of Ann's belongings to her future husband's home. Only one thing slightly blighted Ann's pleasure during those few short weeks leading up to her wedding, and that was Sir Philip's total avoidance of the Grange.

She saw him once only during this hectic period, and then by pure chance, when she called at her future home, bringing with her some of her possessions, and the Baronet just happened to be paying Charles a morning visit at the time. He had written a letter to them both, of course, offering his sincerest congratulations, and had presented them with a beautiful silver tray as a wedding gift.

It had to be said that on that particular morning he had seemed urbanity itself, as gracious and affable as ever. Yet Ann couldn't help wondering whether he was quite as contented with life as he had appeared. If his ease of manner had been no ruse, then she had greatly misjudged the situation, and Beth's refusal to marry him had not troubled him in the least. She simply couldn't believe this was so!

The future Mrs Bathurst had been so right to question Philip's demeanour, for it had been no easy task for him to maintain the pretence of affable contentment during those weeks after his disastrous proposal of marriage.

It wasn't that he had deliberately gone out of his way to avoid any encounter with Beth. In fact, they had chanced to meet on three separate occasions: twice whilst both had been out riding, and once in Markham. On all occasions, although she had done little to prolong the encounters, Beth's behaviour towards him had been affable enough. Nevertheless he couldn't help feeling that his presence at the Grange might not be so welcome, until Beth had recovered fully from what he could only assume must surely have been offence and embarrassment at his marriage proposal.

* * *

Consequently, on the morning of the wedding, Philip couldn't help wondering how she would behave towards him when there was little possibility of avoiding each other for several hours. He quickly discovered that his slight misgivings were totally unfounded, for Beth's behaviour was of the most genial from the outset.

Although she did not go out of her way to avoid him at all, Beth did spend quite some little time in private conversation with Viscount Blackwood. Philip wasn't unduly disturbed by it. Not only was he fairly certain now that the only reason his lordship had delayed his departure from the area was in order to be on hand should his good friend Charles Bathurst have need of his services as a groomsman, a task he had ably carried out that day, but also he was fairly certain now that Beth looked upon his lordship as a friend only. Philip was further heartened when she betrayed no qualms whatsoever when he sat himself beside her at the wedding breakfast, held at the Bathursts' home.

'I know Ann was concerned about not wishing to appear the grand lady of the manor once she had married Charles,' Beth confided, leaning slightly towards him and speaking in an undertone. 'Personally I think she worries unnecessarily over trifles. Besides, it's all gone very smoothly indeed, considering she wasn't granted that much time to organise everything. I think it was sensible of them both to keep it a small affair too, don't you?'

He nodded, feeling another surge of gratification at this further display of complete ease on her part in his company. Determined it should continue, he said, 'Neither of them, so I understand, have any immediate family living. Large weddings are all very well, but one is obliged to invite so many people one's never seen in years, or has any real desire to see either, come to that. But I don't think Ann need trouble herself about her social position. From the first she fitted in very well, and is well liked.'

'Yes, I liked her from the first. I shall dearly miss her,' Beth admitted softly. 'I shall miss Lord Blackwood's frequent visits too. He tells me he's returning to London in the morning by hired carriage.'

'Yes, so I understand,' Philip responded, hoping he had not betrayed the relief he could not help feeling.

Although having by this time surprisingly come to like the Viscount very well, Philip couldn't deny that it had given him a severe shock to discover that he too had proposed to Beth. He might have experienced a degree of relief and satisfaction to know that the Viscount's suit had also not prospered, if he hadn't made such a mull of his own.

Swiftly suppressing the sudden swell of mingled bitter regret and shame that always afflicted him whenever he considered his doomed proposal, he returned to the present, and said, 'I understand, too, that Charles and his new bride will be remaining here for the next few weeks, and travelling to the capital in early spring.'

Beth nodded, not appearing altogether happy. 'And I cannot help but be suspicious about it. Although Ann has denied it vehemently, I still strongly suspect she's remaining in the locale because she's concerned about me being at the Grange on my own. It wouldn't surprise me in the least if she doesn't suggest in the near future that I accompany them to the capital so that she can see to it that I am safely deposited with Aunt Hetta.' She shrugged. 'Well, I suppose it would be agreeable to have company on the journey. So long as she doesn't suggest I accompany them both to Paris in the late spring! I should certainly draw a line at that!'

'You are indeed going to miss her greatly, though, Beth,' he remarked with a sympathetic smile. 'I hope you won't be too lonely at the Grange.'

She surprisingly chuckled. 'I don't think there's much chance of that, Philip. As soon as Rudge has returned me there later today, he's going into the village to collect my pup from the widowed lady. I rather fancy I'll have my hands full for quite some little time to come taking care of him.'

He reached for one of hers and held it in his own. 'Friends again?' he queried gently.

'I hope we shall always be that,' she answered, not attempting to break free from the gentle hold, and little realising that ice-blue eyes were studying the touching interlude intently.

Then Viscount Blackwood turned immediately towards the radiantly happy lady seated on his left at the foot of the table, and easily captured her full attention by a few whispered words.

The following morning, as he sat in his library, doing his utmost to deal with estate matters, Philip found his concentration straying time and again. Eventually admitting defeat, he tossed the paper he had been attempting to read down on the desk.

How on earth was it possible to put one's mind to anything when one's personal life was in such turmoil? He quickly recalled suffering much the same sorts of problems when he had returned to the Court after Eugenie's death, half a decade ago. Only this time it seemed so very much worse.

Burying his face in his hands, he could only wonder

at himself for making such a mess of it all. Why, oh, why hadn't he told Beth the truth, explained exactly how he felt, instead of resorting to such a ridiculous stratagem? The truth of the matter was, of course, he had been too afraid of what her answer might be: that she would declare she could never return his love and that she could only ever look upon him as a brother. Well, she had certainly proved that yesterday, displaying that same sibling affection towards him she'd shown throughout her life. Dear Lord! Could anything be more soul destroying!

The click of the door succeeded in penetrating his despondency, and Philip removed his hands to discover his butler taking a step into the room.

'I'm sorry to disturb you, sir, but Viscount Blackwood has called and begs a few minutes of your time.'

Nodding assent, Philip rose at once to his feet and went to stand before the hearth, wondering what on earth could possibly have prompted the visit. Farewells had been exchanged the previous evening, just prior to his returning to the Court. Slight fears that something untoward had occurred were immediately alleviated by his lordship's entry in the room. His mien was not that of a gentleman with a troubled mind, even though he refused refreshment and the offer of a seat.

'Good of you to see me, Staveley. I've no intention of detaining you for long as I've a post-chaise-and-four outside awaiting my return. But the devil of it is I felt I couldn't leave for London without speaking to you first. Although I have to say,' he continued, smiling ruefully, 'it goes against the grain for me to do so. I'm not one to interfere in the lives of others as a rule.'

More intrigued than anything else, Philip too remained standing. 'You find me positively agog with curiosity, Blackwood. What is so important that you felt the need to delay your departure?'

The Viscount grasped one of the high-backed chairs, and leaned against it, appearing totally at ease. 'Yesterday, I was led to believe that you also had proposed marriage to Beth and that your suit had not prospered either.'

'Who told you that…? Beth?' Philip asked, understandably not altogether pleased that his lack of success was becoming common knowledge, and not reticent to show it either in his expression or his voice.

The Viscount wasn't slow to set him straight on the matter. 'No, it was Ann. And I might add she's as puzzled as I am to understand just why you were unsuccessful.'

Philip released his breath in a long sigh. 'For the same reason as you were, I should suppose.'

'I shouldn't imagine so,' his lordship countered in a trice. 'Beth was honest enough to admit that she wasn't in love with me. I admire her for it, and for her many other fine qualities, too. Although I confess I felt obliged to offer her the protection of my name because we spent an entire night together, I swear to you, Staveley, I didn't so much as attempt to seduce her.'

Philip stared across at the other man levelly, silently appreciating for perhaps the first time just how much his opinion of his lordship had changed during recent weeks. 'You imagine I didn't know that?'

The Viscount's slight smile betrayed no hint of cynicism this time. 'On the contrary, I was sure you did, otherwise I would have received a visit from you. All the same, I still felt honour-bound to offer her the protection of my name. You, on the other hand, were prompted by no such reason.'

'No,' Philip agreed sombrely. 'That wasn't why I asked her.'

'No, I thought not,' his lordship returned. 'Which begs the question, does it not, just why you were refused.'

'As I've said before, for the same reason you were.' Philip raised a hand to run his fingers through his hair, an action that might easily have been taken for a gesture of defeat. 'Beth looks upon me as a brother, nothing more.'

This was surprisingly greeted with a deep rumble of masculine laughter. 'God, Staveley, for an intelligent man you can be damnably dull-witted over certain things, seemingly. I am one-hundred-percent certain that was not the reason she refused you.'

And with that astounding admission his lordship swung round on his heels, but checked as he reached the door. 'I cannot possibly advise you on what you should do now, but I shall tell you this. Beth said something else to me that day I proposed to her, which happens to be very true. She said that had I truly been in love with her, I wouldn't have taken no for an answer. So why have you?'

Feeling slightly stunned, Philip watched his lordship execute a faintly ironic bow and depart. Could it be true? he wondered. Could it, by some miracle, be true? Did Beth truly love him? There was only one way he was going to discover for himself.

Going out into the hall, he called for his horse to be saddled at once.

Chapter Fourteen

Beth paused in the letter she was composing to her aunt, Lady Henrietta Barfield, in order to favour her loyal Rudge with a considering look, as he carried the basket of logs across to the hearth.

To say that he was displaying less than his usual enthusiasm for his daily duties would not have been an exaggeration in the least, and it wasn't too difficult a task to guess the reason why. Unless she was much mistaken, Master Rudge had been only too willing to accept far more of the kind widowed lady's hospitality than she herself had done when she had called at the cottage on that bitterly cold day in December. To give him his due, though, Rudge at least had somehow managed to find his way back to the Grange, unharmed, with her latest acquisition safely tucked beneath his coat.

She transferred her gaze to the young dog, which had seemed to have lost none of its enthusiasm for her society during the weeks since their first encounter. Now happily doing battle with an old slipper, he had positioned himself within inches of where she sat. She couldn't in all honesty say his looks had improved to any significant degree during their weeks apart, though he had grown considerably larger, and resembled the animal that prowled the blacksmith's premises even more closely now.

After replenishing the fire, Rudge rose slowly to his feet to discover his mistress still thoughtfully considering the animal at her feet. 'You know, Miss Beth, I 'ave to say I reckon that's a dashed queer cur for a lady like you to be owning.'

Beth was successful in suppressing a betraying smile, and sounded quite serious as she said, 'I cannot imagine why you should think so. I would never consider housing one of those pampered lapdogs my Aunt Hetta favours. Besides, the reason for having a dog in the first place was to act as a deterrent to any would-be burglar. And I believe he'll prove more than equal to the task when he's older.'

'You may be right in that, miss. But I still think 'ee's a right queer dog for a lady to own,' the servant responded, before rubbing a hand back and forth across his chin. 'And, you know, 'ee reminds me of another I've seen around these parts.'

'And so he should,' Beth returned, nowhere near as successful this time in suppressing a wicked grin. 'You've paid more than one visit to our local blacksmith, after all.'

It took a moment only for the manservant to appreciate fully what he was being told. 'Oh, my gawd!' He clapped a hand over his eyes. 'You don't mean to say that great lolloping cur at the forge be the sire!'

If this knowledge was not bad enough, the sudden vigorous application of the front-door knocker appeared to have a more disturbing effect upon him. 'Now who be that a-pounding on the front door as though the devil 'imself were at 'is heels.'

'I've absolutely no idea. And neither will you have until you've answered it,' Beth responded, returning to the letter she was writing.

The masculine voice that was soon afterwards exchanging pleasantries with her manservant in the hall was sufficient to prepare her for Sir Philip's entry into the room a few moments later. The pup's immediate reaction surprised Beth even more than Philip's unexpected arrival. After turning its head on one side, as though considering the stranger, it went gambolling across the room, easily capturing the visitor's attention by its persistent yaps and its blatant disregard for a pair of highly polished top boots.

Bending low, Philip easily captured the animal with one swoop of his hand, and almost sent Beth into hoops of laughter as he studied the creature more closely. Had he ever been tempted to sport a quizzing-glass, Beth would have wagered he would have raised it at that moment for effect, for she could almost hear him muttering 'good gad!' under his breath.

'Yes, I'm sure you're a pleasant young fellow, and I look forward to becoming better acquainted with you in the very near future,' Philip announced, holding the pup at arm's length in order to prevent it from licking his face. 'None the less, for the present I very much fear you will be more of a hindrance than anything else, as I fully intend to have a serious talk with your mistress.'

Swinging round on his heels, Philip didn't waste time in placing the pup in the servant's capable hands. 'Be so good as to take the creature away, Rudge. I wish to be private with your mistress.'

Automatically complying, Rudge closed the door quietly behind him, which for some obscure reason had the effect of slightly irritating Beth. She wasn't perfectly sure what nettled her more: Rudge's immediate response to the command, or Sir Philip's diabolical nerve in issuing it in the first place!

Consequently, instead of adhering to accepted standards of polite behaviour by offering her visitor refreshment, she remained seated at the escritoire and reached for the quill once again in order to finish her letter to her aunt.

'So what is it that you wish to discuss with me?' she finally asked, after he had gone across to the decanters and quite brazenly helped himself to wine, without offering to pour her a glass.

'Quite simply, my dear, I am here to discover precisely why you refuse to marry me.'

So unexpected was his response that Beth's hand shook slightly, the result of which sent droplets of ink splattering across the page. 'Oh, now look what you've made me do!'

'I'm still waiting for an answer, Beth,' he told her calmly, after watching her rise from the chair and attempt to repair the damage to her letter. 'And please don't again try to fob me off with any of that niffy-naffy nonsense about not marrying a man because he feels honour-bound to propose. That's not why you refused me, and you know it!'

At this unusually brusque tone she turned round very slowly to face him for the very first time, uncertainty and disquiet easily discernible in her expression. Philip took a deliberate step towards her, his own expression revealing his determination to get to the truth.

'You may have refused Blackwood for that reason. And because you don't love him. But that isn't why you refused me, is it…? Is it, Beth?'

Like a child caught red-handed in some wilful act, she shook her head dumbly, the muscles in her neck working as she swallowed some constricting lump in her throat.

'No,' she admitted at last, her voice barely above a whisper.

'Then why, Beth…why?' The rapid rise and fall of her breast was a sure sign of distress. His resolve, none the less, remained firm. He sensed that if he were to weaken now, he would never be granted another chance to discover the truth from her own lips.

He took a further step towards her. 'Be sure I shall not leave until I know the answer.' He stared down at her intently, his gaze mercilessly holding hers captive. 'And you know I shall know if you lie.'

So close was he that he distinctly heard the breath catch in her throat a moment before she swung away to grasp the mantel-shelf as though for support, much as she had done when last he had been in the room. Except he sensed that on this occasion she was battling with far more than just anger.

'God damn, you, Staveley!' she cursed him, her voice shaking with raw emotion. 'Isn't it enough that you've always had my heart? Must you torture it as well!'

Heroically fighting back the tears, she swung round, fists clenched, to face him again. 'Yes, I love you…I've always loved you,' she at last admitted. 'Why do you suppose I so readily agreed to attend that wretched seminary in Bath all those years ago?' She didn't wait for a response. 'For once I was happy to heed my aunt's advice when she warned me that no gentleman of breeding and refinement would ever consider allying himself to any female who refused to comport herself like a lady. And I tried so damnably hard to achieve those standards of accepted behaviour to please you. But it availed me nothing!' She was unable to keep the bitterness out of her voice. 'The next thing I knew you'd fallen head over heels in love with my cousin.'

Hard though it had been to confess those inmost thoughts, those most private of feelings, Beth found some relief in having bared her soul, and was now determined that he should know all.

'Why do you suppose I fled to Spain? To be with my father?' She raised one brow in a mocking arch. 'Well, I suppose in part it was. But the main reason was because I couldn't bear even the thought of witnessing your engagement, let alone perjuring my soul by wishing you both joy. I wished you both anything but! I think I truly hated you both at the time.'

If he found these facts even remotely disquieting, he certainly betrayed no sign of it as he calmly consumed the contents of his glass, before going across to stand before the window.

If anything, he had the air of a man who retained complete mastery over his emotions. He even sounded remarkably composed as he said, 'A very understandable reaction in the circumstances, and one that was, thankfully, not long lasting, I sincerely hope. It explains a great deal, but not quite all. So I must return to my original question—why did you refuse my offer of marriage?'

He had sounded so smugly satisfied that had he been within reach Beth wasn't at all certain she could have withstood the temptation to box his ears. As it was, it was as much as she could do not to gape at him for displaying such a total lack of sensitivity.

'Well, why do you suppose?' she demanded, finding some solace in an unexpected surge of annoyance. 'I'm not made of stone, you know. How do you imagine I should feel knowing the man I'd married wished with all his heart that I were someone else? That every time he held me in his arms he was imagining…wishing with all his heart…that I was a certain other very special lady.'

Once again Beth swung away to grip the mantelshelf, feeling emotionally drained, yet determined still to be totally frank. 'I'm my father's daughter, Philip. I've too much pride to be considered merely second best. I shall never allow myself to be a mere substitute for Eugenie, never, do you understand!'

'Oh, my darling girl, you couldn't be more wrong.'

The sudden bark of laughter that followed the astonishing, and softly spoken, admission was his most surprising reaction of all, and one that had Beth staring across the room at him in total bewilderment, as he turned his back on her to rest a hand on the window frame.

His sigh was clearly one of deep regret, as was the tone of his voice when he said, 'I should have explained before. Perhaps not directly after your return here, when you seemed faintly distant. Of course I can appreciate the reason for your behaviour now. Later, though, after that wonderful rapport we so enjoyed years ago had begun to re-establish itself, I should have confided in you. But I suppose it was something I preferred not to remember. It was in the past, after all. It has little bearing on my life now.'

Beth waited to hear more. When he continued to stare out of the window in silence, curiosity got the better of her and she found herself saying, 'I'm sorry, Philip, I don't perfectly understand what you're trying to tell me.'

A further long silence, then, 'Like everyone else, I suppose, you assumed I buried myself at Staveley Court after Eugenie's death nursing a broken heart?'

Philip turned his head to see an expression on her face that was answer enough. 'Of course you did. It was a con-

clusion most everyone drew, and one that I have always
been content never to rectify. Dear old Uncle Waldo was
perhaps the only one who ever guessed the truth. Omni-
potent demon that he is, he knew that at three-and-twenty
I was too young to know my own mind, that love and in-
fatuation are often confused. Whether I ever truly loved
Eugenie, I honestly could not say. All I do know is that
even before the engagement was made official in that
spring of '09, I was already having doubts about my
choice of bride. Physically she was perfection—the most
beautiful girl I'd ever seen, will possibly ever see. But I
began to realise that there was little else to commend
Eugenie. I began to find her faintly…shallow. All the
same I felt honour-bound to go through with it, and the
wedding planned for the following year.'

Four long strides took him over to the drinks' table,
where once again he helped himself, tossing the wine
down his throat in one swallow, further proof had she
needed it that he wasn't finding these confessions an
easy task.

'No doubt you know all the details concerning the
accident,' he continued softly. 'What you cannot possibly
know is how I felt when I stood there watching Eugenie's
lifeless body being carried on that rough wooden hurdle
back into your aunt and uncle's house. Of course I felt
saddened that such a beautiful girl had died so young. But
alongside this feeling of regret was a strong sense of relief,
knowing that I wouldn't now be called upon to go through
with the wedding. And I felt so damnably ashamed about
the way I felt, but I simply couldn't help it. That's why I
buried myself for so long at Staveley Court. The world
could continue to believe I was nursing a broken heart—
better that than betray my dark, despicable secret.'

Beth was beside him in a trice, placing her hand

gently on one sleeve of his jacket. 'Oh, Philip, I don't know what to say…except perhaps you shouldn't punish yourself any more.'

Capturing her hand, he studied the finely boned, tapering fingers. 'I shall perhaps always carry the burden of guilt, Beth. But my life now is no longer in bad kilter. Someone came back into it, and quickly began to put almost everything right.'

Releasing her hand, he raised both of his to circle her neck and gently force her chin up with his thumbs so that he could stare down into those azure eyes now full of dawning wonder.

'I shall not pretend, Beth, that at some point since your return I suddenly fell head over heels in love with you. And I thank the Lord for it!' he declared with feeling. 'It's no secret that I've always adored you, and my deep affection for you has withstood the test of time. Believe me, my darling girl, you will never be a substitute for someone else. I want you, and only you, to be my wife, the mother of my children, my life's companion.'

It seemed strange at first experiencing the pressure of his lips against hers, simply because his rare, chaste salutes of bygone years bore no resemblance to the persuasive seduction he was practising now. And it worked! Not many moments had passed before Beth found herself automatically responding to the gentle pressure of his mouth as it forced her lips apart, and delighting in the awaking sensations of desire as his arms slipped about her, melding her every contour to his hard-muscled frame.

Wholly satisfied by these initial reactions to his gentle lovemaking, Philip finally released her, and drew her across to the sofa, where he once again held her a very willing captive in the crook of his arm.

'We shall be married as soon as it can be arranged,'

he declared. 'A special licence would provide the ideal solution.'

Beth was more than happy to fall in with his wishes. All the same she couldn't resist resorting to the teasing rapport they'd enjoyed for so long. 'My, my, such unseemly haste, sir! There's enough gossip circulating about me still, let me remind you. Heaven only knows what the tattle-mongers will make of our hasty union when they get wind of it.'

'Unseemly haste…?' he echoed, slanting a mocking look down at her. 'We've wasted too many years already, my girl! And as for the gossips—they can damned well think what they like!'

This was music to her ears. 'So you truly didn't propose to me before simply because you wished to offer the protection of your name?'

'Of course I didn't,' he confirmed, slightly shame-faced. 'Why the devil I didn't simply tell you the truth then, I'll never know.' He sighed. 'I suppose I feared you just might still look upon me as a brother. After all, you've never once given me any reason to suspect your feelings for me went any deeper.'

If only he knew just how much of a strain it had been to retain control over her emotions! It had been hard before her period abroad; harder still since her return. Yes, there was some justification for him thinking as he did, she was silently obliged to acknowledge. Seemingly she had succeeded far better than she had imagined. He began speaking again, easily capturing her full attention.

'I thought if I could persuade you to marry me, then in time you'd accept me as a husband.' His eyes glinted wickedly. 'But you've already proved to me how greatly I've underestimated your affection for me.'

Beth was more than ready to verify this, but after-wards, as she rested her head against his shoulder, she couldn't resist discovering just when he had decided he truly wished to marry her.

'Loath though I am to admit to it, Beth, that was Lord Blackwood's doing. Curse him! It wasn't until I thought you'd captured his interest that I realised just how much you meant to me,' he freely admitted. 'I couldn't bear even the thought of you being married to another man.'

A light tap on the parlour door prepared them for Rudge's re-entry into the room. For the sake of appear-ance, Beth eased herself a little distance away from her future husband; whereas Philip himself merely raised a questioning brow as the servant edged reluctantly towards the sofa.

'Sorry to disturb you, sir...Miss Beth. But the house-keeper's getting into a right state. Swears that if that there 'ound stays in the kitchen much longer, she fears he'll do serious damage to the door.'

'Oh, let him come back through, Rudge,' Beth ordered, dismissing him with a nod, before concentrat-ing once more on the man sitting beside her. 'You do realise, don't you, Philip, that I have responsibilities that I simply cannot ignore? For a start I won't send that pup back to the widow lady. It would be most unfair. Besides, I haven't had a dog for such a long time, and I've grown rather attached to him already.'

She peered up through her lashes, something that she hadn't done in many a long year. 'And then, of course, there's Rudge. I'd have to bring him with me to the Court, as well. His attitude being what it is, he wouldn't find it at all easy attaining a position with someone else.'

'You can stop your wheedling, my girl!' he chided

lovingly. 'I've already told you I consider Rudge would make a first-rate head groom. And as far as the animal's concerned...' He paused to study the pup as it came scampering over to the sofa. 'I dare swear most of my family and friends will consider I've run mad to allow such a creature free rein at the Court, but no doubt I'll grow accustomed to his odd looks in time.'

Beth bestowed a radiant smile upon her future husband. 'Now I'm positive you must truly love me, if you're willing to do that!'

Chapter Fifteen

February 1815

The landlord of the Travellers Rest could hardly believe his ears, or great good fortune, come to that, when he detected what sounded suspiciously like a carriage drawing up outside his hostelry.

His homely wayside tavern was no bustling posting-house, nor was it situated on one of the busy coaching routes. None the less, over the years he and his wife had made a success of running the inn. It had earned itself the reputation for good basic accommodation—whole-some food and clean, aired bedding—and was now very well patronised, during those months when travel became more widespread, by those who preferred peace and quiet to the continual noise at a busy coaching house.

This, however, was February, a month when trade was sadly very slack. Not only that, it had been snowing steadily for the past two hours, making it increasingly difficult to negotiate the narrow country lanes, therefore he was not expecting too many of even his most loyal local patrons from the village to brave the elements on such an evening.

As he went out into the entrance porch, he was overjoyed to discover his hearing was not faulty. A postchaise-and-four had come to a halt directly outside, and one of the post-boys, having already slipped from his mount, was approaching.

'His lordship assured me we'd get accommodation 'ere for the night,' he said, after hurriedly seeking the relative shelter of the porch.

Mine host's smile faded at this. A good reputation his inn might have earned itself during the past decade, but all the same, it was a rare occurrence indeed for members of the nobility to patronise his establishment, and those few who had over the years, more often than not, had proved difficult customers—demanding and faultfinding. Unfortunately, though, he was hardly in a position to be turning away custom, no matter how trying they might turn out to be. Even a complaining patron was better than none at all!

None the less, mine host decided it might be prudent not to seem too eager for patronage. 'A lord, eh? And which lord might that be? Or be you 'aving a little joke, m'lad?'

'He most certainly is not,' a refined voice drawled, and a moment later a tall gentleman, dressed from head to toe in the height of fashion, stepped down from the hired carriage.

As he swept past, the hem of his fur-lined cloak brushed against the landlord's legs, and there was a distinct odour of pomade emanating from beneath the rim of his expensive beaver hat. The innkeeper's eyes sparkled with a gleam of avarice as he followed the unknown into the tap. Whoever the gentleman was, he certainly had style and, if appearances were anything to go by, was undoubtedly plump in the pocket. His curiosity was swiftly satisfied.

'I am Lord Blackwood,' the gentleman announced, after a swift, and sweeping appraisal of the interior. 'I require a room for myself and my servant, and of course accommodation for the post-boys and the horses. You are still in a position to provide for these needs, I assume?'

'No trouble at all, sir,' the landlord confirmed, before something swiftly occurred to him. 'Would I be right in thinking, sir—er—m'lord, that you've put up here afore?'

'Indeed you would. But it was very many years ago, so I beg you not to waste time attempting to recall me to mind. I have changed somewhat in both appearance and behaviour. Which ought to please you, my good man. I was something of a hell-raiser in my youth. Now I am well on the way to cultivating a preference for peace and quiet and my creature comforts.'

After a further cursory glance about him, my lord remarked, 'You still have no private parlour, I see.'

'Well, sir, when the need arises we always open the back room for such purposes. But this being February, and not many people about on the roads, as yer might say, we don't bother to light a fire in there as a rule. But we can have it ready for your lordship by morning,' he offered apologetically

'That will do very well. In the meantime my servant and I shall dine in here, and take the table over there in the corner by the inglenook—not that I suppose for a moment the place will become crowded on such a night as this.'

Although he could have wished it might be quite otherwise, the landlord was obliged to agree, before he listed what his good lady wife would be able to present his lordship for supper.

'Excellent! I shall look forward to it. In the meantime I shall require two tankards of your finest ale, landlord. And I'm positive also that you can provide me with all the ingredients necessary to make a hot toddy, which I shall prepare myself.'

This request had the landlord peering up at the black-haired stranger more closely. His lordship, however, was oblivious to the closer scrutiny as he removed his hat and coat, and tossed them both on a chair. His attention was then drawn by the arrival of a small man with a decided limp.

'Ah, Clegg! Put the bags down over there. The landlord no doubt will have them conveyed to our rooms in due course. You'll sup with me this evening. But first, come and sit yourself down by the fire and join me in a tankard of ale.'

It would have been difficult to say whether the landlord or the servant was more surprised by this command. 'But, m'lord, it would suit me fine to share with the post-boys,' the servant assured his master once he had overcome the shock.

'I dare say it would,' his lordship responded, sounding distinctly bored. 'But it wouldn't suit me. I too vividly recall the last time I was obliged to take shelter from a snowstorm. Had it not been for the principles of a truly exceptional young woman, I might so easily have been obliged to relinquish my bachelor state. This time I fully intend to take every precaution by keeping you close in order to protect me. Besides, I have things I wish to discuss with you.'

The servant's response was to chuckle merrily, as though at some private joke. The landlord, however, was more puzzled than anything else by the exchange. Consequently, after carrying two tankards of his famous home-brewed ale across to his distinguished guest's table, he hurried through to the back of his premises to instruct his daughter to have two bedchambers made ready, and to consult with his spouse, who betrayed no apprehension whatsoever when informed she'd be catering for a member of the aristocracy.

'So what's a-worrying you?' she asked, when he continued to frown heavily down at her. 'As long as 'ee pays his shot before 'ee leaves, and there's no reason to suppose 'ee won't, 'ee can dine with his servant, or anyone 'ee wants, for all I care.'

'No, it ain't that, Bess. It's just that I can't place 'im. Yet I know 'ee's stayed 'ere afore now. 'Ee even asked for stuff to make 'ot toddies. And I bet 'ee takes it with rum an' all.' He shook his head, clearly perplexed. 'Reminds me o' someone, but I just can't bring to mind who.'

'Didn't 'ee give a name.'

'Blackmore…Black…something or other.'

'Well, you'd best not tarry. Go get the things 'ee's asked for,' she advised, ever practical. 'The better the service, the more generous 'ee's likely to be with 'is money.'

Heeding the advice, mine host didn't delay hurrying back through to the tap to discover his lordship perusing an edition of the *Morning Post*, which he'd evidently brought with him from wherever he'd commenced his journey.

'It would be rum you be wanting for the toddies, milord?'

'Never make them with anything else,' was the prompt response. 'Leave the tray on the counter, landlord, and I'll help myself.'

His lordship then gave a start and his eyes became riveted on a certain article on the printed page. 'By heavens, Clegg!' he exclaimed, clearly diverted. 'He's only gone and done it, by gad! Sir Philip Staveley and Miss Bethany Ashworth,' he read out loud, 'only daughter of the late Colonel Augustus Ashworth, were married at a private ceremony conducted at St Edward's Church... in the county of Somerset...so on and so forth.'

He gave a whoop of laughter. 'He gets himself leg-shackled, and then boldly announces it to the world at large! Well done, Staveley! What I'd give to be in London when he brings his delightful bride up to town! Which I'm sure he will do in a month or two. Unfortunately I have responsibilities, and my presence for the foreseeable future is required elsewhere. So I shall merely satisfy myself in the knowledge that I have been, in some small part, instrumental in bringing about such a perfect union.'

Tossing the paper aside, his lordship rose from his chair to grasp the poker and then thrust it into the fire. 'I shall need to be careful in the future, though, Clegg,' he announced, his expression at its most sardonic. 'I don't wish to sully my hitherto well-earned reputation by being considered altruistic, although I suppose just one good turn will soon be forgotten.'

'You've done more than one person a good turn in recent weeks, m'lord,' the servant wasn't slow to remind him.

Black brows rose in two perfectly mocking arches. 'I sincerely trust you're not referring to yourself, Clegg? You've had an easy time of it in my employ thus far. But you just wait until we reach the Manor. You'll discover then just how hard a taskmaster I can be. In the meantime you will join the Seventh Viscount Blackwood in a hot toddy to celebrate Sir Philip and Miss Ashworth's happy union.'

At this the landlord returned to his wife to reveal all

he had discovered, and was somewhat surprised by her modest show of interest. 'But, Bessy, don't you realise who 'ee is? Don't you recall all that scandal over Merryfield way some years back? Folk swore it were the young son that murdered 'is father and brother. I 'eard 'ee were taken up to stand trial, but escaped. Weren't seen for years. But 'ee be back now, right enough, sitting in our tap, as calmly as yer please!'

'Well, what of it?' his wife returned, totally unconcerned. 'Stands to reason, then, 'ee couldn't 'ave done it, otherwise 'ee wouldn't 'ave come back into these parts. Mind, I never believed it in the first place. And another thing, don't you forget it were none other than that there young Master Sebastian Blackwood 'imself that first made this place of ours so popular with travellers. Now I ain't saying 'ee weren't wild, and there's no denying those females 'ee brought 'ere from time to time were no ladies. But 'ee always paid 'is shot.'

The landlady paused for a moment in her pastry making, frowning slightly. 'All the same, to be on the safe side we'd best lock the bedchamber door when we retire. And make sure you lock our daughter's chamber too!'

* * * * *

"Is that for me?" Trey asked.

Cardin Worth cocked her head to the side and considered how much better the day already seemed. "Good morning to you, too."

When she didn't hold out the second cup of coffee for him to take, he came closer. She sipped from her heavy white mug, hiding her grin and her giddy rush of nerves behind it.

But when he stopped in front of her, she made the mistake of lowering her gaze from his face to the exposed strip of his chest. It was either give him his cup of coffee or bury her nose against him and breathe in. She remembered so clearly how he smelled. How he tasted.

She gave him his coffee.

After taking a quick gulp, he smiled and said, "Good morning, Cardin. I hope the floor wasn't too hard for you."

The hardness of the floor hadn't been the problem. She shook her head. "Are you kidding? I slept like a baby, swaddled in my sleeping bag."

"In my sleeping bag, you mean."

If he wanted to get technical, yeah. "Thanks for the loaner. It made sleeping on the floor almost bearable." As had the warmth of his spooned body, she thought, then quickly changed the subject. "I saw you have a loaf of bread and some eggs. Would you like me to cook breakfast?"

He lowered his coffee mug slowly, his gaze as warm as the sun on her shoulders, as the ceramic heating her hands. "I didn't bring you out here to wait on me."

"You didn't bring me out here at all. I volunteered to come."

"To help me get ready for the race. Not to serve me."

"It's just breakfast, Trey. And coffee." Even if last night it had been more. Even if the way he was looking at her made her want to climb back into that sleeping bag. "I work much better when my stomach's not growling. I thought it might be the same for you."

"It is, but I'll cook. You made the coffee."

"That's because I can't work at all without caffeine."

"If I'd known that, I would've put on a pot as soon I got up."

"What time *did* you get up?" Judging by the sun's position, she swore it couldn't be any later than seven now. And, yeah, they'd agreed to start working at six.

"Maybe four?" he guessed, giving her a lazy smile.

"But it was almost two..." She let the sentence dangle, finishing the thought privately. She was quite sure he knew exactly what time they'd finally fallen asleep after he'd made love to her.

The question facing her now was where did this relationship—if you could even call it *that*—go from here?

* * * * *

*Cardin and Trey are about to find out that
great sex is only the beginning….
Don't miss the fireworks!
Get ready for
A LONG, HARD RIDE
by Alison Kent
Available March 2009,
wherever Blaze books are sold.*